The Disappeared

by

Sibel Hodge

First published in 2018 by Bloodhound Books

www.bloodhoundbooks.com

Print ISBN 978-1-912604-74-6

The Devil whispered in my ear, 'You're not strong enough to withstand the storm.'

Today, I whispered in the Devil's ear, 'I am the storm.'
~ *Unknown*

PROLOGUE

Mason Palmer didn't know he had less than two hours to live when he walked into the ramshackle building. It looked more like a truck stop, really, than an airport. One old, concrete square building with a mismatch of tiles on the floor, worn smooth, and a wooden-beamed roof, but it wasn't an international airport and it served its purpose. In the remote, rural area of Lagossa, it was used only for the light aircraft service taking passengers to and from the capital of Galao.

The check-in area was a battered, old plastic desk with cigarette burns dotted on the top. The young woman behind it scanned the sparse waiting room, looking like she'd rather be anywhere else but here. There was no queue, which was hardly surprising given there was only one flight out of there all afternoon—a six-seater plane that would whisk Mason away.

The woman smiled as he approached the desk. 'Hello, Mr Palmer. Nice to see you again.'

After his second visit, she'd remembered his name. This part of the world didn't get many tourists now—the backpackers wanting to discover rural Africa were long gone, the safaris had never operated this far north, and the international reporters either didn't care or didn't dare risk it, so his white skin stood out amongst the darker tones of the locals.

Mason handed over his passport and smiled at her, but his heart wasn't in it. He was too busy thinking about getting home to England. Putting his plan into action. Escaping. 'Thank you, Adjoua.' Mason remembered her name too. He was used to memorising names—he thought his patients deserved a personal touch.

'Going back home for your two weeks' holiday?' She bent over her desk and filled in Mason's details on a form.

'Yes.' He glanced out of the floor-to-ceiling glass windows to his right, to the small plane already on the runway. Two passengers were climbing aboard, a young white man and woman. A member of the airport staff, dressed in a khaki jumpsuit, was filling the plane with fuel.

In twelve hours, he'd be back with Nicole. He'd tell her everything. They'd work out what to do.

Adjoua smiled again as she held out a hand-written boarding pass for his onward flight from the capital. 'Have a good journey. I'll see you again soon.'

He nodded, although it was unlikely he'd ever see this place again. Not after what he was about to do.

Mason took the pass from her and walked towards the doors that led to the runway carved out of the African bush, the tarmac bleached by the sun.

He was almost at the door when a hand clamped on to his shoulder.

'Mr Palmer, we need to speak with you,' a voice said, firm and insistent.

A shiver of fear coursed through Mason. His heart pounded.

They knew.

Mason swallowed quickly, turned around and came face to face with a medium sized man who sported closely cropped black hair, greying at the edges. He wore suit trousers and a short-sleeved checked shirt. His skin was so dark and smooth, it shone like polished ebony. Either side of him were two taller men in black police uniforms, their hands resting on handguns in holsters at their waists.

'I don't understand,' Mason said, forcing an affable smile. 'I'm going to miss my flight.' He tilted his head towards the plane outside.

'The plane can wait.' Checked Shirt smiled. 'Come with us. Let's clear a few things up.' He swung his arm towards a doorway on the opposite side of the check-in desk. It was a casual gesture, his voice was soft and friendly, but this wasn't a request.

Mason nodded, sweat pricking at his forehead. He thought about running, but that would be futile. He'd be shot dead before he got halfway to the front doors. And in this part of Africa, where corruption and incompetence were rife, they could make his body disappear easily.

He needed to play along. Deny everything. He could still get out of here.

Checked Shirt led the way towards the pitted and pockmarked wooden door. Mason followed, the two officers crowding behind him. With one push on his back, he found himself in a cramped office. A window was open behind the desk, but it did little to cool the stifling African mid-day heat oozing inside.

Checked Shirt rounded the desk, sat down. He nodded to his colleagues. Mason glanced behind him at the two officers who stood shoulder to shoulder, blocking the doorway

One of them reached out and took Mason's hold-all from his hand.

'Empty your pockets, Mr Palmer,' Checked Shirt said.

Mason hesitated for a moment, eyeing his hold-all. Then he did as requested, rummaging in his cargo trousers for his wallet and mobile phone before placing them on the desk.

Checked Shirt took Mason's phone and handed it to the guard with the hold-all before nodding to the other guard, who roughly pulled Mason's arms upwards to pat him down. When he was satisfied Mason had nothing on his person, he stopped.

Another nod to the guards from Checked Shirt sent the uniformed men out of the room.

'*Sit*, Mr Palmer.' Checked Shirt indicated to the grey plastic chair on the opposite side of the desk.

Mason sat and placed his hands in his lap, trying to appear casual. He was used to working under pressure. This was no different, he told himself. Even so, his linen shirt stuck to the sweat on his neck, and he edged a finger under the collar to loosen it. He swallowed down the lump in his throat and tried to ignore the rising panic. 'I'm sorry, but I have no idea what this is about.'

The man sat back in his chair, interlaced his fingers and placed them on his stomach. The friendly, amiable smile was still in place. 'Let's stop with the pretence, shall we? I know it was you. I know you were there. And I know what you did.'

'I really don't have a clue what you're talking about.' Mason shook his head.

Checked Shirt sighed gently, as if Mason was an errant school child and he really didn't want to discipline him. 'What equipment do you have?'

'Equipment? I don't have any. All my equipment is at the hospital.' His gaze drifted to the open window. Beyond that was bush land, a small one-lane dusty track that led to the town of Lagossa, to the makeshift hospital, to escape.

'I have your phone, but do you have a tablet, video recorder, laptop?' Checked Shirt asked. 'They will find it in your bag anyway.'

'There's a laptop and video recorder. In my bag. But I really don't know what–'

'Are there copies anywhere?'

Mason gave a laugh of disbelief and thought it sounded convincing to his ears. 'Copies of what? I think you must've mistaken me for a journalist. I'm a doctor here. I work for Health International, an NGO who–'

Checked Shirt held a hand up to silence Mason, staring at him like a snake eyeing up a mouse. 'I know who you are.' He leaned forward, elbows on the desk, his dark brown eyes boring into Mason's. 'This is what's going to happen. You will get on that plane, and you will leave Narumbe. You will never return to this country. And you will never speak of what you did or what you saw. You are being given a chance, Mr Palmer. But if you disobey these instructions, there will be consequences. Do you understand?'

Mason's heart rate hit treble figures. 'I really don't know–'

'Your wife Nicole is very pretty, isn't she?' He slowly licked his lips. 'If anything should happen to her, it would be a great shame. A very great shame. Don't you think?' He tilted his head, his voice still calm and soft, the smile still in place, which made the threat even scarier for Mason.

Mason closed his eyes for a moment, picturing his wife, fear rippling through him.

'Do you understand?' Checked Shirt asked.

Mason opened his eyes. 'Yes, I understand.'

The door opened behind them. One officer walked towards the desk and placed Mason's hold-all on it before nodding at Checked Shirt.

Checked Shirt stood and handed Mason the bag. 'I'm glad you see sense. Now, let's go. You have a plane to catch.'

Mason took his bag and walked past the other officer now stationed outside the door. He took one look behind him and saw Checked Shirt sit back at the desk, a mobile phone to his ear. As he strode towards the glass door to the runway, the officers trailing behind him, he clenched his free hand into a fist to stop it from shaking. The place was eerily empty now, no sign of Adjoua or any staff, apart from the man outside still filling the plane with fuel.

Mason slipped through the door, the heat and sun burning his skin like acid, not daring to look behind him. He tried to breathe slowly, tried to calm his racing pulse as he walked up the steps to the plane.

When he got inside, he spotted the man and woman who were waiting in their seats, chatting softly. He sat in an empty seat in front of them and looked out of the window, towards the airport. Through the glass façade, he watched one of the police officers watching the plane. Mason glanced down and saw the man who was refuelling remove the pump from the plane and nod in the officer's direction. The officer nodded back, then turned around and walked away. Checked Shirt emerged from the office and the officer spoke with him, just a brief exchange before they headed to the front door of the airport building that led to the dusty track into town.

Mason wiped the sweat from his brow with the back of his hand, his mind racing.

One hour and ten minutes later, as the plane was flying over a dense area of bush, all radio communication with the plane was lost. It never arrived at its destination in Galao.

TEN MONTHS LATER...

Chapter 1

It was just an envelope. Brown, cheap, indistinguishable from any other. The kind used by millions of people every day. But the contents had the power to detonate shards of pain through my chest like an atomic bomb.

I almost didn't open it then. I scooped it up with the rest of the post on the door mat and brought it into the kitchen. A hundred things ran through my head as I dumped it on the worktop, then picked up my banana smoothie, downing the last of it. I needed to finish planning the World Explorers theme that would start next month, where my class of Year 1 children would learn about the continents and oceans. Then after half term, I'd have to prepare the next stage, learning about artists from around the world. I was thinking of getting them to study Van Gogh, Klee, Rothko, and Pollock.

That's what I did all the time, these days, think about work. Throwing myself into it like a mad woman stopped me from thinking about Mason and the empty house and the memories and hollowness left inside me. I practised a lot of denial. Maybe it wasn't healthy, but there you go. It was the only way to get me through the minutes and hours.

I glanced at the clock. Six forty-five am. I could be at the school by seven-fifteen, make a start on some new ideas for Phonics and PE. But I didn't leave the house. For some reason, I picked up the post.

I flicked through a white envelope – bank statement – a brown envelope – bill – white, with the name of a loan company on the front that I tossed into the bin without opening. Then I came to another brown one. Maybe it was the fact my name and address had been written in block capital letters that piqued my curiosity. Most of my mail had computer generated labels or window envelopes that showed my postal details.

I slipped my forefinger underneath the flap and ripped it open.

As I slid the photo out, it didn't really register what I was seeing initially. Yes, of course, I knew it was of my husband, but I couldn't comprehend what that meant for a moment.

It was in colour, printed on good quality paper, but those details barely registered at first.

I frowned, my heart slamming to a sudden stop. What the hell? Why would someone send me a photo of Mason?

But before I could even think of possible answers, my gaze was already drinking in the details. His hair was longer than I'd ever seen it before, curling up at the edges of his shirt collar. A beard covered a face that was thin and gaunt. He sat at an outside café table, holding a newspaper across his chest.

I brought the photo closer to my eyes, studied the name of the newspaper, read the date on it. Two days earlier. It felt like my brain was melting inside my head. That couldn't be right. Mason was dead.

I slumped down onto a chair, my legs suddenly refusing to hold me upright. The photo slid from my grasp and rested face up on the kitchen table. I leaned my elbows on the glass top and pressed my hands to my lips as a prickle of…I don't know – surprise, shock, incomprehension – danced over my scalp.

What was this? Someone's idea of a sick joke?

The more I stared, the more I noticed other things. It was obviously a selfie, his arm outstretched before him holding the phone. There were flecks of grey in his hair that had never been there before. Lines graced the corners of his eyes. He looked older, but…how could that be?

I tried to think of the rational possibilities of how someone could've got hold of this and sent it to me, but I couldn't make sense of it.

I licked my lips, my mouth dry, eyes wide and fixated on that piece of shiny paper.

Why would someone send this to me? For what purpose – to hurt me? I had no enemies that I knew of.

Tears welled in my eyes. The loss I'd been trying so hard to block out suddenly hit me again with all the force of a wrecking ball. If I was honest with myself, and I didn't like to be – hence the denial – I had to admit that the gaping hole he'd left in my life was still as fresh and tangible as the day I'd heard about the plane crash.

I wiped the tears away with the back of my trembling hand, trying to think why anyone would do this to me. Then I had another thought. Maybe there was a letter inside the envelope. Something that would explain what was going on.

I picked it up and swept my hand through its insides. Empty. I looked at the back of the envelope, hoping for a return address, but there was no writing there at all. It was postmarked Barcelona with yesterday's date.

I picked up the photo again and turned it over. On the back of it, someone had written a message.

"Everything stinks 'til it's finished."

I will contact you again soon. You mustn't tell anyone about this.

A shard of ice spiked my heart. It didn't make sense, unless you'd lived with Mason for ten years. Unless you knew the stupid private in-jokes and catch phrases and sayings that build up in a relationship that only you both know about.

I was catapulted back through time. It was our second wedding anniversary. We'd had a champagne breakfast – smoked salmon blinis, champagne, the works. A short while afterwards, we'd noticed the drains at the back of the house had completely blocked up and overflowed, leaving a disgusting mess on the patio. Horrified, I'd called a drain specialist to come out, but it was a bank holiday and they were backed up – literally – with jobs. Well, we couldn't just leave it there, stinking to high heaven, because we were going on holiday the next day. Not to mention all the bacteria multiplying on our paving slabs. So, we'd donned rubber gloves and grabbed a hosepipe and pieces of flexible plastic piping and got to work clearing the drains with equal parts disgust and laughter as we joked about it.

When we'd finally managed to unblock everything, he'd said to me in a mock serious voice, 'Everything stinks 'til it's finished.' It was a quote from Dr Seuss, an author we'd both loved as kids, which, of course, made me fall about laughing. And ever since that day, it was a quote that had stuck. Whenever we had a horrible job to do, or something wasn't going right, we'd said it to each other.

I stared at the photo again. Mason had sent it to me.

And yet, that was impossible.

Chapter 2

I parked in the staff car park at the front of the primary school where I taught, totally unable to recall the journey there. Too many thoughts had been crowding my head for me to take in the roads busy with rush-hour traffic.

I headed past the enrichment play area towards the front door and punched in the code to the keypad, just like I'd done a million times, but it beeped and a red light shone.

I tried again, getting it right this time. The door clicked, and I walked down the corridor, past the staffroom, to my classroom. I stepped inside, trying to think about what needed doing. Half of my brain was working on necessities. *What exercises shall I do for the warm up before gymnastics glass? I could do the beans again; the children love it when they have to act out Mexican or jumping beans.* The other half was on the photo and the message. Writing I recognised as Mason's, his messy, doctorly scrawl. Writing I'd seen hundreds of times on notes he'd given me, left at home when he was on shift at the hospital, birthday and Valentine's cards, writing that signed the register at our wedding eight years before.

A sob escaped my lips, and I placed my hand over my mouth to stifle it. This didn't make any sense. It was insane to think he'd sent it.

I sat in my chair behind my desk at the front of the classroom and stared into thin air, my head spinning. What was I supposed to do about it? Was someone just playing a nasty joke? Was this the start of someone harassing me? Or would he send another message soon?

No, of course there would be no message. Mason was *dead.*

But they never found the plane, a voice in my head repeated.

So what? another voice said. *If he was alive, where has he been for the last ten months?* And why was he only contacting me now? Why all this mystery? No. If Mason was alive, he'd have called me. He would've come home.

I took my laptop from my messenger bag and placed it on my desk, booting it up and chewing on my thumbnail.

I typed in *plane crash Narumbe.*

It only brought up fifteen hits, which contained the brief report I'd read after the crash had happened and was simply repeated verbatim in various online newspapers. It was hardly big news internationally, and I assumed it was simply a repeat of the official statement the Narumbean government had put out.

Four people are presumed dead after a Piper Cherokee light aircraft is believed to have crashed in dense jungle on Friday. The plane had left the rural airport at Lagossa and was en route to the capital of Galao when it disappeared from GPS tracking systems and radio contact was lost. Authorities do not believe there are any survivors.

At this time, the government does not consider it safe to attempt to locate and recover the wreckage due to an uprising of rebel militia in the immediate area…

There were no new articles. No reports telling me the plane had been found. Nothing that mentioned some miraculous news of survivors who'd suddenly appeared. And besides, if there was any breaking information, surely the Narumbean authorities would've been in contact with me.

I sat back in the chair and stared at the screen blankly, paralysed with shock.

A knock sounded on my door before Cheryl opened it and walked in, holding two mugs of coffee. Her curly grey hair was loose over her shoulders. She wore a flowing flowery skirt, a loose chambray blouse and Birkenstocks, looking more like an aging hippie than a Head Mistress. Cheryl wasn't just my boss, she was also a good friend. Even though she was twenty years older than me, we'd hit it off as soon as I'd started working here fifteen years ago.

'Morning.' She grinned, then gave me an odd look. 'Are you okay? You look like you've seen a ghost.'

I just stared at her, my mouth half hanging open. A ghost. Yes. Cheryl didn't know how spot on she was. But a ghost couldn't write messages and send photos.

She walked towards my desk and put one mug down in front of me. 'I saw you rushing past the staff room and thought you'd want this.'

'Yeah. Um…thanks.' I made no move to take it. My hands were trembling so much, I'd have had trouble picking it up, even if I wanted to.

She frowned, the lines on her forehead increasing. 'What's wrong? Are you not feeling well?'

'Um…' I thought about telling her what had happened. But the message stabbed at my brain. *You mustn't tell anyone about this.*

The words evaporated in my mouth.

She came around the desk and looked at the laptop, seeing the old news reports. Crouching over me, she put her arm around me. 'I'm so sorry, my dear. I know some days must be harder than others.'

I let her hug me from her awkwardly bent position, not knowing what to say, letting her think it was just a case of grief hitting me again.

I would've cried if I wasn't so stunned by it all. The smoothie I'd had earlier churned threateningly in my stomach.

She pulled back, her eyes scanning my face with sympathy. 'Do you want to take the day off? I can cover your classes.'

I shook my head. 'There's so much to do. And we've got parents' evening tonight. I need to be here for that. I need to…' I trailed off, my gaze straying to the headlines on the screen.

She sat on the edge of my desk. 'Yes, but maybe you just need a bit of time out. I mean, you were back at work a couple of weeks after his death. I know you felt like it would help you stop thinking about things, but maybe it was too soon. It's like you've been on a mission to just keep going, and there's bound to be some moments when you step back and everything catches up with you.'

I loved teaching, loved my kids, loved helping them learn and grow, hopefully giving them the building blocks of tools that would turn them into good, happy individuals. But she was right. I had poured everything I had into work to stop myself falling. It was the only crutch I had to keep me upright.

'Seriously, I can cover everything. Go home, take some *you* time. This'll all be here tomorrow. You need to help yourself first before you help other people.'

'Yes, but I need to set up for the parents' evening later. I need to–'

'I'll do it.' She leaned in conspiratorially. 'And it won't hurt the children not to stick to a teaching plan for one day. We'll do some art projects. Read. It will be fun. And actually, you'd be doing me favour. I've been too busy with appraisals and budgets to get in the classroom for a long time. I miss it.'

I hesitated for a moment. I knew it would be impossible to concentrate on anything properly after this.

She put her hand on my shoulder and bent her head to look me square in the eyes. 'You don't have to deal with everything on your own.'

I nodded. Knew she was right. 'Okay, just one day off. But I'll be back at six-thirty for parents' evening.'

'That's settled, then. I'll see you later.' She took my hand and pulled me up gently, turned me around, hands on my shoulders, and walked me towards the door.

'Thank you,' I said.

'It's nothing. And if you need to talk, you know I'm always here.'

In the past ten months, I'd never cried on her shoulder, even in my darkest moments. I'd never rambled on about Mason and how unfair life was and how much I missed him. I kept things inside and let them fester away – I always had, ever since I was a kid. I found it hard to open up and bare my soul to people, even to Cheryl, my one genuine friend who I knew had my back. And this was something I definitely couldn't tell her.

Not until I knew what the hell was going on.

Chapter 3

I drove back home again in a blur. Of course this wasn't real. It was out-of-this-world-crazy for me to believe Mason was alive and had sent that photo to me. Someone was indeed playing a cruel, twisted prank. But the irrational part of my brain ignored all that, and a kernel of hope blossomed inside.

I sat at the kitchen table in the same spot I'd been in earlier and pulled the photograph from my bag, stared at it.

At the top of the right-hand frame was the edge of an awning that displayed the café's name which I hadn't noticed before because I'd been too busy looking at Mason. It read *Cafelito*, and I knew the place. I'd been there before with Mason during a long weekend break to Barcelona about five years ago, before everything had started its downward trajectory. We'd sat there several times, eating tapas and crepes. We'd people-watched from the bistro tables outside and laughed and held hands and drank wine at lunchtime before going back to the hotel to have sex. We'd walked the city, taking in the sites, shopped, laughed.

I picked up the photo again and stared. What was happening? And why didn't he just come to the house if he was alive? Why not call from wherever he'd been for the last ten months? Perhaps he'd been in hospital in Africa, pulled from the wreckage of the plane in a remote area of the bush with no phones or internet.

Well, how did he manage to take a selfie and send it through the post? And how did he get to Barcelona?

Nothing made sense. I looked at the name of the newspaper he was holding – *The Independent* – and read the headline: *Egypt's Deadliest Terror Attack at Mosque*. I pulled up their website, assuming the photo had to be a fake.

I chewed on my lip then gasped when I saw the exact same headline on the online version of the newspaper.

So...think...what's going on?

At some point, Mason had survived the plane crash and gone to Barcelona?

Never mind the *how.* The question I couldn't shake was *why. Why* hadn't he contacted me until now?

I stood and paced the floor, chewing on a thumbnail, trying to make sense of something so senseless. Part of me felt an overwhelming anger. How could he do this to me? Let me think he was dead. What kind of person did that to their spouse?

Yes, things had been difficult between us. The four years of fertility treatment and IVF had taken their toll on both of us. We'd grown distant, and that was my fault. In the end, I'd pushed him away. I'd been in a bad place back then. The all-consuming need for a baby had turned my love for him into something not quite hatred, but more like blame...anger. Although it was myself I really blamed, but I took it out on him. My whole life I'd never believed I was good enough. And not being able to give Mason the child he wanted didn't just compound that thought again, it was the last straw for me.

When the treatment had failed again and again, the tsunami of emotions that are so hard to explain to someone who's never experienced infertility – all the agonising dashed prayers, the death of dreams, the raw hopelessness – were all heaped on his shoulders from me. I knew I was turning into someone I didn't recognise, someone I didn't even like. Although he'd been supportive at first, I'd turned my back on him. I couldn't explain what was going on inside me because I didn't understand it myself. Even at the height of my desperate need for a child, I knew I was becoming increasingly irrational and horrible to be around, but I was still powerless to stop it. I'd felt he could never really understand me anymore because he wasn't a woman. He was a man who could compartmentalise. Who could take a step back and say that it wasn't meant to be and move on with his life. I should've been able to do the same, but I couldn't. Again, I'd dived into work instead. Concentrated on the children I *could* have every day. I'd pushed him away. And instead of leaving me, he'd done the same, searching for a new job far from Addenbrooke's Hospital where he worked as a general surgeon. He'd taken a job with Health International, an NGO who provided health aid to victims of war and natural disasters. He came home for R and R for two weeks out of every five, and he thought the time apart would do us good. Maybe he hadn't wanted to admit it to me either, but I think he'd felt desperate to escape what I'd become, and that the challenge would make him feel alive again. Instead, it killed him. Literally. Or so I thought.

He was right, of course. We'd needed a break. I think he was hoping it would give me time to work through my own feelings without him, because I was the only one who could help me, and he'd felt powerless to help me himself. So, he'd stepped away from the mess our personal lives had become and thrown himself into the new job in Narumbe.

At the time, I would've preferred it if he'd just left me, but as the months went by, the distance and space started to heal me. I began to realise how much I missed him. How messed up I'd become in my quest for a baby. How I still had something important in my life – him – and I had to let my dreams wither and die if I wanted to hold everything together. In the recent months before his death, our relationship had slowly started to improve. We'd begun to find *us* in all of it again. So there had to be good reason why he hadn't contacted me until now, because no matter how bad things had got between us, Mason wasn't a cruel person. He'd never have put me through the last ten months believing he was dead on purpose. And he'd never left me when he could've easily walked away for good.

As bizarre as it seemed, the photo and message all pointed to Mason still being alive. And I couldn't just sit here and wait for him to contact me again. No. I'd go mad in the meantime.

I thought about calling Cheryl and telling her what had happened, but Mason's words permeated my head again.

You mustn't tell anyone about this.

I still didn't understand what had happened, what was happening now, but somehow, I had to try to find out.

Chapter 4

Moussa Damba sat back in his softly padded chair and sucked on the Gurkha His Majesty's Reserve cigar. He exhaled a cloud of blue-grey smoke out slowly, savouring the taste. Each cigar had a price tag of $750, containing aged tobacco – eighteen years old. And they said Africa was a backward country! You could get anything here for a price.

He surveyed the plush garden in front of him from the cover of his veranda and took a sip of cognac. Finest Louis XIII de Rémy Martin, of course. He liked the fine things in life. Maybe he'd sold his soul to the devil, but the devil paid well. He almost laughed at his own joke but settled for a wide grin instead. His life was good. Everything was going to plan.

He'd had a privileged background. His family was very well off; his father a lawyer, his mother a teacher, and they'd lived in a plush area of Galao – commonly referred to as the Paris of Africa – with its five-star hotels, fine restaurants, designer shops and luxurious properties. Miles away from the slums and shanties in the north of the country. But he'd always been strong-willed. As a child, he constantly found himself getting into trouble. Stealing, bullying the other children, it was all a buzz to him. When his father had insisted he join the police force to curb his increasingly criminal behaviour, he laughed in his face. Moussa didn't like being told what to do, following orders. He liked to be the one in control. But as the job progressed, he realised that the benefits that came with it were better than wasting time with petty crime. He made more money in bribes than he ever did selling stolen goods. And as he'd worked his way up, the power of his position was the most intoxicating thing in the world.

Like an addict, he craved more of it. He could do exactly as he pleased, and it was all legal.

He was now head of the secret police and the president's right-hand man. The fixer. The adviser. But the president was getting fat and lazy and greedy, and Moussa had always been cunning. He'd learned over the years that time and patience were the keys to getting what you wanted. He glanced at the garden again. Cultivation, that was the word he was looking for. You cultivated power and opportunity, just like plants and seeds. And it was *his* time now.

His ruminations were annoyingly interrupted by the arrival of Chief Inspector Bakari Sumano. As the second highest in command of the secret police, Sumano would usually be a force to be reckoned with. But Sumano didn't work for President Koffi. Not anymore. Sumano worked for him. Cultivation, see? And when the moment was ripe for plucking, President Koffi would be ousted, killed, and Moussa would take over the country. He'd insert himself in the top spot, and everyone would be begging for it to happen.

Sumano stood in his full uniform, a sheen of sweat from the relentless heat covering his forehead. 'We have a problem, sir.'

Moussa drank the final dregs of his cognac and held his glass up in the air. His maid, Fanta, was hovering, as always, in the background, ready to do Moussa's bidding. She was young, pretty. Grateful. And so she should be. Working for him was as far as she'd ever get in this life. She should consider it an honour.

He waited until she'd refilled his cognac before turning to Sumano and smiling. 'Problems are just a challenge waiting to happen.'

'The plane crash.'

'What about it?'

'Our rebels found it. In the middle of dense bush.'

'So? It's too late to save them now.' Moussa threw back his head and laughed.

Sumano cleared his throat. Looked at the cognac longingly. He'd be lucky to get some of it. Moussa didn't like to share with anyone.

When it was obvious Sumano hadn't told his boss everything he'd wanted to say, Moussa snapped, 'Get on with it.'

'When the plane went down, it stayed almost intact. The bodies were still inside, strapped into the seats.'

'And why do I care about this?' Moussa was bored with this conversation already. He stared at Fanta, wanting to hear her beg again like last night. He licked his lips with anticipation.

'Because there were only two passengers on the plane,'

Moussa looked up at Sumano sharply, frowning. 'What?'

'The English man. Mason Palmer. He was not on the plane.'

'That's not possible!' Moussa shot out of his chair and stood face to face with Sumano. Although Sumano towered over Moussa, he shrank noticeably with fear. Even if Sumano hadn't witnessed first-hand some of the things Moussa had done, his reputation alone was enough to reduce even the biggest man to a shrinking, quivering wreck. No one wanted Moussa's attention focused on themselves for too long. 'You saw him get on the plane, didn't you?'

Sumano swallowed hard. 'Yes, sir.'

'So…' Moussa was thinking. His reptilian mind was always thinking. Life was like a chess game. It paid to be one step ahead of everyone else. 'A predator took his remains – leopard or lion.'

Sumano shook his head. 'There was no trace of him. No trace of any of his bones, and both the other bodies are still there. A predator hasn't found them yet. And there was no sign of his luggage. He wasn't on the plane.'

Moussa's eyes bulged from his head. 'So, where the hell did he go?'

Sumano swallowed nervously. 'I don't know.'

'Well, find out what happened to him! We cannot risk this coming out. Not now, not when I'm so close. Do you understand?' His usually calm façade began to crack. Everything he'd worked towards, every goal he'd had, could be ruined if they didn't find Mason Palmer.

Chapter 5

I walked towards Palmer's Travel Agent on the High Street in Haverhill. Mason's younger brother had started the business fifteen years ago, and although it had done well initially, he was barely hanging on these days. The internet had been good for many things, but booking holidays and flights online had almost killed Aiden's livelihood.

I stepped inside and saw Aiden at his desk at the far end of the narrow shop, speaking on the phone. Although he was the owner, he'd had to lay off two staff in recent years, so he did everything with the help of Mel, who'd been with him since the beginning.

Mel was at her desk, chatting to a couple seated in front of her about the Maldives, her pen waving around in the air animatedly. She smiled at me and turned back to her clients.

Aiden had a tense expression on his face that changed when he saw me. If you didn't know they were brothers, you'd never have put Mason and Aiden together as siblings. Where Mason was tall and slim built, Aiden was short and overweight. Mason had a full head of thick hair and Aiden's had been receding since his early twenties. Mason was olive-skinned and brown-eyed, Aiden was blond with blue eyes.

Aiden grinned and indicated the chair in front of him with a sweep of his hand.

I sat and fidgeted with my hands until he'd finished his call.

He hung up then came around to my side of the desk, hugged me. 'Nice to see you, Nicole. Sorry about that. I'm just sorting out last minute arrangements for a two-day travel conference I'm going to tomorrow in London. Fingers crossed it will bring in some much-needed business.' He raised his eyebrows with hope.

'Anyway, enough of me.' He smiled. 'Have you got a day off work today?'

'No, I…' I'd rehearsed my lines on the way over here. I couldn't be specific. Couldn't come right out and say, *I think Mason is alive.* I would sound insane for starters, and Mason's warning still reverberated in my head. 'Um…' I glanced towards Mel, who was still engrossed in her conversation. Back to Aiden. I licked my lips. 'Look, I've been thinking about things, and…can you tell me again what happened when you went out to Narumbe after the plane crash?' When we'd heard the news, I'd been too distraught to go out there and speak to the government officials myself and sort out the death certificate. Aiden had been kind enough to go on my behalf, but they hadn't had much information to give him. Mason had got on the plane. The plane had crashed due to what they said was a bird strike and subsequent engine failure. It had never been found. Still…if Mason was alive, had they lied to us? And if so, why?

He sat down, his forehead pinched with a worried frown. 'Are you sure you want to go over this?'

'Yes. It's just that we didn't really talk about it at the time.'

'You didn't want to talk about it,' he said, but his tone wasn't unkind. It was true.

'I know.' You see, this is what I mean about blocking and denial. 'But I need to know what happened out there. What they told you. I think…I think I'm ready to hear it now.'

'Okay. Let's go in the back.' He stood and led me along a tight corridor. To the right was his office, to the left a small kitchen that he walked into. 'Do you want a tea or coffee?' He opened a cupboard and poked his finger around some boxes of tea. 'I've got PG or some weird herbal concoction Mel likes.'

'No, I'm fine, thanks.'

He closed the cupboard and sat down at a small plastic table along one wall. I sat opposite.

Aiden clasped his hands together and looked down at them. 'When I went out to Narumbe, I met with a government official.

I can't remember his name now. Mossy, or...something like that. He took me out to the medical centre and the airport at Lagossa, because I wanted to see where Mason had been. And he said that's where Mason had taken the flight from. The plane took off with no problems. He said it had been checked beforehand by the pilot, and everything was fine. And then...' He rubbed his hand across his forehead and looked up at me. 'About an hour into the journey, just as they were over a dense area of jungle, the pilot said they were being attacked by a bird strike, and shortly afterwards, radio contact with the plane stopped suddenly. He said it must've been a freak accident. A swarm of birds had flown into the engine.'

I chewed on my lip. 'Right.'

'He also said they couldn't look for the wreckage. It was too dangerous to go out to that part of the country because the area was used as a base for the rebels who wanted to overthrow the government.'

I nodded slowly. The rebel militia and fighting were the reason Mason was there in the first place. His first posting for Health International had been just after the trouble started, and reports came pouring in of villages being massacred and set fire to, innocent people being raped and murdered. He'd been tasked with setting up a medical centre in the north of the country for all the casualties.

I leaned my elbows on the table. 'But if they never found the plane...it's possible that...I mean, how do they know it actually crashed? Or, if it did crash, how do they know there weren't any survivors?'

He looked at me with sympathy. 'Because it was in the middle of nowhere. I saw a satellite map of the area where the plane lost contact. It was all thick trees and bush for miles on end. If anyone managed to survive, which would've been highly unlikely, they would've been killed by the rebels or eaten by a lion or died of dehydration before they made it to the nearest village.'

'Is that what they told you?'

'Well, yes.' He shrugged helplessly. 'It stands to reason, I suppose. Anyway, they issued a death certificate because they were certain everyone on board had been killed. They wouldn't have done that otherwise, would they?'

The Narumbean authorities had declared Mason and the other people on board the plane as legally dead in absentia of their bodies, because the circumstances surrounding their disappearance overwhelmingly supported the belief that they couldn't have survived the crash.

Even though I wanted desperately to tell Aiden about the photo and message, I couldn't go against Mason's warning. But somehow, Mason must have walked out of that jungle alive.

Then I had a thought. After the plane crashed, I'd been in contact with Pam and Eric Long, the parents of Susan and Jeff Long, a brother and sister who were also on the plane and had been backpacking around Africa during their gap year until the trouble in Narumbe got so bad, they decided they were going to move on to Botswana. Pam and Eric were the only ones who knew what I was going through, and we'd corresponded for a while via email and phone, trying to support each other through our mutual grief. If there were survivors, surely they would've heard something. I had to call them. Find out if they were aware of anything new.

Aiden reached out and took my hand in his, ripping me away from my hundred-mile-an-hour thoughts. He gave me a solemn smile. 'I know it's going to be the anniversary soon. Do you want to think about doing something?'

Mason hadn't yet had a funeral. There were no remains to repatriate, nothing tangible to put to rest, and maybe that had made my blocking and denial easier. I'd had a small memorial service in the New Forest, a place Mason and I had both loved. When we'd been talking once about what we wanted the other to do when we died, I'd always said I wanted to be cremated and my ashes scattered in the sea. Mason had opted for cremation and a scattering of his ashes in the New Forest. It was where he'd proposed to me. I'd also planted a tree in our back garden, a symbol I thought showed life springing from death. But I'd never given Mason a proper goodbye. Mostly because I didn't want to admit it was final. And maybe, now, it wasn't.

'We could do another memorial service or something?' Aiden suggested.

'No,' I said. It came out too sharply. 'Look, is there anything you're not telling me?'

Aiden looked at me oddly. 'Like what?'

Like Mason is still alive. Like somehow you know about it too?

I studied his face to see if he was hiding something, but it just seemed full of concern, not deceit.

'Are you okay?' he asked.

I hated that question. People had been asking it for the last ten months. But I took a breath, tried to smile. 'Yes, I'm okay.' I stood up abruptly.

Aiden stood, too, smoothed down his tie. 'I know it's not easy. It hasn't been easy for me, either. But…have you thought about having a break? I could book somewhere for you. A holiday to get away from things. Mates rates.' He smiled. 'Since it happened, you've just thrown yourself into work and…you know, maybe you're burning yourself out.'

'Thank you, but I'm okay. Really. I just need to…' I pointed towards the door vaguely. 'I'm just going to go home. Relax. Read a book or something.'

'All right. But let me know if you change your mind.'

I hugged him and left, my mind already distracted by the next thing I needed to do.

Chapter 6

I pulled onto my driveway and hurried from the car. Once inside, I found my Filofax in the kitchen drawer, flicked through it until I found the mobile number for Pam Long.

The phone rang loudly in my ear as the international dialling tone kicked in. The Longs were British but had retired to France a few years back. I paced the floor, impatiently waiting for her to pick up.

'Hi, Nicole,' she said, her voice sounding brighter than the last time I'd spoken to her two months ago. 'How are you doing?'

'Um…not so good at the moment, really.'

'I know what you mean. Some days, it hits you really bad, doesn't it? Just when you think things are finally getting easier.'

'Yes. But, listen…have you heard anything recently from officials in Narumbe?'

There was a moment's pause before Pam asked in a surprised voice, 'Like what, love?'

Like your daughter and son are still alive?

'Just…any new information. I mean, have you heard that they found the plane or if there were…' I was about to say, "any survivors", but stopped myself just in time.

'No, we haven't heard a thing. We're not expecting to, really. When we went out to Narumbe to speak with officials, they said it was too dangerous to try to recover the bodies because of the rebels. And the situation out there is a lot worse now, apparently.'

'I know, but I just thought, maybe…' I exhaled with frustration. It was obvious they hadn't heard from Susan or Jeff. Of course not. 'I'm sorry. It's nothing,' I said. 'I'm just being stupid.' 'If I do hear anything, of course you'll be the first person I call. I want to bring them back home, too. Have a proper burial, as I'm sure you do.'

'Yes. Look, I've got to go. Sorry to bother you.'

'You're not a bother, love. Any time you need to talk, you're always welcome to call, you know that.'

I thanked her again and hung up. There was one other thing I could try. *If* Mason had been still alive all this time, then it meant he'd survived the crash. It sounded impossible, but I wouldn't accept defeat yet. There had to be a logical reason for everything. What that reason was was totally escaping me. But maybe his boss knew.

Isabelle Moore was the director of Health International. I'd met her only once, when Mason and I had been invited to a cocktail party at her house when he was home for New Year. The next time we'd spoken via phone was when she'd sent her condolences and told me she was doing everything possible to find out what had happened in Narumbe, followed by her extending an invitation for me to go out there and speak with the government officials, if I wanted to. I'd passed that responsibility onto Aiden.

I flicked the pages of my Filofax and found her contact numbers. Health International's head office was in London, and I tried her direct office line first.

'Isabelle Moore,' she answered with a cultivated, soft voice.

'Hi, Isabelle, this is Nicole Palmer.'

'Oh, hello, Nicole. How are you?'

'I'm fine, thanks.' Which was obviously a lie. I was in turmoil. Everything I thought I knew had turned upside down in the space of a few hours. Before she could say anything else, I asked, 'Have you heard anything from Narumbe recently?'

'No. I'm afraid not. Unfortunately, it doesn't look likely we'll be able to recover Mason's remains in the near future. The rebel uprising appears to be getting worse.'

'But it's possible there could've been survivors, isn't it? How do they know unless they find the wreckage?'

She paused for a moment, and when she spoke, there was sympathy in her voice. 'I'm sorry, Nicole, but no one could've survived that crash. My contact out there says the plane would've been crushed.'

'Can I speak to them? Your contact? Can you give me their number?'

'Well…yes, I suppose so. But…are you sure you want to put yourself through this? I don't want to sound harsh, but Mason is dead, Nicole. Maybe it would be best for you to try to move on.'

It did sound harsh to me. When I'd met her, she'd come across as direct and quite blunt, even. Then again, in the position she held, I guessed she was used to getting terrible news about death on a daily basis, maybe talking about it so dispassionately was her way of blocking it out. She had to be cold. Couldn't get through her working days without being so.

'I just need the number. Please.'

'Okay. Hold on a moment.' I pictured her scrolling through her phone as the seconds turned into a minute,

'Do you have a pen?' she said, finally getting back to me.

'Yes.'

'It's a mobile number.' She read it out.

I scribbled it down. 'Thank you.'

'His name is Adama. He worked closely with Mason, setting up the medical centre, getting government permissions, organising supplies. Adama is a great help to us in making sure things run smoothly at the centre.'

'Thanks. Um…did Mason ever mention anything…any problems of any kind?'

'Problems?' She sighed softly. 'We go into war-torn countries and deal with horrific things on a daily basis. There are always problems.'

'Yes, I understand that. But did he ever say anything…I don't know…' I cast around for the right words to say without giving any of my suspicions away. 'Did he ever mention anything specific?'

'No, of course not.'

'When did you last speak to Mason before the crash?'

'Well, let me think now…we didn't speak on day-to-day matters. Mason was managing the centre successfully, and there were no problems with any staff. Adama was assisting us on the ground. It must've been at some point in the first week of his shift when he gave me a progress report.'

I tried to think of Mason's colleague's name, the other doctor who was in charge when Mason came home on leave, but I only remembered the first name. 'Do you also have a phone number for Jean-Luc? I'm sorry, I can't remember his surname.'

'Jean-Luc Martin? Yes, of course.'

Another interminable pause. And then: 'Here we are.'

I wrote that down too, thanked Isabelle and hung up.

I dialled Jean-Luc first. There was no answer, which didn't surprise me. He would be working in the makeshift medical centre that Mason had set up, probably rushed off his feet, inundated with sights and situations that Mason had described to me during his rest periods but which I'd tried to blank out because they were so atrocious. I left a message on his voicemail and called Adama. Again, there was no answer, and no facility this time to leave a message. I saved both numbers to my phone and then stared at it, willing it to ring back. I couldn't keep still as I waited, but at the same time, I couldn't concentrate on anything. I needed to do something physical to get rid of the nervous energy surging through me. My chest was so tight and my heart kept fluttering irregularly. If I sat there and did nothing, I'd either have a heart attack or go mad.

I changed into my running gear and tucked my phone into my pocket. Then I ran out of my cul-de-sac and down the hill, heading towards the main road in Linton. I did a loop of the village and tried to concentrate timing my breath to my footsteps pounding the road. In. Out. In. Out. I want to clear my mind in a kind of meditation, but it wasn't working. Instead, images of Mason flooded in, bloody and smashed up, crawling out of the mangled plane wreckage. But when I tried to picture what might've happened next, I drew a blank that made me want to scream.

I ran harder, until my lungs burned and my hamstrings cramped and I'd pushed myself to exhaustion. Then I walked the last leg home. When I got inside, I stretched out my calves, my pants of breath echoing around the lonely hallway. I was just about to do my quads when the phone rang in my pocket, making me jump.

I slid it out, and Jean-Luc's name flashed up on my screen.

'Hello, Jean-Luc. Thank you for calling me back,' I said breathlessly.

'Hello, Nicole? Is that you?' he asked in a heavy French accent. Although Health International was based in the UK, their medical staff came from all over the world. I'd never actually met him, although Mason had told me a lot about him during our phone calls or when he was home on leave. 'There is a delay on the line. These international calls, you know how they are. Especially out here. We might get cut off.'

'That's okay. I–'

'I'm sorry, I meant to call you before now and see how you were doing. And then we had a crisis here and time ran away with me and…anyway, I'm sorry. Mason was a very nice man. It was a big honour and privilege to work with him.'

'Thank you.' I stifled back a sob. 'Um…the reason I'm calling…I just wanted to know…have you heard anything? About Mason?'

'No. What do you mean? About the crash?'

'Yes. Or, just anything.'

'The last thing I heard was that they wouldn't try to recover the plane because the rebels had taken over that area. Unfortunately, finding and repatriating three causalities isn't a priority out here at the moment with everything going on, and that area is unsafe.'

I blew out a disappointed breath. 'Did Mason ever speak about anything that happened out there? Anything that was bothering him or…I don't know.' The trouble was, I didn't know what to ask exactly because I didn't have a clue what was going on.

There was a static pause on the other end of the phone and then: 'Well, I was on leave for a week before he left. I got back the day before he was due to fly out on his own R and R. I barely had time to talk to him. There were a lot of casualties from a recent massacre in a village, and it was crazy around here.'

'Was there anything out of the ordinary that happened?'

He sighed. 'Sometimes, I think the whole world is out of the ordinary. When you see what we see on a daily basis…' He paused. 'What is this about?' His voice was gentle but concerned.

'I don't really know.' *I think he could still be alive. I think there's something wrong about what I've been told. Be careful, Nicole, don't give away too much.* 'Maybe it's just that things have been playing on my mind. It would be nice to hear what he'd been doing before…you know. In his last days.' I walked into the kitchen and looked at the photo sitting beside my laptop. Swallowed. Took a breath.

'I don't think I can really help you. Like I said, I was only there the day before he left and it was very busy.'

'Yes, of course. Well…thank you for your time.'

'Have you spoken to Adama? He was close to Mason. Closer than me, I'm sorry to say now. They were good friends.'

'I've tried to call him, but I'll try again.'

'Okay. Good. Well…'

'Yes, thanks again.'

I hung up and sank to the chair at the kitchen table, the kernel of hope I'd had catching fire and combusting into dust.

No one could've survived the plane crash. It was a light aircraft, nothing more than thin metal. It was confirmed that the plane was flying at 8,000 feet. Mason and everyone on board would've been crushed to smithereens when it went down. They were all dead, just like we'd been told.

And someone was playing a twisted joke on me. That had to be the only logical explanation.

Chapter 7

It seemed that all the grief I'd been holding at bay for ten months unleashed, like a dam exploding. It was a jolt so powerful and painful, I could barely breathe. All I could do was let it out in loud, shoulder-shaking sobs.

I don't know how long I sat and cried for, but sometime later, my mobile rang, startling me out of my sobs. It was Cheryl.

'Hello, dear,' she said. 'I was just checking on you. Seeing if you're up to parents' evening. I can sit in for you, if you need some more time. The children's workbooks are in the office, aren't they?'

I took a deep breath and looked at the clock on the wall, realising parents' evening would be starting in less than an hour. I had to get a grip on myself. I couldn't let people down. 'Thanks, Cheryl, but I'll be okay. I'll be there.' My nose and eyes were swollen from crying, and it sounded as if I had a cold.

'If you're sure. I'll see you soon.'

I hurried up the stairs, into the master bedroom. I stripped off my clothes, stepped in the shower and scrubbed my tear-stained face under a blast of hot water as I tried to work out who would be so cruel as to play this kind of a twisted joke, but I could only come up with one person who might've had a grudge against me.

My primary school was situated in a mixed catchment area that included many kids in social housing with a high rate of unemployment and parents claiming benefits. Fights between children, and even the parents, were not unheard of. Many parents think their child can do no wrong, and discipline can sometimes be poor or nonexistent at home. Of course, dealing with this is a part of my job, one I liked to think of as a challenge, but sometimes, it can get out of hand. I'd had instances of certain parents becoming livid when I'd had to tell their child off and had become threatening or defensive when I'd tried to discuss their child's behaviour. There was one occasion three weeks ago when I'd had to speak to a single parent called Angela Taylor. Her son, Robbie, had picked up another child and thrown them on the ground, mimicking a martial arts film he'd seen. After disciplining him, I'd spoken to Angela because the other child could've been seriously injured, and, unsurprisingly, it had caused a huge disruption in class for the other kids. To say Angela wasn't happy with me would be an understatement. She wouldn't accept Robbie was in the wrong. *'Nah, my Robbie wouldn't do that', 'I don't believe you', 'You're lying about my son because of the other hoity toity lot you've got in your class! You're just picking on him'*, she'd said. And when I pressed on, she'd made excuses for him: *'They're just mucking about', 'It's what boys do', 'It's not like he's taking a knife to school, is it?'*. She said I should watch myself, because no one messed with her family, and even though the threat was only a casual, verbal warning, and I hadn't thought too much about it at the time or taken it particularly seriously, it took on a new importance now. It actually wasn't the first time Angela had threatened a member of staff. When Robbie was in the playground one day, he'd been told off by a teaching assistant for punching one of the girls in his year, and when Angela had been spoken to about it, she'd threatened to punch the teaching assistant as well. A week after that, the teaching assistant had received numerous silent phone calls at home, taxis and takeaways turning up that she'd never ordered, and finally, the piece de resistance had been a lump of dog excrement being put through her letterbox. Of course, talk in the staff room had pretty much agreed it was Angela harassing the poor woman, but nothing could ever be proven, and it stopped just as quickly as it had started.

Was this a way of Angela trying to get me back, though? There was only one way to find out and that was to ask her. Surprisingly, despite her hostility towards the staff in general, she always attended parents' evening, even if she was standoffish and defensive.

By the time I rushed into the assembly hall where the teachers' stations had been set up, I spotted Cheryl immediately. She was talking to a colleague in the corner.

I waved at them and walked to my table which had one chair for me placed behind it and two others on the opposite side. A pile of the children's workbooks was already stacked on top for me to show to parents. I wiped my sweaty forehead with the back of my hand and put my folder of student notes on the desk before slumping to the chair and staring into space, my mind racing.

Cheryl appeared in front of me. She placed her hands on the desk and leaned forward with a concerned frown pinching her forehead. I could see her take in my puffy eyes and blotchy face. 'How are you?'

I jerked my head up and tried to smile. 'I'm fine. Thanks.'

'You don't look fine.' She glanced around to make sure none of the other teachers milling around were in earshot. 'I can take over. I know your notes on the students will be meticulous, so it would be no bother for me.'

'No!' I said, sharper and louder than I intended. I took a breath. 'Sorry. No, it's all right, really.' I needed to get to the bottom of what was going on. If I was being threatened or stalked by a parent, I needed to find out and stop it before things escalated.

She considered me for a moment before her gaze wavered, and she nodded and smiled. 'Okay.'

The caretaker, Bob, called her name from the corner of the room. He wanted to bother her about a broken chair or something. Cheryl sighed towards me before rambling over to him.

I opened my folder and flicked through the notes I'd written up, trying to read them to refresh my memory, but my mind was a jumble of conflicting emotions and I couldn't concentrate.

A few minutes later, mums and dads filed into the hall and made their way to the respective teachers.

The mum of a sweet little girl called Emily was first to approach me. I took a deep breath, plastered a wobbly smile on my face and attempted to update her on Emily's progress, her targets to achieve the government's age-related expectations, and some targets for improving reading, writing and maths. Usually, I could reel a child's report off by heart, but I kept faltering and referring to my notes, and at one point, I even got Emily's name wrong. When I searched through the pile of workbooks to find her daughter's, the whole lot ended up falling to the floor with a loud *slap* that echoed in the large assembly hall. All eyes turned my way for a few moments before settling back to their own conversations.

My cheeks flushed red as I apologised, and Emily's mum helped me pick up all the books and rearrange them neatly on the desk.

'I'm sorry,' I said for what was probably the fifth time.

'It's okay.' She gave me a tight smile as if she couldn't believe this incompetent person was actually teaching her child.

My meeting with the next parent went a little better as I forced myself to concentrate. But during a conversation with the third parent, I was halfway through explaining how good her son was at art, when I spotted Angela enter the hall. It stopped me in mid-flow.

She was dressed in a short, tight skirt and low vest top that exposed a lot of cleavage and was more appropriate for a clubbing session than a parent-teacher evening, but it wasn't her clothes that held my attention; it was the sneer on her face as she stared at me.

I don't normally get flustered, even when I've got a class full of unruly five to six-year-olds, but still, I don't like confrontation and knew this could potentially be a big one. I snatched my gaze away from Angela as she started speaking to another parent and tried to ignore her loud high-pitched laugh that I was sure was meant to unnerve me.

I was just answering a few questions from the parent in front of me when Angela approached my desk, looking pointedly at her watch.

My heart did a double tap in my chest as the parent got up to leave, and Robbie's mum sat down with a force that slid the chair away from the desk.

I made myself breathe and smile, as if she wasn't bothering me in the slightest. 'Hello, Miss Taylor.'

'Mrs *Palmer.*' She nodded a reply, a sarcastic-sounding emphasis on my surname.

I didn't really know how to begin, so I decided to just dive right in. 'I'm sorry if we got off on the wrong foot regarding Robbie's behaviour with Callum.'

'Too right we did. You can't go round accusing my boy of hurting other kids when he didn't even do anything wrong. They were just playing.' She gave me a sullen look, sarcastic raised eyebrows and a shake of her head that reminded me of Robbie.

'I'm not going to go over that incident again. Both I and the school have followed procedures with you and Robbie about the matter, but…I did want to talk about something else. Did you send me something through the post in an attempt to try and upset me?'

'What?' Her eyebrows pitched higher.

I repeated myself. 'Did you send me something in the post because you're still angry about the incident involving Robbie?'

She snorted. 'Like what?'

I glanced around the room. Everyone was deep into their own conversations. 'A photo.'

'I don't have a clue what you're talking about.' She clicked her tongue against her teeth and rolled her eyes.

I studied her face, but I couldn't tell if she was lying or not. It had to be her, though. It was the only thing that made any sense.

'I'll have to report it as harassment, if you do it again,' I pressed on, knowing I should shut up and take this to Cheryl with my suspicions, make it official.

She rested her elbows on the desk and leaned so close I could smell both cigarette smoke and alcohol on her breath. 'First, you accuse my son of being violent and then you accuse me of harassment!' she shrieked, her loud voice causing others to look over. 'You've got a bloody cheek.'

'When I spoke to you about Robbie before, you said I should watch myself because no one messes with your family. Is sending me a personal photo that you knew would hurt me, your way of trying to get back at me? Are you doing this to punish me?' My own voice cracked higher.

'Right. That's it.' She stood up, slapping her hand on the desk. 'I want Robbie taken out of your class, right now. You've got no business accusing us of all sorts of rubbish,' she shouted, then looked around. 'Where's the head? I'm going to put in a complaint about you. Ah, there she is.' She swivelled round, one hand leaning on the front of the desk as Cheryl approached.

Cheryl cast a confused glance between me and Angela. 'Is everything okay?'

'No. It's not okay,' Angela barked out, swinging her forefinger in my direction. '*She's* accusing me of harassment. Who the fuck does she think she is? First, my Robbie, and now me. The stuck-up bitch!'

Everyone had stopped talking now and were staring openly at us.

Cheryl held her hands up in a placatory gesture. 'Angela, you need to calm down. Let's talk about this in my office, shall we? And please watch your language.'

'No. I will not *calm down*!' She put a hand on her hip and shook her head. 'I want Robbie taken out of *her* class immediately. She's got a grudge against him, and I'm not having that. I won't be sending him back to school until I hear he's got a new teacher. And if she doesn't stop picking on him, *I'll* be the one making accusations of harassment, do you hear?' And with that she stalked out of the room, her stilettos clacking loudly on the floor.

Then I burst into tears, my whole body shaking with a build up of adrenaline. It took a good few minutes for people to stop gawping and get back to their conversations.

In that time, Cheryl spoke softly to me, touching me on the shoulder. 'Come on, let's talk in private.' She walked towards the doorway, down the corridor and to her office.

I followed her inside, and she perched on the edge of her desk.

'What's going on?'

I wiped my face. 'God, I'm so embarrassed. Everyone just saw that.' I took a deep breath and tried to compose myself.

'Something bad must've happened with her, so what is it?'

'I don't even really understand it myself.' I paused. 'You remember the incident with Robbie a while back? After Angela was spoken to, she told me to watch my back? Well, I thought she might be harassing me, so I asked her about it.'

'Harassing you how?'

'I thought she might have sent me something in the post.'

'What was it?' A horrified look appeared on her face. 'Not dog shit again?'

I shook my head. Opened my mouth to speak. Shut it again when I remembered the warning. But then realised that if it *was* Angela who'd sent the photo, the warning was just telling me to be quiet so she could scare me and get away with a campaign of harassment against me. 'I think she sent me a photo of Mason, knowing it would upset me. I think she's still annoyed with me for punishing Robbie for what he did to Callum.' My words came out all jittery.

'Why didn't you come to me about it?'

'I don't know.' I threw my hands in the air, feeling myself choking up. 'I suppose I wanted to ask her directly before involving you. We both know it's not the first time she's done something like that. She denied it, anyway. And now I look like a lunatic.'

She rested her hands on my shoulder, her lips pressed together with sympathy. 'I agree it wasn't the best way to handle things, but this isn't like you, crying, losing control, raising your voice.' She paused. 'I think maybe it would be a good idea to take some more time off. You only took two weeks' compassionate leave after Mason's death. Why don't you take a further week or so? I can arrange for a supply teacher to come in. Then I can try and sort things out with Angela in the meantime and get everything calmed down.'

I shook my head and sniffed. 'I should be able to handle this without losing it.'

'But maybe you're not handling things as well as you thought. I'm not worried about dealing with Angela, but I am worried about you.' She tilted her head, watching me carefully, reached out and clutched my hand. 'Maybe it would be a good idea to speak to a grief counsellor.'

I opened my mouth to protest. It wouldn't help. Talking about Mason hurt like hell, which is why I refused to try any kind of counselling. Besides, healing came from within. Not from someone who had never met either him or me and couldn't really care less about us. It seemed too much effort to try to voice that to Cheryl so I shut my mouth again. Maybe Cheryl was right about one thing, though. The photo had swirled up a jumble of emotions that I'd tried so hard to bury. And obviously failed.

'Do you want to report the incident to the police? If it's the start of harassment, you should get it logged with them like we did before.'

'No. I…let's hope this is the end of it.'

'All right. Well, why don't you go home now? I'll cover for you here. And I don't want to see you at work for at least another week.'

'Okay.'

She smiled. 'I'll check in with you soon. And let me know if you get anything further sent to you. I'm here to support you, and you don't have to deal with this on your own.'

I nodded. 'I'm so sorry about all this.'

She hugged me before I left, and I drove home, still shaking. I was certain Angela was involved. And I knew how she'd done it now. There were photos of our Barcelona trip on Facebook. Mason didn't use social media, but I did, although I hadn't been on it since Mason had died. I couldn't handle seeing the photos of us together or other people's messages of concern and shock. I'd had enough of my own to deal with.

But Angela must've somehow got hold of a photo from Facebook and Photoshopped it. Made Mason look older, thinner, superimposed a recent newspaper on it. She must've somehow copied his writing too.

I parked on the driveway of my house and got out, looking around the quiet cul-de-sac in case Angela was waiting for me here, but there was no one around and all was quiet.

I fumbled with the key in the lock and pushed the door open, rushing into the kitchen and pouring a glass of red wine. I drank a big gulp, then opened the bi-folding doors that led to the patio and took the glass and my messenger bag outside. The recent unseasonable spring heatwave had made it too stiflingly hot to sit in the kitchen, and I needed some air.

I sat at the teak patio table and pulled the photo of Mason I'd been sent and my laptop from the bag. I took another swallow of wine before logging onto Facebook. After pulling up my page, I blinked back a fresh wave of tears as I saw the last posts on there, all the condolence messages from people. I took a deep breath. Held it. Exhaled slowly.

Okay, let's do this.

I clicked on my albums and brought up the Barcelona photos. Then I clicked through each one; me eating gelato on La Rambla, Mason sitting on the edge of a fountain in Placa Catalunya, me in the Gothic Quarter, him at a flamenco show, toasting up a glass of wine. The pain in my heart overwhelmed me, but I forced myself to keep looking. The answer must be here. There were fifty-five shots, but none were taken at *Cafelito*. I didn't remember ever seeing a photo of Mason taking a selfie in the past, either. He always thought they were ridiculous and made him too self-conscious. So how could Angela, or anyone else, have got hold of it and Photoshopped it if it didn't even exist?

I picked up the photo I'd been sent again and stared at it. The more I looked, the more I sensed the photo hadn't been manipulated. It looked so *real*. Mason was wearing a short-sleeved shirt and shorts, and in the background, there was a couple walking along the plaza in light spring clothes. We'd visited in December, when it was chilly and we'd worn jeans and winter coats and boots.

Back then, Mason didn't look like he did in this photo, either. I'd never seen him with a beard. Never seen his hair this long. He'd never been as thin as this in all the time I'd known him. There was no way this photo could belong to our trip.

And what about the cryptic message? Mason and I were the only people who could've possibly known that obscure Dr Seuss line was personal to us. I'd never told anyone, and I was pretty sure Mason wouldn't have; he'd always been private about our life, especially with what had been going on with the IVF causing problems between us.

I began to feel sick, for more reasons than one. I'd been utterly wrong to accuse Angela. The photo *was* real. And that could only mean one thing.

Mason really was alive and trying to contact me.

Chapter 8

Adama bowed to Allah, kneeling on the prayer mat inside his small home built of mud brick. He went through his usual ritual, reciting the prayer words he knew by heart. When he finished, he offered up a silent prayer of his own.

'Please let Allah save us from war. From poverty. From evil.'

But Adama was losing faith. Things were changing for the worse. His country was dying. *People* were dying or disappearing.

He blinked back the tears. He'd tried to do his best to help, but he was just one man in a small network of similar-minded friends. President Koffi was blinded by money. He was too wrapped up comfortably inside his palatial mansion to care about the destruction and devastation the rebels were causing. His money was guaranteed from high places. Narumbe had something the big men wanted and that wouldn't change, no matter who was in power.

Money and greed. The true root of all evil. While his brothers and sisters were living in poverty, President Koffi was being paid handsomely. Adama knew Moussa Damba was plotting a coup. Knew that the rebels were working for him in an effort to gain a foothold, ready to strike when the time was right. This country needed change desperately, but Moussa would not change anything. He was making promises he wouldn't keep. He'd slip right into the President's mansion and put his feet up on the coffee table as if he'd been there all along.

Adama stood and felt the hopelessness wash over him once again. He thought of the women arriving at the medical centre – raped, beaten, mutilated by the rebels. He thought of the children, missing, stolen. He thought of the men – murdered so they couldn't fight back and mess with Moussa's plan. And he thought again about the fat cats in the West, the ones who were really in control of Africa.

Life was painful. He didn't realise then just how painful it could be.

Forty minutes later, after his rickety door burst open and two members of the secret police came for him, after they'd blindfolded him and taken him to an unknown location, after he'd been forced into a chair, his arms and legs tied to it with thick rope, he realised true pain.

Adama trembled from head to toe behind the blindfold of material that scratched his skin. He breathed heavily through his mouth, trying to quell the fear burning inside the pit of his stomach.

There was no warning when the first blow struck him on the side of his head. A fist hit hard enough to knock him onto his side, the chair clattering on the floor beneath him, banging his shoulder against rough concrete. There was barely any time before he was hoisted up again and another blow hit him, this time from behind.

Adama's head flew forward onto his chest. 'No! Please, no! I haven't done anything.' He struggled violently against the rope.

The next strike sent pain erupting through his spine between his shoulder blades, like a firework against his skin, as his captors used a whip.

Adama pleaded and whimpered, but the whip rained down on his back, his arms, his torso, the crack against skin followed by Adama's shrieking cry of pain. But no one would ever hear him down there.

The officers whipped Adama until he was almost too far gone he couldn't cry out anymore. Then Moussa nodded at them to stop.

Adama's head lolled against his chest, saliva dripping from his chin, his body soaked with sweat and blood and racked with pain.

Moussa ripped off the blindfold, then leaned against the concrete wall opposite and crossed his arms casually over his chest. He watched Adama gulp in air and blink rapidly as his eyes adjusted to the searing white light from the spotlight rigged up above his head, glaring down at him.

'Where is Mason Palmer?' Moussa asked.

Adama sucked in the dusty, dry air. He tried to fight the pain ricocheting through his body, but it was no use. And he knew it would only get worse.

'I…I don't know what you mean. He died…in a plane crash.'

Moussa clicked his teeth with his tongue. 'Unfortunately not. And you are trying my patience. Where did you take Mason Palmer? We know he was not on that plane before it took off. It could only have been you that helped him.'

Adama thought back to that day. 'I don't…understand what you mean. I took him to the airport. As far as I knew he was on that plane. I am being honest, sir.'

'Did he give you what he took?'

Adama shook his head manically. 'He didn't give me anything. I don't know what you're talking about. Really, I have no idea.'

'But you were friends.'

'Not friends. Colleagues, maybe. I helped set up the medical centre.'

'Yes. I know all about you.' Moussa stepped away from the wall and walked closer to Adama. 'I know about your little *group*,' he hissed.

Adama let out a small whimper. 'I have no group. I am just one man.'

Moussa picked up a pair of rusty pliers from a table in the corner of the room. He stopped in front of Adama and attached the pliers to his right nipple, clenching down hard and twisting.

Adama let out a blood-curdling scream.

Moussa bent over so his face was inches from Adama's. 'If you tell me the truth, I will let you go. If you don't…well…I will rip off bits and pieces of you, one by one.'

Salty tears streamed down Adama's cheeks as he fought the sickening wave of hurt. He could tell Moussa everything he knew.

He could betray a trust, a friend, the children and his country, but he knew he was a dead man anyway. It was only a matter of time. He was utterly helpless and alone, and no one would come to his rescue. He just hoped he could endure the pain before they killed him.

'I don't know anything!' Adama cried out. 'I took him to the airport, and then I came home. I didn't see him again. I didn't know he wasn't on the plane. This is the truth.'

Moussa ripped off his nipple and held it up for Adama to see.

Adama panted hard, trying to brace himself against the new onslaught of agony.

'And what about his wife, hmmm? Does she know where he is? Has she been hiding him all this time?'

'I don't…I don't know his wife. I don't know what happened. He…must…he must've got on the plane.'

Moussa stood upright, bringing the pliers in front of his face, staring at Adama's nipple with fascination. 'Nothing will jeopardise my takeover of this country. Nothing will jeopardise the business interests of my country. You have one final chance to tell me. And if you do, I will treat you well. I will make sure you are rewarded. If not, you will disappear.' He clicked his fingers to signify it could happen in an instant. 'It is your choice. Everything is up to you.'

But Adama knew that choices were an illusion. He'd known that even as a little boy. 'I don't know anything,' Adama repeated quietly.

'Then you have made your choice.'

Chapter 9

I stared into space as I sat in the garden, thinking, wondering, hoping, waiting for Adama to call me back. I needed to find out if there really was something tangible that could prove Mason wasn't dead. Even though my heart had already accepted he was alive, my head was resisting the idea. There was still the possibility this was some kind of elaborately sick joke someone was playing.

My world tilted and shook as I picked up the photo again and stared at it, my fingertip tracing his face. And that's when I realised something important. If Mason was alive, he'd need money to live on. I'd always handled our joint bank accounts online, because Mason was too busy working long hospital shifts. I hadn't noticed any strange withdrawals in the last ten months, but then again, I had noticed much around me at all. I hadn't yet got around to cancelling his debit and credit cards, so it was possible he had used them without me knowing.

I put the photo down and called up our internet banking page on my laptop, my knee jittering up and down impatiently as I logged on and sipped more wine.

I clicked on "statements" and went back month-by-month from today's date, scrutinising the entries meticulously. There was the mortgage payment, buildings and contents insurance, direct debits for utilities, supermarket payments for groceries, many everyday payments. Nothing out of the ordinary. Nothing I hadn't paid for myself.

When I'd gone back ten months, to just before Mason had died, I saw some purchases he'd made. The deal with Health International was that Mason would use his credit card for any work and travel expenses and then claim them with a monthly expense report.

Something inside my chest squeezed tight as I read through the entries, picturing him at Heathrow Airport on the day he'd left to go to Narumbe via Paris for the last stint before the plane crash, buying a coffee in Starbucks, a sandwich from Pret A Manger. And then there was nothing for the three weeks he was in Narumbe. His accommodation and food were all paid for. But then something made me peer closer to the screen. Made me blink to refocus my eyes.

Dated two days before he was due to fly home for his R and R was an entry that read: *Cloudbox £99*. It was the only payment he'd made during his whole time in Narumbe.

Cloudbox? I had no idea what that was, but sometimes, companies weren't always listed on statements with the same name they used online. I thought back, my thumb and forefinger tugging at my lower lip, but it didn't mean anything to me.

I opened another tab and typed "Cloudbox" in the search bar. A website with the same name came up as the first hit. I clicked on it and it took me to the login page. I scanned the header banner and found an "About Us" link which took me to a blurb about Cloudbox being a technology company who built powerful tools for personal and business needs...whatever the hell that meant. But as I read further, at the sales pitch which said they had over 500 million customers who could use Cloudbox on any device, anywhere in the world, I realised what it was. A file hosting service that offered cloud storage and file synchronisation. Cheryl had been talking about using something similar at school for our documents so we'd never lose anything if our computers crashed.

This definitely wasn't something I'd paid for, so it had to have been Mason.

I went back to the home page of the website and typed his email address into the login bar. Then I typed in a generic password he favoured for online accounts.

A box reading, "Invalid email or password" popped up.

I tried another password of his I knew – our wedding date.

Same response.

I tried his email address with *Whiskey4* – the name of his first pet and our house number, another generic password he used.

Invalid email or password.

Damn.

I tried some more combinations, our wedding date with various versions of our names, but it still wouldn't let me in.

Next, I logged onto Yahoo Mail to retrieve his email account, because I definitely knew his password for that, and it was possible he'd been sent a joining email from Cloudbox and had kept it.

When I logged on, page upon page of spam and work-related unopened emails flooded the screen; adverts for equipment and pharmaceuticals, invitations to medical conferences. Ten month's worth of correspondence.

It took over two hours to go through everything, double-checking some, deleting others straight away if I could tell what they were from the subject line. But there was no email from Cloudbox. Nothing relevant that could tell me where Mason might've been for the last ten months.

Then I had a brainwave. I went back to the Cloudbox site and looked at the login again, realising I'd missed the words the first time that said, "Forgotten Your Password?"

I clicked on it. Typed in Mason's email address and clicked submit. Then I switched tabs and checked on his Yahoo Mail account.

A message that said, "Password resetting instructions from Cloudbox" had arrived.

I clicked on the link which took me to the Cloudbox login page again, set up a new password, and I was in.

It brought me to Mason's home page. I clicked on "Files", but there was nothing there.

I frowned at the screen. Why had he set up a cloud storage site, two days before he'd left Africa, but not added anything to it? Or had he added something and then deleted it?

I stared at the screen, chewing on my lower lip until I tasted blood. Then I picked up my phone and dialled Adama's number again. It rang with no reply, but it gave me another idea.

I logged onto Mason's mobile phone account, but because I'd cancelled his contract several months ago, it wouldn't let me in any longer. I had the same provider for my phone, so I rang and asked to speak to a supervisor. After an interminable wait, I explained that I needed copies of my husband's bills.

'Yes, we can do that. How far back do you need them for?'

I told them the month's span for the whole time he'd been working in Africa until I'd cancelled it.

'I can email them to you, but it might take a little while.'

'That would be really helpful, thank you.'

While I waited, I tried to piece things together. *If* Mason was still alive, what did that mean? He'd been rescued from the plane wreckage by some remote tribe and been recovering all this time? But if so, why the need for this kind of mysterious secrecy?

I tried Adama again. Still no reply.

Next, I went to our office desk in the lounge and opened up the folder where I kept personal documents, birth certificates, my passport, Mason's death certificate given to Aiden from the Narumbean government, and the letter I'd originally received from them about the crash. I read through it again...

Dear Mrs Palmer,

It is with regret that I must inform you of the death of your husband due to a plane crash in Narumbe on 15th September 2017. The light aircraft he was travelling on left Lagossa Airport at 2.10 pm and was en route to the capital Galao with two other passengers and pilot when all contact was lost with the plane one hour into the flight. It is believed to have suffered engine failure from a bird strike, causing the plane to go down in dense bush land in the central area of the country, which, unfortunately at present, is controlled by a rebel militia. Therefore, it is considered highly unsafe to attempt to investigate, locate the wreckage, and recover the bodies for repatriation. The plane was flying at an altitude of 8000 feet and we are certain there were no survivors.

We will shortly be issuing a death certificate in absentia. If you, or a chosen representative, would like to visit Narumbe to take ownership of the certificate or speak with me, you are most welcome to do so. Alternatively, I can arrange for the certificate to be posted.

We would like to thank Mason Palmer for his medical service to our country in this time of civil unrest.

If you have any further questions, please don't hesitate to contact me.

Our condolences and thoughts are with you at this sad time.

Kind regards,

Moussa Damba
Head of Police
Interior Ministry
Narumbe

There was a contact number on the top corner of the letter. I dialled and paced as I waited for the call to be picked up. A woman answered, speaking in French.

'I'm sorry, do you speak English?' I asked.

'Leetle.'

'Can I speak to Moussa Damba, please?'

'Une minute.'

There was a click and a wait, and then a female voice said, 'This is Moussa Damba's assistant. How can I help you?'

'Hello. My name is Nicole Palmer. My husband died in a plane crash in Narumbe ten months ago. Mr Damba wrote to me and spoke with my brother-in-law, Aiden Palmer, regarding the death certificate when he came out there. Is it possible to speak with Mr Damba himself about it?' There was silence on the line, and I thought we'd been disconnected. 'Hello? Are you still there?'

'Yes. Please hold the line while I see if he is free.'

More waiting and then I was finally put through. 'Hello, Mrs Palmer. This is Moussa Damba speaking.' His voice was soft and friendly. 'Once again, I'm very sorry for your loss. What can I do for you?'

'Thank you. I've just been wondering whether you've managed to locate the plane yet? Or if you have any new information? I know you said before that the area it went down in was occupied by rebels, but has there been any change in that situation?'

'I'm sorry, but the plane has never been located. As I explained to your brother-in-law at the time, the rebel factions operating in that area make it impossible to facilitate any kind of search for the wreckage. I do not expect the situation to change in the near future.'

'Right.' I rubbed at my forehead, throbbing with tension. Maybe I was heading off on some ridiculous, wild goose chase, because I just desperately wanted to believe Mason was really alive. But wanting something to be true didn't make it so. It was still entirely possible someone, for some reason, wanted to hurt me. 'Okay. Well, thank you for your time.'

'You are most welcome. And if anything changes, I will, of course, inform you.'

We said our goodbyes, and I went back to my laptop outside in the garden, sat in front of it and refreshed my email page. The mobile phone company's message had come through.

I clicked on the attachment, a PDF file containing the monthly statements I'd requested, and scrolled down until I got to the month of Mason's last shift in Narumbe. I examined the calls, most of which were made to me and two mobile numbers that I double checked belonged to Adama and Jean-Luc. A third number was listed, a British mobile phone he'd called six times that month which belonged to Isabelle. The last time Mason had called it was the day before he was due to fly home. Just after that, the last call he ever made, was at two-eighteen pm – another call to Adama which lasted forty-five seconds.

But that must've been wrong. There was an error somewhere. Mason's flight took off at two-ten pm; there was no way he would've been calling from the air. Even if he could've got a mobile phone signal up there, it surely would've interfered with the plane's instruments and Mason would've had his phone on flight mode. Unless the time of the flight's take off was wrong. Or the entry on the phone bill.

I hurried back into the lounge, phone in hand, to the letter from Moussa Damba explaining the circumstances of Mason's death. I skipped over the *It is with regret that I must inform you of the death of your husband*, until I reached the flight details... *The light aircraft he was travelling on left Lagossa Airport at 2.10 pm and was en route to the capital Galao.*

I stared at the letter. It didn't make sense, unless...unless, what? The only thing I could think of was that Mason hadn't been on that plane.

I picked up my mobile phone and tried Adama again. Still no answer. If anyone would know something, it must be him, the last person Mason had called.

I cupped a hand to my mouth as I stared at the words swimming together on the page, getting more and more confused. Mason had called Isabelle the day before his flight, but her words rang in my head from our previous conversation. She'd said she'd last spoken to him when he first started his new three-week shift out there to give him a progress report, but that wasn't right.

Was it an error on her part? Or had she lied to me? And did she know more than she'd told me?

Chapter 10

Moussa Damba dialled the number in Zurich and waited for it to connect. There were many geographic miles between himself and the recipient of the call, but in terms of goals, they were as close as brothers.

'Hello,' Julian Bolliger answered.

'We have a problem.' Moussa spoke softly into the phone.

'What kind of problem?'

Moussa swallowed. He didn't get nervous often, but he was now. He hated asking for outside help, but this couldn't just be contained on Narumbean soil. He hesitated a moment, then answered.

'Why am I only hearing about this Mason Palmer now?'

'I thought it had been dealt with sufficiently.'

'You assured me that you could handle operations out there,' Bolliger spat down the phone. 'And now you're telling me this… when we're in the middle of something I've spent months building up to?'

'It is not just you who has been working hard for months. I can handle things, and I will, but we need extra help to be brought in. Someone in England.'

'How much does his wife know?'

'I'm not sure. She seems suspicious, asking questions. This is why I need your help. I think we should send some people to find out what she knows and who she's talking to.'

The line was silent for a moment before the man said, 'I'll get my people on it. This cannot get out. Not now. Not ever.'

'Thank you.' The words were foreign to Moussa. He wasn't used to thanking people, and it grated on him, made him feel less of a man.

'Keep me updated,' Bolliger snapped.

'And you too.'

Moussa hung up the phone and called for Fanta. The only way to get rid of the impotent anger was to hurt someone.

Chapter 11

Julian Bolliger hung up and stared down at the city of Zurich from his floor-to-ceiling office window. He felt more at home here than he did in his multi-million Swiss Franc mansion. He'd never been married and had no time for demanding relationships, even though he'd been named most eligible Swiss bachelor several times. He had his dalliances with women, of course. He had needs like any other man. But he was a workaholic. Most of his arousal came from money and power. Nothing could beat the climax of counting the numbers on his portfolio.

His family had built the company up from scratch into the billion-pound venture it was today. Even as a small boy, he would accompany his father to work, trawling the huge building, staring in awe at everything. He was primed to take over before he was even born. Everyone knew the name Bolliger, but he would turn the company into a goliath. When the forthcoming merger he'd just officially announced took place, he'd be in control of the biggest industry corporation in the world. Nothing would get in his way.

He clenched his jaw and scowled, thinking about Moussa Damba. The stupid imbecile. He'd assured Julian all had been taken care of. When Damba had originally approached him with his new plans for Narumbe, Julian hadn't been surprised. This was Africa after all; corruption was rife, coups were a way of life. It didn't matter who was in charge, as far as Julian was concerned. The arrangement would still be the same. What mattered was the price Bolliger would pay for the merchandise would be significantly less with Damba in charge, and it would keep on coming. Damba would get his own power and line his pockets well, and Julian would be further in profit. It was win-win for both of them.

But now all his hard work was being threatened, and he couldn't have that. There was far too much to lose.

He strode over to his desk and picked up the phone.

Chapter 12

I was halfway through dialling Isabelle's mobile number when I stopped. This was a conversation we needed to have in person. If she was hiding something from me, or lying, then it would be easier for me to tell face to face.

I glanced at my watch. It was already midnight. Where had the time gone? Was it really only seventeen hours before that I'd been plunged into this…this…whatever it was?

It would have to wait until morning, although I had no idea how I was possibly going to get any sleep. I was far too jittery, filled with equal amounts of excitement at the prospect of Mason being alive and fear that I was going mad. I climbed into bed, rolled over and hugged the pillow on his side. His smell had long since dissipated, but it felt comforting somehow. I kept my mobile phone and landline handset on the bed next to me, in case Mason called, but as the minutes ticked by in the darkness and the dawn light slowly started to break, the hope I'd felt earlier was replaced with doubt.

Emotionally drained but spurred on by a need to find answers, I finally got out of bed at six am. I just hoped Isabelle would be there when I arrived, but I didn't want to tip her off by letting her know I was on my way.

I dressed hastily, stuffed a cereal bar and a bottle of water into my bag, as well as the photo of Mason, my laptop and my phone.

I drove to the park and ride bus stop outside Cambridge city centre, left my car there and caught the bus to the station. Then I took the train into London and switched to the underground. I didn't know exactly where the office was, but it wouldn't be hard to find. I headed left out of Regent's Park tube station and strode up the road until I came to a glass-fronted building with their brand name emblazoned on a brass plaque.

The receptionist was a young woman with a headset on. Her smile lit up the minimalist décor of the lobby as I approached.

'Can I help you?'

'I'd like to see Isabelle Moore, please.'

'Do you have an appointment?'

'No, but it's very important that I speak to her. My name's Nicole Palmer. My husband used to work for HI.'

The smile slipped. 'Ah, yes. I'm so sorry about what happened to him. Let me speak with Isabelle. She's only just got in.' She dialled a number and told Isabelle I was here, then she glanced up at me and said, 'Okay, thanks.' After ending the call, she told me Isabelle would be right down and indicated to a sofa.

I couldn't sit, though. I was too fired up, too on edge. Instead, I picked up a leaflet from the coffee table advertising Health International's charitable work and read:

Health International provides health aid to victims of war and natural disasters, entering war-torn countries with the permission of authorities. Founded in 1980, HI now has four operational centres in Europe and ten delegate offices around the world. In 2000 it spent over $250 million on its programs and sent 2,213 volunteers into the field.

In addition to acute disasters, HI also provides aid in chronic emergencies and assists in many long-term health projects…

A memory slammed into my head. Mason coming home from another ridiculously long shift at Addenbrooke's Hospital, exhausted and frustrated at the funding cuts, the lack of resources, the overwhelming malaise of the NHS. And maybe he could've put up with it all, like he'd done for the last fifteen years, if it hadn't been for me. I'd pushed him away, and he'd ended up on another continent, trying to help others while trying to find himself again and give us space. I was most likely responsible for whatever had happened to him out there.

My stomach twisted with guilt and I felt sick.

Isabelle calling my name jerked me out of my thoughts. I turned and she was behind me, her head tilted with a confused smile on her face, probably wondering why I was there. I bet she wasn't half as confused as me, though.

She was a very attractive woman. I knew she was in her late forties but looked thirty-five at a push. Her mum was French and her dad Spanish, and she'd inherited beautiful Mediterranean olive skin and green eyes. She had a smattering of freckles across her face, shoulder length black curls and an envious figure.

'Nicole, are you okay?' She rested her hand on my shoulder, her forehead bunched with what looked like concern.

I avoided the question. 'Can I talk to you in private?'

She studied me for a moment. 'Of course. Come this way.' She walked past the reception desk towards a set of double doors which she pushed through, then we strolled along a bright corridor until we arrived at a large conference room. A mahogany table lay in the middle of it with enough chairs to seat thirty people. She sat at the head of the table, crossed her legs and smoothed her grey pencil skirt down. 'What can I do for you? I'm afraid I haven't heard anymore about the plane,' she said quickly, as if she was pre-empting any blame I might lay at her feet.

I sat opposite her. 'I spoke to Jean-Luc, and I've been trying to speak with Adama, but I can't get hold of him.'

She tilted her head again slightly, the bridge of her nose pinched, not in a frown, but with a look of concentration. 'Sometimes, the phone system is erratic out there.'

'When I talked to you yesterday, you said you last spoke to Mason during the first week of his final shift in Narumbe. Was that right?'

'I think so.' Her gaze roamed my face.

'Well, I've just been going through his phone records, and it shows that you spoke with him the day before he was…before he disappeared. Can you tell me what it was about?'

Her reaction was subtle, but I was positive it was there – the tightening of her mouth, her eyes widening a fraction, blinking faster than normal. But she hardly missed a beat before she said, 'Well, it would've been work related. I can't remember exactly what we spoke about, it was ten months ago.'

'Right.' I carried on scanning her face, pretty sure she was lying. 'How did he seem?'

She licked her lips, uncrossed her legs then recrossed them the other way, as if stalling for time. 'From what I can remember, he was fine. Busy, of course, but otherwise the medical centre was doing its job well.'

'So, there were no problems he mentioned to you?'

She gave a small shake of her head and tucked a stray black curl behind her ear. 'Not that I recall, no. I've already told you this.'

I looked at her hand and saw the almost imperceptible tremor in it. Looked back to her face, straight into her eyes. 'Were you having an affair with him?'

'Of course not. How could you think such a thing? I can assure you, our relationship was purely professional.'

I continued staring into her eyes. Something was off about what she was telling me, I was certain of it.

She broke eye contact first, looking away, standing up. 'I'm sorry, but I don't think I can help you any further, and I'm …' she glanced at her watch, 'expecting an important conference call in five minutes. You don't know how difficult it is keeping on top of fund raising.' She smiled stiffly.

'Yes, of course.' I rose too.

She headed towards the door, throwing the next words over her shoulder. 'Like I said on the phone, if I find out any more about the plane, I'll let you know. I'm sure you'd like to bring him home, if you can.'

'Yes,' I said, not really listening any more, trying instead to work out exactly what she could be hiding and why.

Chapter 13

Isabelle walked me to the front doors, although I got the impression it wasn't because she wanted to say a formal goodbye, more to make sure I left the building.

Her hand was icy cold in mine as she shook it and said, 'Take care,' her voice sounding strained.

I felt her eyes on my back as I walked away and turned in the opposite direction of the tube station. I had no idea where I was heading, but I wanted to walk and think about what all of this meant. As I threaded through the throngs of people on the busy London street, I still couldn't make anything fit a rational explanation.

Was the photo real? Or had Isabelle been having an affair with my husband and had sent it to me to hurt me somehow? Because she was jealous? I suppose Mason could've told her about the Dr Seuss quote, which would enable her to have written the message on the back. She was definitely lying about something, but I wasn't convinced it was to do with an affair. When you considered the phone call Mason had made to Adama after the plane had taken off, it seemed more likely Mason hadn't even been on that plane when it went down. I still couldn't work out why he hadn't contacted me until now, though. How could he have let me think he was dead, for God's sake? Go through the interminable grief and guilt of the last ten months? There had to be a bloody good reason.

I stepped through the entrance of Regent's Park and walked towards a nearby bench. I stared into the distance, not really seeing anything. In my mind, I was visualising Mason; the way he laughed, loud and deep and slightly dirty. His hands, both strong and gentle at the same time. Hands that saved lives and caressed my body. How he always gave people his rapt attention when they talked, like they were the most interesting thing in the world – that rare quality of really being able to listen. How he was so passionate about always wanting to help people.

I blinked back the tears threatening to form and then my phone rang. I dug it out of my bag and saw the country code for Narumbe prefixed on the screen. I pressed at the green button, held the phone to my ear.

'You need to stop. You are in danger. Do not trust Moussa Damba.' The voice was muffled, the line crackling, but the accent was distinctly French.

'What do you mean? Who are you?' I was talking to thin air. Whoever it was had abruptly ended the call.

I stared at my phone, a shiver of fear dancing up my spine as I reran the words through my head again. Had I really heard them right? Why would I be in danger?

As I looked up, I spotted a man on a bench about twenty metres further along the path. He was dressed casually in jeans and a hoodie. It was hard to place an age on him, but he was looking right at me. For a second, maybe even half a second, his gaze locked on mine before he turned his head in the other direction so I could no longer see his face.

Was he watching me? Yes, people catch your eye all the time, people look, stare, especially in a city. There was no reason to think he was suspicious, except for the strange look in his eyes, something chilling, something that seemed to stare right into my soul.

The man stood up and walked away. I watched his retreating back until he'd rounded a corner and disappeared, then I shook my head. Of course he wasn't watching me. I was just spooked by the call.

You are in danger.

I glanced around, taking everyone in – a grandmother pushing a child in a buggy, a dad and son playing bat and ball, a student-looking girl sitting cross-legged on the grass reading a textbook and smoking, a teenager walking a dog, a business man wearing sunglasses tapping away on a tablet. No one was paying me any attention, but still, I didn't want to hang around.

I rose slowly, slung my bag diagonally across my body and walked back to the entrance. As I joined the rest of the crowds on the pavement, I scanned for anyone looking suspicious, but that was ridiculous – there were plenty of strange people wandering around in London, and if someone was following me, the real danger would sneak up from behind.

Chapter 14

I parked on my drive, got out of the car and scanned up and down the cul-de-sac warily. There was no one hanging around. I recognised a few of my neighbour's cars on their driveways, the others would be out at work. There was a white van parked at the entrance to the cul-de-sac, most likely some kind of workman doing plumbing or decorating for a neighbour.

I went inside, kicked off my trainers in the hallway and headed into the kitchen at the back of the house. My stomach cramped with the need for food, but I ignored it. I couldn't think about eating. Not now. All I could think of was how personal the note was to me. The only thing that made sense was that it *had* to have come from Mason. And that's when it hit me. Mason must've got mixed up in something that happened in Narumbe. Something so bad, he'd been in hiding for ten months. Hiding, even, from me.

I dug my phone from my bag and hit redial on my mobile, hoping to speak to whoever had called earlier to warn me off.

The number rang and rang, and just as I was about to hang up a voice answered in French.

'Bonjour? Metro Bar and Hotel.'

I started to speak, then stopped myself. Mason had spoken of this bar. He'd been there a few times with Jean-Luc when they'd had some down time. It was in the nearest town to the medical centre. The voice sounded different to whomever had called earlier, and if I was in danger, it would be stupid to alert whoever was on the other end of the line that someone had tried to warn me.

I hung up. I had no other leads to try to follow now to find out where Mason was. All I could do was wait for him to make contact with me again, but the wait was interminable, and I spent the afternoon alternating between looking at my phone to see if Mason had emailed me and chewing on my nails until they were red raw.

The doorbell rang sometime later, making me flinch. For a moment, I sat frozen at the kitchen table, unsure what to do, wondering if it was either the man from the park or Mason.

Slowly, I inched towards the front door. A silhouette was in shadow against the obscured glass, but it wasn't a man. It was Cheryl.

I opened it and tried to smile, but my emotions overwhelmed me, and my face refused to cooperate.

'Hi.' Cheryl's smile was warm and, for some reason, made tears spring into my eyes. 'I just wanted to pop by and see if you're okay.'

Cheryl was one of the few friends I had. I didn't open up to people easily. I didn't let people in without a fight. I knew it stemmed from my relationship with my mum, which was complex, as I'm sure it is for most people. Mum was what I would describe as a social climber, always wanting to be someone she wasn't and have something she couldn't, which in turn made her bitter. She'd grown up on a council estate in a poor family and aspired to be a rich, lady of the manor. Instead, she'd met my dad, also from what some would call the wrong side of the tracks, whose only aspirations in life were to put a roof over his head, be happy, and provide for his family.

Over the years, she gave him hell, because whatever he did was never good enough to give her the things she wanted most – flashy cars, designer clothes, transatlantic holidays, a perception of richness. When I was born, she'd tried to push her aspirations onto me, smothering me by pushing me into being the best at everything: the most popular kid in school – no way was that happening – the prettiest – I was average looking, still am – the best at ballet classes – I was too clumsy. Over and over, she drummed into me that I wasn't good enough, showing her displeasure whenever I didn't come up to scratch with frequent jibes, until after all her failed attempts at trying to improve me and make me popular so the world would take notice of her, my confidence was stripped away, and I started to become more and more introverted, which only seemed to get worse as I got older.

I'm sure psychoanalysts would have a field day with me, but I didn't need analysing. I always felt it was quite obvious what my problems were. There were two clear issues: One: I couldn't open up to people for fear of being hurt, rebuffed, etc. And two, and more importantly, I kept things inside because if I bared my soul, the person with fears and disappointments and weaknesses, people would never like the real me. So, I kept problems bottled up inside. Pretended I was strong. Dealt with things myself because I was the only one I could rely on. I knew it was a coping mechanism, and not a very healthy one. It was one of my biggest weaknesses, and even Mason hadn't been able to change me.

But for once, I wasn't strong. For once, I didn't want my own company, and I couldn't face being in this empty house alone just waiting for Mason to get in touch again, with the constant whirring of my thoughts hurling me into chaos and ripping my stomach lining to shreds. So, I plastered on my best smile and invited Cheryl inside.

She followed me into the lounge. I flopped onto the sofa, tucked my knees underneath me and avoided her gaze. I really wanted to tell her what was going on, but if there was a possibility I was in danger, then she could be too. So, I had to keep this secret hidden.

'I'm so sorry about yesterday. I completely messed up,' I said. 'I made a mistake about Angela. About everything. I was confused. I'm not thinking straight at the moment. And I'm so embarrassed about it all.'

She reached out and touched my hand, gave it a reassuring squeeze.

'You were right. Everything is just really hitting me all of a sudden.' I flopped my head into my hands, tears pricking at my eyes.

'Oh, love.' She put her arm around my shoulder. 'I hate to see you like this. I think you're having some kind of delayed grief. Which is not surprising, really. You haven't had a chance to bring him home and bury him yet, which must make it so hard to put some kind of finality on things so you can start to heal.'

I dropped my hands, wiped my cheeks. 'Am I in trouble at work?'

'No. I explained to Angela that you were going through a difficult time. She was still ranting about getting Robbie into another class, but I told her that would be impossible. She backed down, and it all seems to have blown over.'

'Good. I know I shouldn't have dealt with it like that. I should've come to you about it first. I handled it all wrong. I was just–'

'No. Let's not say anymore about any of this. We'll just move on from it. I know you weren't acting like your usual self.' She squeezed my hand.

I forced a smile back at her, grateful she'd accepted my explanation and didn't press me for further details on the photo I'd told her about last night and who might've sent it if it hadn't been Angela.

'But … I do really think it would help you to speak to a counsellor.' She let go of my hand and looked at me intensely for a moment before diving into her handbag. 'Here.' She handed me a business card. 'I spoke to her after my divorce. She's very good. Helped me immensely.'

'Yes. Maybe I will do that.' I took the card and stared at it, knowing it wasn't a counsellor I needed, it was a psychic who could tell me where Mason was right now. 'Thanks.'

'Now that's out of the way, how about we order a takeaway and crack open a bottle of wine? I bet you haven't bothered to eat, have you?'

Chapter 15

Blade was already waiting for Isabelle Moore when she arrived home at exactly six forty-three pm. Blade wasn't his real name, of course. He'd earned the nickname years ago for his creative preference for using a knife.

Isabelle lived alone, which was handy. But even if she'd been married with kids, he would've just found another way. He had clear instructions, and he always followed them to the letter, even if he liked to add a touch of initiative to his work.

In this case, his orders were to find out how much Nicole Palmer knew and whether she was in touch with her husband. From the bugs and cameras Blade's associate, Frankie, had planted in Nicole's house that morning – while Blade had been following her to Health International's offices – nothing interesting had come to light yet, and he wasn't convinced she knew anything. But Blade thought Isabelle looked guilty as hell about something as she'd watched Nicole walk away from the building's front doors. Their conversation could only have been to do with Mason Palmer, which meant perhaps Isabelle knew something about Mason's whereabouts that she was keeping hidden.

Isabelle had a nice barn conversion on the edge of Old Knebworth, a village some people would call quaint but he'd call boring-as-fuck. It was all rustic wood with high ceilings, detached, with a curving driveway set back from the road. Health International was supposed to be a non-profit organization, but Blade didn't believe all those happy-clappy do-gooders weren't siphoning money for themselves. He was pretty sure, judging from her house, that Isabelle was lining her own pockets. There were very few people who turned down access to the amount of money she raised, and pretty pound notes were a temptation for most people.

He picked up a photo of Isabelle from a bookcase in the lounge at the back of the house with his gloved hand. She was actually quite hot. She had that sexy older woman thing going on which reminded him of the wife of a rival gang boss he'd offed in Spain. He grinned to himself, remembering the details. She'd been a good-looking bird, but not when Blade had finished with her. Those had been the days, when he'd been an enforcer for the Hopper Gang. It hadn't been about any particular loyalty to the Hopper brothers for Blade, although the money had been good. No, he did it for the thrill, and the pleasure, giving him an excuse to murder and torture at will, perfecting some of the techniques he used now.

He licked his lips and put the photo back down as he heard a key enter the lock at the front door.

He took up position behind the door and clutched his double-edged stiletto knife. It was his favourite weapon – a Fairbairn-Sykes fighting knife with a long, slender blade and a needle-sharp point, perfect for deep penetration into a rib or an eye.

He listened to Isabelle's footsteps in the hallway and waited patiently, his back against the wall. His breathing was calm. His heart rate steady. He was used to waiting.

Man, he loved his job.

He heard her enter the kitchen, then the sound of glass chinking on the granite worktop and the fridge opening. He pictured her pouring a glass of wine, taking a sip.

Her footsteps came closer. The door swung inwards, and she entered the room without noticing him.

He punched her hard in the kidney, and she fell forwards, splaying out onto the carpeted floor, the breath audibly expelling from her lungs in a *whoosh*, the wine glass hitting the carpet and spraying an arc of white liquid.

She moaned in agony and tried to get up, but he didn't give her the chance, quickly straddling her back, sinking his entire heavy six-foot-two frame into her as he sat astride her.

She cried out as he grabbed her arms and plasti-cuffed them together behind her back. She tried to struggle her body beneath him, but it was pointless.

'Please,' she whimpered. 'Don't hurt me. I have money upstairs. Jewellery. I haven't seen you. I can't identify you. Please take it and leave me alone.'

He leaned forward at the waist and put his mouth to her ear, his breath caressing her skin. 'I haven't come for that.'

The smell of her, something musky and sweet got him hard. He ground himself into her back.

She froze. 'No. Please. Not that.'

'You and me are going to have a little chat. If you tell me the truth, I'll let you go.' He ran his fingers through her hair softly, stroking down the right side of her neck, lower, his fingertips skimming the outline of her breast. 'Do you understand?'

Her breath came in sharp pants as she whimpered. She nodded her head vigorously. 'Yes. But *please* don't hurt me.' Her voice was whiney now, and Blade hated that. He hated begging. It made him see red.

'Just so we're completely clear …' He trailed off and whipped the knife around, bringing it in front of her face.

She moaned wildly, her body trembling beneath him. She tried to buck him off, but she was no match for his weight pressing her down into the carpet.

He grabbed her long hair and yanked her head backwards with one hand, touched the tip of the sharp blade to her cheekbone with the other.

'If I think you're lying, I'll cut out your eye.' He drew a light circle on the skin around her eye with the tip of the blade, not hard enough to cut her, but chilling nevertheless.

'What … what do you want?'

Blade pressed the knife to her lips. 'Shush. I ask the questions. If you co-operate, I'll let you go.'

She made a squeaking sound and nodded rapidly.

'You met with Nicole Palmer.'

'Y … yes.'

'What did you talk about?'

'She just … um … she asked about her husband.'

'*What* about him?'

Tears slid down her cheeks as she said, 'She wanted to know what Mason had spoken to me about a few days before the plane crash.'

'Explain.'

A sob escaped from her lips before she said, 'I haven't told anyone. I can't risk it getting out. My priority is medical aid, and I didn't want our permissions to be revoked.'

'Haven't told anyone *what*?'

'About what Mason told me. Moussa Damba. His involvement. I … I think that's why you're here?'

'So, you've just kept it to yourself all this time?'

'Yes. Yes!'

Blade snorted. 'You know, I'm not sure whether to believe you, Isabelle.'

'It's true. We don't get involved in government issues. We can't afford to. When Mason told me what was going on, I said we couldn't do anything about it. I told him to keep quiet.'

'And what did you tell Nicole?'

'I didn't tell her anything. I said I couldn't remember what I spoke to him about. I didn't want to rock the boat.'

'Is she in contact with him?'

'I don't … I don't know what you mean.'

He dug the blade into her cheek.

She shrieked.

'Did she tell you where he was?'

'He's dead!' She twisted her head away. 'Mason's dead.'

He released the grip on her hair a little and stroked her face with the knife. 'Are you sure about that?'

'Yes. *Yes*.' She jerked her head and clamped her teeth onto the exposed wrist of his knife hand, in the area between where his glove finished and the sleeve of his hoodie had ridden up.

Blade tried to yank his arm away, but her teeth bore down hard. His knife wouldn't reach her from this angle.

'You stupid fucking bitch.' He released her hair and punched her in the back of the head.

She let go of his wrist, whimpering and shaking beneath him. His skin throbbed. She'd fucking pay for that.

He shifted his weight to the side then turned her over onto her back, her arms tight beneath her. Then he straddled her once more.

She looked up at him with absolute terror in her eyes, lying rigid. Now, *that* look was hot.

'You shouldn't have done that. I was asking nicely.' He pressed the blade to her throat. 'What else did you talk about with Nicole?'

'Nothing. I swear.'

'Because if I find out you're lying …' He grinned down at her, licking his lips.

'Honestly, I'm telling you the truth. I've kept it to myself all this time. I didn't tell anyone what Mason told me, and then he died, and I … Please, let me go. I won't say a word. I won't. I've proved that.'

'Do you know what? I think you're telling the truth. But the rules have changed now. I think after the stunt you pulled you *owe* me, so …' He trailed the knife over her collar bone, down towards her heaving chest. He sliced through the buttons on her sexy silk blouse one by one, gradually exposing the luscious tanned skin beneath.

Chapter 16

After Cheryl left at just gone midnight, I climbed into bed and stared at the ceiling, willing Mason to call, to email, to … *do something*. I kept picking up my mobile phone, checking the screen to make sure I still had a signal or to see if I had a new message alert, but … nothing.

I knew for certain then, with the phone call from the Metro Bar, that this wasn't a hoax. Mason was really out there. Alive.

I must've finally drifted off to sleep in the early hours, because I woke to the sound of my ringtone.

I grabbed my mobile from next to my pillow, my heart thumping with anticipation, but it was just my dad calling.

'Hi, dear,' he said briskly. 'I just wanted to phone before I head off to the airport to remind you that you don't need to water the plants this time. Molly from next door is doing it for me.'

'Oh, yeah. Right. Have a nice holiday,' I replied, disappointment flooding through me as I rubbed a twitchy hand across my face. Even though it was nice to hear his voice, I wanted to get Dad off the phone. My relationship with him wasn't like that with my mum. He'd always been kind, fair, caring, and although he never told me he loved me growing up, in the way many older generations of parents hadn't particularly, I knew that he did.

'Thanks. I'm looking forward to sampling new cuisine. I've been trying to make Thai red curry, but it tasted awful. I hope the local food's nicer than that.' He laughed. Dad had only discovered foreign holidays after Mum died fifteen years ago, and he'd retired with a reasonable pension from his job as a foreman at Vauxhall's car factory. When I was young, it was family camping trips to Devon and Cornwall for us, which Mum despised and had moaned incessantly about. Now he was off to Thailand for two weeks with his local gardening club. Mum would be turning in her grave, green with jealousy that Dad was getting to do all the things she'd henpecked him about when she was alive.

'That'll be nice.' My gaze drifted towards the alarm clock on my bedside table. Eight am. How had I even managed to sleep?

'Are you all right? You sound a bit away with the fairies.'

'Um … yes. Actually, I have to go. I'll be late for school,' I lied.

'Okay, dear. Well, I'll see you when I get back.'

I said my goodbyes and hung up, then looked at my screen. No new emails or private messages. No calls I'd slept through. No texts.

I blew out a frustrated breath and threw back the tangled sheets. After showering, I felt more awake but no less of a nervous wreck.

I opened the curtains in the lounge and looked up and down the street, searching for the postman, breathy with anticipation in case the contact would come again in the form of a letter or another photo. If Mason was in trouble, if he'd been hiding for some reason, he must've realised that our emails could be intercepted and watched, which was why he'd posted the photo. In this digital age, where most communication was done online, who would think to monitor the snail mail?

My gaze scanned the few cars that belong to my neighbours and the white van parked at the end of the street that had been there yesterday. The postman was usually early, but there was no sign of him. I made a cup of tea, just for something to do with my hands to distract me, and took the cup to the lounge sofa beneath the window so I could position myself for easy viewing.

Then I mounted a vigil, nervous anticipation barrelling through my veins.

An agonising hour later, I shot off the sofa as soon as I saw the postman delivering to my neighbour four houses along. I waited behind the front door, chewing on my thumbnail, eyes firmly locked onto the letterbox.

When the envelopes came clattering through, even though I'd been expecting it, it still made me jump.

I kneeled on the floor and scooped everything up; junk mail, junk mail, a letter from my car insurance company and a small brown envelope addressed in the same block capital letters.

I ripped it open and pulled out a single piece of paper. Another note.

Meet me at Jesus Green today. The last bench next to the Lido at the same time we got married.

Can't wait to see you again and explain everything.

I've missed you SO much XX

I blew out the breath I'd been clutching inside and pressed a hand to my racing heart, reading and rereading it again.

The same time we got married. Midday.

I stood up and tucked the letter into the pocket of my dressing gown then pressed my palms together as if in prayer, a wide smile stretching my cheeks.

Chapter 17

Blade sat in the back of the van parked at the end of Nicole's close and watched the live feed from the cameras in the lounge, kitchen, and master bedroom. So far, nothing interesting had happened. She'd made a cup of tea, sat looking out the lounge window, and mumbled to herself a lot. The only thing of note was that she kept checking her phone, but he knew from his associate, Frankie, who was monitoring her calls and emails, that Mason hadn't been in touch with her.

Blade had gone over the footage from last night, recorded while he was busy with the delicious Isabelle. Nothing much had happened then, either. Nicole's conversation with her boss, who didn't appear to know anything, was mundane gossipy chit-chat. Whatever Nicole knew about Mason and his whereabouts, she was keeping to herself.

Fuck it. He couldn't wait much longer. It was time to bring her in for a nice little chat.

Chapter 18

Mason Palmer stood at his hotel window that overlooked the River Cam and the Lido on Jesus Green, his stomach coiled tight as he watched for Nicole's approach. It would all be over soon. After all this waiting, they'd finally be together again. He'd chosen this location away from the house in case one of his neighbours recognised him before he could do what he had to. He couldn't have anyone else finding out he was still alive until the final moment when it was too late for them to react.

He wiped his sweating palms on his jeans for the fourth time and let his mind wander back to Africa; to what he'd seen, what they didn't want him to expose, being ordered into the office at the airport by Moussa Damba and them confiscating his equipment. It had all been a strange experience. The police officer who'd patted him down had checked the leg pocket of his cargo trousers but, surprisingly, didn't reveal to Damba Mason's British phone nestled inside. The other phone that Mason had handed over freely had been a cheap phone with a local SIM card, used only for emergencies. Mason was told later by Adama that the officer had been one of Adama's inside men. But sadly, Moussa had later suspected him of working with Adama's group and had him killed. After Moussa had let Mason go, he'd thought he was home and free. They wouldn't have found anything on his laptop and video recorder because Mason had already removed the evidence and uploaded everything to a cloud.

But after he'd climbed aboard the plane and taken a window seat, he'd looked back at the airport, at the other tall police officer he knew was Moussa's right-hand man – Chief Inspector Sumano – staring at the plane through the glass doors. He'd witnessed Sumano's almost imperceptible nod at the man in the green overalls filling the plane with fuel and knew for certain something bad was about to happen. Moussa would never risk it coming out. So, he'd waited until Sumano had turned away and left, waited until the man in the overalls had walked into the small hangar with his back to Mason. When he'd told the pilot doing his pre-flight checks that he had an emergency he needed to deal with and couldn't take the flight after all, his heart had hammered in his chest in case the pilot was in on it too.

At that time, he'd thought maybe they would be waiting for him in the capital of Galao to intercept him when he arrived and kill him there. He had no idea then they were about to murder three innocent people by tampering with the plane to bring it down, but afterwards, it made sense. It was a better strategy for a foreign aid worker to die in a plane crash than disappear or be murdered, because others would start asking questions, like they did about the French journalist who'd disappeared.

He'd felt like he was having a heart attack as he climbed down the steps, hurried along to the side of the building and hidden in the bush before calling Adama to come and collect him.

Adama helped "the disappeared" all the time. He had a heart of pure gold, that man. The fake passport Adama had arranged was a work of art, not that Mason knew anything about false documents in his previous life, but it was a masterpiece of a copy. Adama had smuggled him across the unmanned back roads that skirted around the border checkpoint into Mali. From there, he'd taken a plane to Paris. All he could think of was *escape*, getting out of the country and getting to Nicole so he could keep her safe. But before he'd even left Mali, Adama had told him the plane had gone down and his plan had to change.

In the last ten months, while they'd been getting everything ready, he'd almost reached out and contacted her so many times but had stopped himself at the last minute. It was torture.

He couldn't let anything happen to her. Not until he could keep her safe. And the only way to ensure her safety in the meantime was to let her, and them, think he was dead.

He watched the people in the park, his breath jagged, his nerves jangling, waiting for that first glimpse of her. A mum was handing her son fistfuls of birdseed to feed the swans that had gathered on the river bank. The boy threw them high in the air, laughing every time the birds pecked at the seeds after they'd fallen to the ground. A cyclist rode past them on the path skirting the river. An elderly man walked his Jack Russell, stopping every few metres for the dog to sniff at the benches. Children played noisily in the Lido's swimming pool.

He thought about the first time he ever saw his wife. Nicole was the gorgeous girl next door, quite literally. When he caught a glimpse of the removal van arriving to unload furniture to the newly-sold house next to him, he had no way of knowing exactly what it was delivering into his life. He'd watched out of the window as his new neighbour arrived in her car, stopped and talked to the removal men before heading into the house, her back straight and an intense look of concentration on her face, poised with a natural beauty. Even then, she'd looked both vulnerable and strong, with a hint of the untouchable about her. She had an outer shell that she vigorously defended, finding it hard to let people in. She was a giver. But she couldn't handle taking in return. And maybe that was the reason he was in this mess now, although he would never blame Nicole for that.

Their relationship had developed slowly, chatting outside whenever they saw each other, until he'd dared to invite her to his house for a drink. They were friends first, for six months, and getting to know each other slowly with no pressure or expectations had been more arousing and heady than if they'd dived right in. He recognised her cautious nature, gave her space, and eventually, she opened up to him. She had a good sense of humour. She'd laughed a lot back then. When he'd been away for a week attending a medical conference in the States, she'd missed him so much that she realised this was *it*. This was love. Mason had felt it from almost the beginning. They had a bond, and throughout everything, their bond was unbreakable.

His heart stopped as he saw Nicole walk towards the bench nearest to the Lido from the right-hand side of the path. When it kick-started again, it beat fast and hard with longing. She wore black Capri trousers with a coral coloured gypsy-style top that he'd always found so sexy on her and cork-heeled wedges. He grabbed his baseball cap and sunglasses, not that he thought he'd need a disguise now, but the habits of the last few months were hard to shake off. It paid to be cautious, even though there was no way they could suspect anything.

He slipped the cap over his hair and watched Nicole sit on the bench and look around. He felt a twinge in his chest. As a doctor, he knew it wasn't his heart. As a romantic, he would describe it as a reaction of love. God, he'd missed her so much. His stomach churned. There was so much explaining to do. The journey for them was only just beginning.

As he put on his sunglasses, he noticed a man in a long leather jacket sit down on the bench next to Nicole. He was tall and wide, built like a rugby player. He had a baseball cap on and wore sunglasses. Mason watched the man casually glance around the park. It was hard to tell from this distance, but Mason thought his lips were moving as if speaking to her. The man was probably just making polite small talk. It was nothing to worry about.

But … something was off. Why was he wearing a long winter jacket when it was almost thirty degrees Celsius out?

He kept his gaze on them, just to be sure, and then he saw the man's hand inside his jacket pocket manoeuvring a little closer to her body.

Fear slammed into Mason's chest. The man had a gun, he was sure of it. And it was pointed at Nicole through his coat.

No. No, no, no. How had they found out she was meeting him? He'd always been so careful.

He stood frozen in horror as the man took Nicole's arm and lifted her up to standing, as she walked away beside him, keeping his hand in his pocket all the time, as her face disappeared from view.

Then instinct kicked in and he ran from the room, down the corridor past the lifts and shouldered open the fire doors, sliding down the stairs three at a time.

Chapter 19

I couldn't stop smiling as I sat on the bench, waiting for Mason. We'd had our fair share of ups and downs over the years, what marriage hasn't? When he'd told me his life was lacking purpose at the hospital and he'd needed a new challenge, I couldn't believe he was seriously considering taking the job for Health International. Apart from the fact that he would be going into war-torn countries and the obvious danger involved, it had felt like he was turning his back on me. That I was the problem. I guess I had been, back then. I'd pushed him into leaving because of the infertility madness I was going through. I couldn't blame him for that, but I'd cried, shouted, tried to persuade him to change his mind. But Mason was as stubborn as I could be. And through the rows and the tears, I'd come to gradually realise that it was something he needed to do. He didn't feel like he was making much of a difference at the hospital. *This* would make a difference, he'd told me.

If he'd said I had to give up teaching, I would've fought him on it and not backed down, so I couldn't stand in his way. If this was something he had to do, then I had to support him, even if I was scared for his safety. His passionate empathy and compassion for others was what had made me fall in love with him in the first place, so I could hardly throw it back in his face. I wasn't ecstatic, but I'd learned to accept it. And as the months went on, I knew it had been the best thing for both of us, giving us the distance I'd needed to put my own turmoil of emotions into perspective.

But it wasn't the bad times we'd gone through that I was thinking about as I glanced around, waiting for my first glimpse of him – they'd evaporated now. It was the happy moments we'd had that came to mind, and there had been plenty. I thought of his romantic proposal during a weekend away in the New Forest. The words he'd carved into an ancient pine tree in the woods. The day before he'd brought me to the spot where he'd planned it happening, he'd left me alone in the old manor house hotel we were staying in on the pretext of getting a supply of wine from the nearby village shop while I relaxed. But really, he'd walked the route he wanted to take me on the following day, knowing I'd love the beauty of it. He'd carved the words into the tree and then left. The following day, when he'd picked up the picnic basket he'd pre-arranged with the hotel and we'd walked there, he'd made a big show of examining the tree, hoping I'd join him and see it. But instead, I'd spotted a small group of wild ponies grazing in the distance and was watching them with delight.

'Hey, come and look at what someone's carved into the bark,' he'd said eventually when I'd made no move towards it.

Dragging my gaze away, I stood next to him reading the words *Will You Marry Me, Nicole?*

I remembered my eyes widening. My mouth falling open. I'd gasped with surprise, a slow smile creeping up my lips. 'Seriously?' I'd asked.

The smile he gave me in return had said it all. 'So … what's your answer?'

I'd wrapped my arms around his neck and kissed him hard saying, 'Yes! Of course, yes!', and he'd twirled me around, giddy with relief.

I looked at my watch now. It was nearly time. A tightness squeezed at my chest, and I didn't know if it was fear or nervous excitement. I couldn't wait to hold him again, smell his familiar smell. Feel his arms wrapped around me. But what if I was wrong and this had been some kind of elaborately sick hoax?

I blew out a breath, trying to keep the ache in my chest at bay, and glanced around.

I barely registered the man who sat next to me at first. I was annoyed with his proximity, though. I'd wanted it to be just Mason and me with no intruding witnesses for our reunion.

I ignored him, until he whispered, 'I have a gun pointed at your waist.'

My head whipped around towards him with surprise, thinking I'd completely misheard what he'd said.

He stared straight ahead with a smile on his face.

I recognised him. It was the same man who'd been looking at me in the park after I'd met with Isabelle.

I glanced down to look at his hands. They were in his pockets. He manoeuvred one closer to me, digging something hard into my thigh.

I gasped. Even though I couldn't actually see it, I knew he was telling the truth.

'You're going to get up and come with me. If you start screaming, if you try to run, if you do anything at all that draws attention to us, I'll shoot you. And then I'll shoot him.' He nodded to a small boy feeding the swans. 'And his mum. And plenty of other people. Do you understand?' He delivered the words casually, as if he was simply chit-chatting about the weather.

The breath caught in my throat. I was too stunned to speak. The shock and fear had turned my brain to mush.

'Do you understand? I'm not going to tell you again.' He turned his face towards me but his eyes were hidden behind sunglasses.

'Yes,' I managed to croak out.

He gave me a smile that chilled my bones, gripped my forearm and pulled me to my feet.

I felt dizzy as he walked beside me, his hand in his jacket pocket. I glanced down, saw the bulge of a gun through it, pointing at me. I swallowed, panic making my throat dry. I looked around, trying to catch someone's eye. There was a jogger heading our way along the path, an old man waiting for his dog to finish sniffing at a tree trunk on the grass to our right, but no one was paying us any attention or looking in our direction.

'Don't even think about it. Don't look at anyone. Don't try to catch someone's eye or there will be many dead people's blood on your hands,' the man said, his voice calm and flat, his body leaning closer to me so I could feel his heat through his leather jacket.

I kept my gaze straight ahead as my heart pounded, and we walked at a fast pace. 'Look, I think you've made a mistake. I don't know what's going on here.'

'No talking.' He jabbed the gun into my waist.

I sucked in a whimper.

We were approaching the park entrance that led to Victoria Avenue. I saw a white van parked up at the side of the road and wondered if it was the same van I'd seen at the end of my street this morning. He marched me up to it, opened the sliding door on the side and gestured for me to get inside.

I hesitated a moment, my eyes wanting to frantically search out the street and the road but not daring to in case he started shooting random people. 'Wait, please don't do this.'

He smiled again, leaned forwards so his body pressed into me against the side panel of the van. The gun ground into my hip, a hard metal lump. He put his arm around the back of my neck, squeezing it tight, his face millimetres from mine so I was forced to look at him.

It felt like every drop of blood drained out of me as he smiled again. To anyone walking past, it would look like we were lovers having an intimate conversation.

'Get in the fucking van or I'll kill you.'

Chapter 20

By the time Mason had barrelled through the doors to the hotel and run across the bridge over the River Cam to Jesus Green, there was no sign of Nicole and the strange man. Mason stood and turned a 360-degree angle. Nothing. He jogged around the park, searching for them, fear lodged in his chest like a knife.

Where the hell were they? That man could've taken her anywhere by now; the park was huge and led onto several different back roads filled with houses. He ran across to the entrance that opened up on Victoria Avenue, looking one way then the other, panic spiking through him. No sign of her.

This couldn't be happening. It was supposed to be so easy. No one should've been watching her now. Enough time had passed to think they'd got away with murder. He and Nicole were supposed to finally get their lives back.

He ran around the park, calling her name, not caring anymore that he was drawing attention to himself, because if that man had an accomplice waiting for him, then he would use himself to draw them out. He would offer to exchange himself for Nicole or try to convince them to let her go.

But as he searched the area, it became apparent that no one was waiting to ambush him and the man and Nicole had vanished.

He ran a hand over his sweaty forehead, his stomach twisting with fear for her. It was his fault they'd taken her.

And he had no idea how to get her back.

Chapter 21

The man pushed me onto a wooden bench seat on the opposite side of the sliding door and sat next to me. He pulled the gun out of his pocket, along with a silencer that he screwed on, pointed it at me. I'd never seen a gun in real life, only in movies, so I didn't know what kind it was – just that it looked huge.

The van sped along the road, the sound of my pulse roaring in my ears muffling out some of the traffic noise. We took a right turn, and I gripped onto the edge of the bench to stop myself being thrown into him.

I was absolutely terrified, but I knew that my only hope of getting away from them was to use some kind of weapon. My handbag was strapped diagonally across my body facing away from him. I frantically tried to think of anything inside that would help me. A notepad, a pack of tissues, a half-eaten packet of mints, my purse, and phone. But I also had a ballpoint pen in there. I moved my hand from the edge of the bench, trying to stop it shaking. If I could quietly lift the popper flap on my bag I could reach my hand in, remove the cap of the pen and wait for the right opportunity to stab him in the eye.

At least, that was the theory. In my head, it sounded, while not a great idea, like the only hope I had. And then what? What if I missed? Stabbing someone was most likely harder than it sounded. By the time I got my hand around in front of me to stab him, he would notice and probably shoot me. I was a primary school teacher, for God's sake, not Wonder Woman.

I chewed on the inside of my mouth, trying out the scenario in my head, but before I could make my mind think properly, he said, 'Give me your bag.'

He took his sunglasses off and put them in his pocket, stared at me.

It seemed as if there was nothing behind his eyes. No empathy, no compassion, nothing. It felt as if something hard had lodged in my throat, stopping me from breathing.

He pointed the gun at my knee. 'Do you know how fucking painful it is to get kneecapped?'

My whole body tensed, readying for the shot of a bullet before I slid my bag off with shaking hands and handed it to him.

He opened the flap and tipped the contents onto the floor of the van, which clattered against the metal. Then he picked up the biro and stared at it thoughtfully. 'I once killed someone with a pen. A hard stab to the heart and that was it.' He grinned with a sadistic malevolence that made my stomach lurch violently.

My gaze darted around. The blood curdled in my veins. How the hell was I going to get out of this? I didn't know where they were taking me, but I knew I wouldn't be returning. I'd seen his face. I could identify him. There was no way he was going to let me live when he'd finished with me.

Behind the driver's cab was a black wire mesh separating it from the van's body, but the mesh was closely woven, so I couldn't get a good glimpse of the driver or where we were, just a flash of brightness behind it.

Above the bench seat were wooden shelves that must've been used for tools but were empty. On the floor to my right lay a pile of dust sheets. I didn't know where they'd got the van from, but it seemed safe to say it had belonged to some kind of workman.

I swallowed and decided maybe I could talk my way out of this. 'What are you going to do with me?' I watched him out of the corner of my eye.

He tucked the biro in his jacket pocket and said, 'Well, that depends on you, gorgeous.' He moved the gun so the silencer slid down the edge of my top, lifting the fabric away from my skin.

I squirmed against the side of the van, trying to get away, but I had nowhere to go.

He leaned over, glanced down at the bra I chosen with care a few hours earlier for Mason. 'I've always had a thing for lace. What colour do you call that? Silver or pewter?'

I held my breath and clamped my eyes closed, my hands rigidly clutching the edge of the bench, fear bubbling beneath my skin.

The cold metal traced up the side of my neck, softly stroking me. A sound I'd never heard from myself before escaped my lips. I forced myself to speak, to try to distract him with my words. 'I don't know what you want. I don't know what's going on here. But you have the wrong person. Please, I'm– '

'Shush.' He whispered, digging the end of the silencer under my chin. 'Say something original. It fucking pisses me off when people just beg and deny and plead. They all say the same thing.' His lips twisted in a humourless smile. 'Go on. Be different from the rest, Nicole.'

I swallowed hard, squeezed my eyes shut even more. A lead block grew in my chest, freezing me in place, and my mind went blank. I was hanging onto life with the tip of my fingers and I couldn't even speak.

'Nothing to say?' He gave a cruel laugh. 'Well, when we get where we're going, I'll make sure you talk plenty. I always do.' His voice exuded chilling confidence.

My eyelids snapped open, and I stared into his eyes.

He removed the gun, leaning away from me, suddenly seeming bored. 'No more talking until we get there.'

As we drove in silence, the city noises began to disappear and we stayed on a straight road for a long time that I thought was probably a motorway.

My mind raced. What could I do to get away? But deep down, I knew there was no getting out of it. I was going to die.

I don't know how much time passed while I desperately tried to think of a way out of the situation. Eventually, the van took a tight left turn, and my torso fell forwards, my feet sliding out, the only thing saving me from sprawling on the floor was my grip on the bench.

Trying to be as surreptitious as possible, I glanced down to my right because my feet had just touched something underneath the lumpy dust sheets. Something hard.

The van sped up, slowed, sped up again. At the next left turn, it became apparent what was hiding under the rags when the edge of a can of spray paint rolled out from underneath. I tore my gaze away and looked straight in front of me, watching the gunman from the corner of my eye. He wasn't looking at me, instead staring straight ahead at the van's side door.

If I could grab hold of the can, I could spray him in the face, catch him off guard, blind him. If I timed it wrong, though, he would kill me. I had no doubt about that.

I clamped my jaw shut and turned my gaze towards the dust sheets.

The van was going fast now, twisting and turning on a winding road. The can edged out a little further, so close I could reach down and touch it.

I clenched my sweating fist and tried to remember to breathe.

Then the van suddenly lurched violently to the left, and the driver slammed on the brakes. There was a loud bang before we jerked to a hard stop.

I was launched to my right, out of my seat, falling onto my hands and knees on top of the dust sheet. The side of my forehead slammed into the mesh grille. I reached my hand under the edge of the dirty sheet and wrapped my fingers around the can of paint.

'Fucking deer ran in the road!' the driver yelled out.

I whipped my head around and saw the gunman on his feet against the side door where he'd been thrown, bracing himself against it with one hand. 'Well, slow the fuck down. You're driving too fast.' He turned his head away from me to shout at the driver through the mesh.

The driver tried to start the van, but the engine had stalled. It was now or never.

I quickly shot up, spun around and sprayed black paint in his face.

He yelped. One arm flew up in front of his face to ward off the attack. His gun hand pointed in my direction.

'What going on?' the driver yelled.

I lurched to the right and kept on spraying. So far so good, except he was still in front of the door and there was no escape.

The driver kept on swearing and turning over the engine.

The gunman shot at me as I carried on spraying. The bullet whizzed past my shoulder. Then he swung his weapon blindly, trying to hit me with it as he protected his face from the constant stream of paint.

His fist caught my outstretched wrist, knocking the can to the floor, giving him some respite, and he launched towards me, his eyes squeezed shut, paint dripping into his mouth.

I darted to my side, but his torso caught me on the shoulder, and I fell to the floor. A split second later, he landed on top of me, trying to grab my arms.

I twisted beneath him and elbowed him in the head, the blow catching him on the side of the temple. He made a grab for my wrist, swinging the gun around towards my head to hit me with it.

I ducked away just in time, and it danced a glancing blow above my ear, which was already ringing from the sound of the shot. I spotted the paint can to my right, a couple of inches out of reach. I stretched towards it, but he grabbed one arm and pinned it above my head. I still had one arm free as I writhed on the ground and slammed the heel of my hand into the underside of his nose. His head jerked up and his grip on me released as he fell into the door and slumped in front of it.

I scrabbled to my feet and kicked him as hard as I could in the balls with every ounce of strength I had, my wedged heels as thick as a brick hitting him in his weakest spot.

He let out a sound like the air being let out of a balloon and collapsed onto his side in a foetal position, clutching his crotch, coughing and retching and trying to breathe, all at the same time.

I kicked again, landing a foot in his mouth, before dodging over his feet and lurching for the door handle.

Then I ran for my life.

Chapter 22

The van was at the side of a grass verge in a country lane with woods either side. A dead deer lay in the road in front of it.

I ran blindly through the trees with no clue as to where I was, stumbling on my wedges. I thought about undoing the buckles and kicking them off, but that would take time, and I couldn't afford to waste precious moments. My arms and legs pumped faster as I dodged tree branches, winding through a forest. I had no idea which direction I should be going in, but through the panic, I had one clear thought: get as far away from here as possible. I didn't dare turn around to see if they were following, and all I could hear was the crashing of my footfalls through the bushes and foliage, my heart banging a bass drum inside, and the hiss of my breath.

Eventually, I emerged at the edge of another country lane. I didn't stop. I just carried on running along the edge of the tarmac, hoping someone would come and take me to safety.

And then what? a voice said in my head. Where would I be safe? They knew my name. They'd know where I lived. I had no clue why they were after me, but it must be to do with Mason and they must've followed me.

I'd been kidnapped and shot at with a gun. What the fuck was going on? Why hadn't Mason turned up? Who were those people, and why did they want me dead? Had Mason spotted them? Or was the photo and message all an elaborate hoax by those men? A trap to get me there so they could kidnap me … I didn't know what the hell to believe anymore. My whole world was spinning out of control. I wanted to get off but didn't know where the stop button was.

My mind raced as I ran. I needed to go to the police and tell them what had happened. But then I had another thought. If it wasn't a trap, if Mason was really alive, he must've been in hiding for ten months. These people were obviously prepared to kill over whatever he was involved in. How did I know who I could trust?

I didn't have time to think about what to do for the best, though, I just had to keep putting as much distance between me and those men as I could. I was tiring, though, as the sudden burst of adrenaline slowed down. I felt sick and weak as I jogged along, desperately thirsty.

No cars came down the lane. I tried to keep on running, but my feet stumbled as my lungs burned. Blood streamed into my eyes from my forehead. I reached up and touched a throbbing egg-sized lump that I must've got from hitting it on the mesh grille when the van screeched to a stop. My foot and ankle also hurt from kicking him so hard in the balls.

Unable to keep up my pace any longer, I slowed to a stop in the road, bent over at the waist and sucked in air for a few moments, rubbing at a stitch in my left-hand side.

After a few moments, I straightened up and looked all round. There were no signs of life, just endless road and woods.

And out of nowhere, I heard the rumbling of an engine in the distance behind me.

Chapter 23

Blade's eyes burned like a motherfucker. He remembered a job he'd done a few years back where a husband had wanted acid thrown in the face of his wife. He bet this was what it felt like.

His bollocks ached like he'd been kicked by a rhino. He wanted to puke. Tears streamed down his cheeks as he tried to blink, but he couldn't manage to open his eyes for long.

Dazed, he scrabbled around on the floor for the dust sheet and wiped his face with it. That fucking idiot Dave. Blade had given him clear instructions to remove everything inside the van, except the sheets that would come in handy for transporting and burying her body. How had the stupid wanker missed a can of paint?

'This is your fucking fault!' Blade shouted out from the back of the van.

But Dave didn't reply. Hopefully, he'd run after the bitch.

Blade wiped frantically at the paint, but he was just smearing it more into his eyes. He grunted with annoyance and felt his way to the side door with his lids shut, climbing out of the van and edging along to the front passenger door. He yanked it open and felt in the centre console for the bottle of water he'd put there earlier.

His hands clasped the plastic, and he unscrewed the lid, poured it over his face, wiping away the paint with the other hand. When the water ran out, he wiped his eyes on the sleeve of his jacket.

He tried blinking, but he couldn't keep his eyes open for more than a fraction of a second before they closed involuntarily, streaming with tears.

His anger boiled over as he waited a minute before trying again. This time, he could keep them open a little longer. When he got hold of Nicole, he was going to torture her longer for this little stunt.

He had no idea how much time passed before he was able to half open his eyes. He looked into the van and realised why Dave hadn't answered him. When he'd been shooting at Nicole while tussling with her, he'd accidentally shot Dave in the back. His head was slumped over the steering wheel, and there was a round patch of blood on his shirt.

Oh, well, tough shit. Dave was a useless bastard anyway.

'Dave!' Blade called out, leaning over the passenger seat and shaking him.

Dave moaned.

'Fuck's sake.' Blade climbed up into the passenger seat and gripped Dave's arm, trying to haul him over the gearstick into the passenger side, but he was too heavy and got wedged against it. 'Fat bastard,' Blade muttered, pulling him again.

This time, Dave's torso flopped towards him. Blade edged backwards and tugged, slowly dragging Dave, ignoring his foot getting stuck on the accelerator pedal. He tried yanking him, but it wasn't working quick enough.

He'd had enough of this shit.

Blade went around to the driver's side, opened the door and leaned in, pushing Dave's body. Eventually, he managed to get Dave in position slumped on the passenger seat and slid behind the wheel, wiping his eyes again with the back of his hand.

There was a huge deer in the road, and the front of the van was dented. Blade turned over the engine but it didn't start.

'Jesus fucking Christ!' he snapped, turning the keys again.

The van made a spluttering sound and then died.

He tried again. The van started.

He drove up the lane, looking left and right into the woods, the sunlight burning his eyes, his nuts on fire. He'd made a monumental fuck up, but there was still time to put it right. She couldn't have got far.

Chapter 24

I stood frozen in the road as I listened to the vehicle approaching, knowing this could be my one chance of getting away, but also knowing that the men in the van could still be looking for me. It took a few seconds for my brain to snap into action and I ducked back into the woods.

I pushed aside the bracken and ferns and found a thick tree about fifty metres from the road, far enough away that the driver wouldn't see me, but close enough to run out and hopefully catch their attention if I realised it wasn't them. I crouched down, peered around. My right eye twitched beneath the lump, and I was breathing so fast I was almost hyperventilating as the vehicle roared closer.

I concentrated on staring at the road through the foliage. And then the white van came into view, travelling slowly.

I jerked back so I was completely hidden from view and held my breath. I heard the van slow to a stop, the engine idling with a whining sound.

I heard a door open. Heard footsteps on tarmac.

I clenched my eyes shut and breathed out as quietly as I could. Panic froze me solid. I'd escaped only for them to find me again.

I waited.

One second.

Two seconds.

I couldn't hear anything else and pictured the gunman peering into the woods.

Three seconds.

Then I heard the door slam shut, and the vehicle screeched off as if the engine was under duress.

I carried on waiting there, until my thighs shook in their crouched position so uncontrollably that I slid to my knees and held onto the tree trunk. I was shivering, but I didn't know if it was from fear, exhaustion or from the sweat cooling on my body.

To be sure they'd gone I carried on waiting until the light faded, worrying that they could be parked up somewhere waiting for me. I only heard one vehicle driving on the lane during that time, but I didn't dare move.

Eventually, I got to my feet, my muscles stiff and painful.

I had no choice but to keep on going. At some point, I'd come to a village or town.

I slid a hand in the pocket of my Capri trousers and breathed a sigh of relief. I was always wary of my bag being stolen, so I kept a small fabric purse with some money in my pocket whenever I went out. It was still there so at least I had some means of paying for a ride back to … where? I couldn't go home now. They would most likely be waiting for me there.

Before I could think things through, I heard the sound of a vehicle. I stood up, keeping my body covered, and peered round the tree. In the distance, I saw a flash of red. It was a small car.

I ran out of the woods and stood in the road, waving my arms wildly.

The car slowed to a stop about ten metres in front of me. The sinking sun bounced off the windscreen and I couldn't see who was driving.

For a heart-stopping moment, I thought it would be them again in a change of vehicle, but then the driver's door opened, and a bewildered-looking young woman stepped out.

'Oh, my God, are you okay?' she asked. 'Have you been in a car accident?'

As I walked towards her, I realised she couldn't have been more than nineteen. 'Thank you for stopping. My … um …' I thought about trying to explain it, but I didn't even know where to begin and I needed to get off this road in case those men came back. By the time I'd told her what had happened, she'd either think I was crazy or we'd both be dead so it was easier to lie. 'Yes. An accident. I left my car. I've been walking, but I don't know where I am. Can you give me a lift, please?'

She frowned at my forehead. 'Of course. Get in. You've got a big bump there. Do you want me to take you to hospital?'

I got in the passenger side and buckled up as she slid behind the wheel. I winced as the pain registered again all over my body from the fight with the gunman.

'Um … no, thanks. I'll be all right.' Even though my head was killing me, I didn't have concussion, and I didn't have time to get it looked at.

'Where shall I drop you, then?'

I glanced around, keeping one eye out for the van.

That was a good question. I didn't even know where the hell I was.

Chapter 25

Mason finally stopped running and bent over, hands on thighs, catching his breath. He'd searched all of the surrounding streets with no sign of Nicole, and now he had to admit defeat. They had most likely had a vehicle at the ready and were long gone. In between searching, he'd repeatedly tried calling her mobile number, but it was switched off.

He had to find out where they'd taken her. The trouble was, he had no clue where to start. They could be anywhere. They'd torture her to find out what she knew about him, and then they'd kill her.

'Jesus Christ,' he muttered to himself, not noticing an elderly woman walking her dog who gave him an odd look and a wide berth.

Was it time to go to the authorities?

Not yet. They had friends in high places. Billions of pounds were at stake. Their reach would be everywhere. He couldn't trust anyone else to keep Nicole safe. So how could he find his wife before it was too late?

He stood upright again on unsteady legs, his eyes still scanning for signs of Nicole and the man who'd kidnapped her, even though he knew it was futile. All he could do was go to their house in Linton and hope those bastards had taken Nicole there to try and draw him out of hiding.

It was a long shot, but it was all he had.

Chapter 26

Blade drove on, his jaw clenching with fury as he accepted the fact Nicole had disappeared. It was very rare that he failed at something, but he seemed to be losing his shit lately. First, Isabelle biting him, and now, Nicole escaping, although for the latter he put the blame squarely on Dave's shoulders.

As if in response, Dave moaned from his unconscious slump. Blade needed to get rid of the van. And Dave, who was now a liability.

His mobile phone rang in his jacket pocket. He pulled it out and looked at the screen. It was the man he was doing this job for. Julian Bolliger.

'How is our problem coming along?' Julian asked.

Blade hesitated. Bolliger had already paid Blade fifty grand upfront, with another hundred when he finished the job. He didn't know Bolliger personally, it was an underworld fixer who'd directed Bolliger to Blade, but he knew Bolliger wouldn't be too impressed to find out what had happened this afternoon. And Blade didn't want a slur on his reputation. So, he lied.

'Everything is under control. I'll have her answers for you shortly. And then I'll eliminate her.'

'Make sure she tells you where her husband is. I need the problem gone within three days.'

'Understood.' Blade glared at the phone after Bolliger hung up. Glared at Dave, who couldn't even understand a direct order to clear the stolen van out or have the common sense to avoid hitting a fucking deer.

Then his boiling anger turned to arousal as he thought about the pain he'd inflict on Nicole Palmer when he got hold of her.

He'd do it slow. Over a few days. Make her scream and beg for mercy.

There were plenty of ways to find her. The tracking software Frankie had remotely put on her phone was useless now, since it was still in the back of the van where he'd dumped the contents of her bag, but the tracker on her car would hopefully lead him to her. And if not, Frankie would be able to find her. These days, no one could stay off the grid completely.

Dave groaned again.

Blade took his gun with the suppressor and fired it into the side of Dave's temple, cursing Dave again for making him clean up after this mess.

Chapter 27

It turned out, I was in Epping Forest. The girl kindly dropped me at Epping Underground Station, and I caught a tube heading towards London. I'd thought about going back to Cambridge, to the park and ride bus stop to get my car, but I'd had a horrible thought that they'd put some kind of tracker on my vehicle, so that was out of the question. They'd probably been tracking my phone too, but that didn't matter now, seeing as it was in the back of the van.

Those men obviously thought I knew something about whatever Mason was involved in, but what? I thought again about going to the police but still didn't want to defy Mason's message not to tell anyone. Plus, what would I tell them? I think my dead husband's alive, and someone tried to kidnap me because they think I know something. I haven't got a clue what, though. It sounded insane.

No. First, I needed to speak to Isabelle again. She definitely knew more than she was telling me. Had she known all along that Mason wasn't even dead?

I got off the tube and took the over ground train to St Pancras, then walked to Kings Cross Station where I stared at the board looking for trains to Knebworth, the nearest station to the village Isabelle lived in.

The train didn't leave for another twenty minutes, so I bought two bottles of water and a bar of chocolate and rushed to the toilets to wash my face. I stared at my haunted reflection. There were bits of leaves in my matted hair, the lump on my forehead was angry red with caked blood. Bruises were already forming on my arms and legs from where I'd been flung around in the van. I looked like I was starring in a scene from *The Walking Dead.*

Gently, I washed the lump, gritting my teeth against the pain, then patted it with a paper towel. I ran my fingers through my hair, removed all the debris, then pulled it over my forehead to disguise the bump. I waited on the platform, trying to rehydrate and get my energy back as I glanced nervously around. It was rush hour, and the place was packed with commuters. How long would it take those men to find out where I was? They were obviously professionals so perhaps not long at all.

When the train arrived, I stepped aboard. I wanted to sit down, my legs barely felt as if they'd hold me up. My gaze scanned the crowds, looking for the gunman. But I thought it was safer to stand in the doorway, all the better to make a quick getaway, just in case. I leaned my back against the glass partition separating the entryway from the body of the train and fought the waves of exhaustion and the throbbing in my head.

By the time I arrived at Knebworth station, I was certain that there had to be a good reason why Mason didn't show up at the meeting place. He must've seen those men following me and disappeared again.

Reality struck that Mason wouldn't be able to contact me again. If he sent another note through the post, it would probably be intercepted by those men and he'd be in grave danger. He wouldn't be able to call me on the mobile number he knew as my phone was in the back of that van. He could still send me an email, though. I was sure those people would already have been monitoring my email address, which was most likely the reason Mason had chosen to communicate by post, but if he emailed a cryptic message again to meet up in a location only we knew, there was no way they could follow me if they didn't know where I was and couldn't work out the location. It was the only thing I could hope for now.

I walked from the train station towards the High Street and spotted a small supermarket that was still open. Hopefully, I'd be able to get a mobile phone there.

I grabbed a basket by the entrance and picked up another bottle of water from the sandwich display. As I searched the aisles for mobile phones, I unscrewed the lid and gulped it down, but it barely took the edge off my parched throat. By the time the bottle was half full, I'd picked up a cheap phone that would do the job, along with a SIM card that had internet access and added that to my basket, my eyes constantly scanning the few local shoppers.

A sudden jolt from behind forced a scared shriek from my mouth. I dropped the basket and turned around, hands up, ready to fight if necessary, but it was only a schoolboy – about fifteen years old – dressed in his uniform, jostling with his mates.

The schoolboy mumbled a laughing apology and sauntered out of the shop, oblivious to the heart attack he'd almost given me.

I took a steadying breath. Blew it out. Then headed for the check out. After I'd made my purchases, I stepped out into the dark night, my heart beating erratically in my chest, and downed the rest of the water before putting the bottle in a nearby bin.

My stomach growled, and a wave of dizziness took over. I leaned against the supermarket's brick wall façade until it passed. I'd barely eaten anything all day, I'd been too nervous to have breakfast with the thought of finally seeing my husband again, and I was running on empty. I needed something warm inside me and to charge the new phone up. There was an Indian restaurant just down the road, so I headed there. Hopefully, I'd be safe in amongst other people, and the curtains were closed at their windows so no one would see me from the outside.

I was shown by a waiter to a table in the corner where I could watch the doorway. There were only a few people inside – a couple eating at a table and an elderly man at the bar loudly ordering a takeaway. While I waited for my food order, I assembled the pay-as-you-go SIM card in the phone. I glanced around and spotted a plug socket by my feet, so plugged it in to charge.

By the time I'd polished off a biryani and naan bread, my hands had stopped shaking. I checked the battery level on the phone. Two little bricks. I logged onto my email account, waiting with breathless anticipation for a message from Mason, my heart plummeting when I found only two spam emails. I couldn't call Adama again, because I couldn't remember the number.

I ground my teeth and contemplated my next move. I'd only been to Isabelle's house once before with Mason, for the New Year's Eve party she'd held, and I just hoped I could remember where it was, although Old Knebworth wasn't a big village. If she wasn't back from work yet, I'd just have to wait on her doorstep until I could get the answers I needed.

I headed towards a taxi rank, a chill hitting me that had nothing to do with the cool night air on my skin. I kept looking behind me periodically to spot if someone was following, my gaze scanning the people passing me, but I saw no one suspicious. There was one person already queuing when I arrived but two cabs pulled up at once, and a few minutes later, I was seated in the back of one, ignoring the chatty driver. And that's when the shock caught up with me, hitting me hard between the eyes as I realised that, miraculously, I'd managed to escape a psychopathic killer by the skin of my teeth.

But if they found me again, I wasn't so sure I'd be that lucky a second time.

Chapter 28

After taking a few wrong turns through the village, the taxi driver began to get frustrated with me because I couldn't remember exactly where I was going. But then I spotted a pub I recognised and knew we'd taken a left after it, up some quiet country lane.

'Here it is,' I said.

The taxi driver pulled to a stop outside Isabelle's front wooden gates. I wondered if I was making a huge mistake. Was I safe with Isabelle? What if she was the one who'd set those men on me? I chewed on my lip, trying to decide whether she could be a cold-blooded killer. Even though I was convinced she knew something, I couldn't see her being involved like that, but still … what if she attacked me? Or those men were inside?

It was too late to back out, so as I handed the driver some of my dwindling money and waited for the change, I asked, 'Would you mind waiting for me?'

He glanced at his watch. 'I can wait five minutes, love.'

'Thanks. If I'm not out in five, can you come and get me?'

He sighed. 'I'm not a personal assistant, you know.'

'Yes, I know, but, please. It's important.'

He shrugged. 'All right.'

I got out of the cab, unlatched the gate and closed it behind me.

Her barn conversion was set back from the road, in the shadows.

I passed her parked Mercedes and looked around for something to use as protection, but there was nothing. My stomach fluttered as I pressed the bell and wondered what she would tell me.

There was no answer. I pressed it again.

Still no response. I knocked on the door, and it swung inwards with an ominous creaking sound.

'Hello? Isabelle ...' I leaned around the partially-open door, but it was too dark to see much, just the shadowy staircase to my right and the hallway in front that led to her lounge at the rear of the property. 'It's Nicole.' I pushed the door open further and stepped inside the property. 'Isabelle? Are you here?'

I stood and listened but could hear no sounds. The hairs on the back of my neck rose, and even though a voice in my head was screaming at me to get out, I still walked up the hallway, because the need to find out what she knew and where Mason might be was greater than my fear.

'Isabelle?' I pressed a button on my new phone, its weak light illuminating the shadows a little. I swung it around and saw the lounge door was closed. 'Hello?'

There was an umbrella hanging from a wooden coat hook to my left. Not much of a weapon, but it would have to do. I took it and held it up against my shoulder, ready to strike someone with it, if I needed to. Ridiculous, really, because if someone was waiting inside, they already knew I was there and could take me by surprise, but my mind wasn't exactly thinking straight at that point. If it was, I would've run. But instead, I walked cautiously towards the closed doorway at the end of the hall, my footsteps silent on the plush carpet, my heart pounding.

Clutching the umbrella in one hand, I pressed down on the handle with my fingertips, the light from my phone clenched in my fist shining on the floor as it moved with me.

The door swung open, and I knew what was inside before my phone had even illuminated the room. It was the smell that gave it away.

That's when I saw her. Lying on her back on the floor, blood covering her body and pooling around her on the carpet. Her head was twisted towards me, her right eye staring blankly in my direction, a dark red gaping hole where her left eye used to be, her mouth wide open in the echo of a scream.

'Oh, my God.' The umbrella and phone fell from my hands to the floor as I stood rooted to the spot, unable to believe the horror of what I was seeing. The contents of my stomach threatened to come back up. I swallowed, trying to force it back down.

Then I heard a noise behind me.

Before I could turn around, someone shouted, 'Police! Do not move.'

Chapter 29

It was fully dark when Mason finally approached his house after parking the car he'd hired from the airport with false documents a few streets away. He tugged his baseball cap over his eyes to hide himself from any of the neighbours who might recognise him and looked at the home he'd shared with Nicole, his heart twisting. There was no time for regrets and melancholy thoughts, though. It was a risk coming here but a risk he had to take if he was going to find his wife again and save her.

There were no lights on in the house, and her car wasn't sitting on the drive. He didn't think she was even inside, but he had to try. There was still no answer from her phone, it was just a dead line, and he had no other ideas of where they might've taken her.

He strode to the front door and unlocked it with his key. For the first time in ten months, he stepped inside his home.

'Nicole?' he called out, his stomach a jumble of nerves.

There was no response. As he rushed from room to room downstairs, desperately crying out her name, the familiar scent of her *Lush* perfume hit him. It was called Karma; he'd bought it for her many times. His heart clenched with fear for his wife as he climbed the stairs and checked the master bedroom, even checking wardrobes, and the en suite. Then the spare two bedrooms.

There was no sign of her.

He leaned against the wall on the landing as his knees threatened to buckle beneath him. He'd tried to do the right thing, and he'd failed to keep her safe. He had no idea where they'd taken her, if she was even alive. Most likely he'd never see her again. Not when they were finished with her.

He slid to the carpeted floor, wrapped his arms around his knees and rested his head on them, sobbing.

Chapter 30

Blade arrived at the disused chalk quarry.

In the summer, the area was popular with locals – teenagers who swam in the murky waters and drank icy cold beers, families who barbequed. Now it would be his associate's final resting place, and it wasn't the first time Blade had used it.

He drove the van along the dusty white track with fields either side of him until he came to a copse of trees. There were several paths that vehicles had eroded over the years in their quest for fun and frolics at the Pit. He took the right fork and drove along until the huge quarry opened up before him on his left-hand side. Even though it was dark, with no one likely to be around now, he drove in a loop, making sure there were no dog walkers, no hikers, no witnesses.

He parked at the edge of the deepest part of the quarry where there was an incline. The opposite edge was shallow, but from here, the cliff fell away in a straight drop.

He turned off the engine and put the gearstick in neutral, then pulled up the handbrake and glanced at Dave, now covered with one of the dust sheets from the rear. Blade got out of the driver's door and peered over the edge.

Perfect.

He wound down the driver's window, opened Dave's door and wound that down also. Then he closed the door, walked back to the driver's side again and took the handbrake off.

He ran to the back of the van and pushed it towards the incline. It edged forwards, gaining momentum, then fell off the cliff.

He leaned over and looked down, waiting until the open windows had filled with water.

Then he took out his mobile and phoned Frankie. Told him to come collect him.

While he waited, he pulled up an app on his phone that provided GPS data from the tracker on Nicole Palmer's car. According to the location given, it was still at the park and ride bus station. She must've guessed they'd been monitoring her movements and not returned to it.

Shit.

As he peered once more over the edge of the quarry, the only sign now of the vehicle just a ripple in the water as it sank into oblivion, his phone buzzed with an alert.

It was from the covert cameras and voice recorders planted in Nicole's house and they'd just been activated. A grin snaked up the corner of his lips.

As he clicked on the first recording box to view the real time footage, his eyes widened with surprise. He was looking at the main prize.

Mason Palmer, alive and in the flesh.

Chapter 31

I watched every second tick by on the clock in the interview room. I was trying to use it for meditation, to focus on that one hand turning around, so I could stop the terror escalating. But it didn't work. I couldn't block out Isabelle's lifeless body from my mind, nor the men who'd kidnapped me.

Someone was prepared to kill over this. I wasn't safe out on the streets. I just prayed I'd be safer in here.

By the time the clock had gone through a cycle of one hour and fifty-two seconds, and two officers dressed in suits entered the room, I'd decided I had to tell all, despite Mason's warning not to. I wasn't equipped for this. And I couldn't keep running. I had no idea where Mason was, and I needed help before those men found me again.

The male officer, who had a tanned face and sandy brown hair greying at his long sideburns, said, 'I'm DI Thornton. This is DS Harris.' He nodded towards his female colleague. She was younger than him, her hair pulled into a messy bun, tendrils escaping at the side of her temple.

They both wore grave expressions as they sat in front of me. DS Harris fiddled with a recording device on the desk between us and announced who was in the room as well as the date and time.

'You're not under arrest at this time, but we are treating you as a person of interest in this murder enquiry. Do you understand?' DI Thornton said.

'Yes,' I managed to croak out, sitting on my hands to stop them shaking.

'What were you doing at Isabelle Moore's house?' he asked.

I swallowed. 'It's a long story.'

'Well, we've got all night.' He sat back in the plastic chair and folded his arms.

I took a deep breath. I knew it would sound crazy to them but that was the least of my worries. 'My husband, Mason, died in a plane crash in Africa ten months ago. He was a doctor, working for an international medical NGO that had set up a clinic there. Then three days ago, I received a photo of Mason in the mail.' I carried on with my story, how I'd spoken to Jean-Luc, Aiden, Moussa Damba, finding the last phone call on Mason's phone records, my conversations with Isabelle, trying to reach Adama, the warning I'd received on the phone, then the second contact from Mason about where to meet. Being kidnapped at gun point, fighting to get away from those men, running for my life, going back to see Isabelle, because I suspected she knew more than she was telling me, finding her dead body.

DI Thornton gave me a suspicious look. 'Right. Let me make sure I've got this straight. The authorities in Narumbe issued a death certificate for your husband?'

'Yes. But the plane has never been found, so how do they know for certain?'

'But they advised you no one could've survived the crash, even though the plane's never been located?'

I swallowed. 'Yes. But–'

'And the other three people on the plane haven't reappeared, because you spoke to their mum, is that right?'

'Yes,' I mumbled and looked down at the desk, knowing how ridiculous it sounded.

'So, they didn't survive the crash, either?'

'It doesn't look like it, no.'

'So, it can't have been your husband sending the photo and notes, right?'

'No. Yes. I don't think he even got on the plane.'

'Where do you think he's been all this time then?' DS Harris asked.

'I don't know. That's what I'm trying to explain.' I blew out a frustrated breath. 'I don't know what is–'

'But then you say that your husband, who, very sadly must be deceased, suddenly contacts you again asking to meet?' DI Thornton asked.

'Yes. And when I went to where he said, the kidnappers must've followed me. A man grabbed me and bundled me into a van. He had a gun, but I managed to escape.'

'By spraying him with paint?' DI Thornton asked, an incredulous tone in his voice.

'Yes. It was self-defence. He was going to kill me, I was sure of it.'

'Why would someone want to kill you?' DI Thornton again.

'I think they were looking for Mason.'

'But he died ten months ago,' DS Harris said. 'So why would they be looking for him?'

'I *told* you, I don't think he was on that plane.'

'Because of the photo and note you were sent?' DI Thornton quirked up one eyebrow.

'Yes.'

'Which could've been sent by anybody. Someone playing a malicious prank on you.'

'Yes, I suppose so, but they couldn't have known the things written on the back of the photo. It was written so only I'd know what it meant.'

'Was it in a foreign language?' DS Harris asked.

'No. Just … you know, couples have private sayings and things that happen to them that make … that you know other people … experiences that …' I couldn't think how to explain myself. I didn't even know what I meant anymore. It all sounded too bizarre. I rubbed at my forehead, catching the lump, and winced.

'And what did it say?' DS Harris asked. 'This note.'

'Um… "Everything stinks 'til it's finished".'

'Why would someone write that?' DI Thornton asked.

'It's a Dr Seuss quote.' I sighed. 'It was personal to us. And then it said, I *will* contact you again soon. You mustn't tell anyone about this.'

'Right. But he couldn't have sent it to you if he'd been in a fatal plane crash in Africa, could he?' DI Thornton asked. He was trying to be sympathetic, but I detected a note of incredulity and impatience in his voice.

I threw my hands in the air, anger bubbling to the surface. My head started spinning. 'You're not listening to me! He *wasn't on the plane.*' I swallowed to get rid of the dry, sour taste in my mouth.

'But the authorities say he was, Nicole,' DS Harris added softly.

'Look, I don't know what's going on. I know it sounds mad, but the photo and note were from Mason. I know it. How do you explain the phone call made from his phone? If the plane took off at two-ten, how could he have made a call at two-eighteen if he was on it?'

DI Thornton ignored the question and said, 'Why didn't you report this abduction, when you managed to get away from the man with a gun? If you thought you were in danger, why didn't you go to the nearest police station?'

I glanced down again. 'I didn't know who I could trust. I was scared. I didn't know what to do. I thought if I could just speak to Isabelle again, then maybe she'd tell me what she really knew, and I could find Mason and find out what's going on.'

'So then you went to her house and killed her?' DI Thornton said, all attempt at sympathy now gone.

My head shot up to look at them. 'You're joking!' It felt like the walls were closing in on me. Like I was suffocating. My forehead throbbed harder.

'It doesn't seem funny from where we're sitting,' DI Thornton said.

'No! You've got it wrong. You can't seriously think I killed her. Why would I? I just went there to speak to her. This is what's happening, though, people are being killed over it. And I received a warning from someone in Narumbe not to trust the government officer, Moussa Damba.'

DI Thornton tapped his fingertips on the desk. 'And what is *it*?' His expression gave nothing away, but he didn't believe me, that much was obvious.

'I don't know. That's what I'm trying to find out!' I put my head in my hands and took several deep breaths before sitting up again, using every ounce of energy not to cry.

DI Thornton studied me carefully for a moment before standing and saying that the interview was suspended and they were leaving the room. Then he turned off the recording equipment and said to me, 'I'll be back in a moment.'

They stepped outside and shut the door. I rested my forehead on the desk and closed my eyes. I didn't open them again until I heard the sound of the door. I was crazy to think they'd understand what was going on. I didn't even understand it myself and I'd been living it. I wondered if I should get a lawyer, but surely that would only make me look guiltier.

DI Thornton returned on his own and started the interview again.

'You have a nasty lump on your forehead there.' He pointed to my head.

My hand went up and touched the painful skin. 'Like I said, I got it when I was fighting with the gunman in the van.'

'Are you sure you don't want to see the force doctor? You could have a concussion or possible head injury.'

They'd already asked me once when I arrived if I wanted medical attention. And although a headache had wormed its way behind my right eye and temple, I didn't want to waste time waiting for a doctor.

'No, it's okay. I just want to find out what's going on here.'

He clasped his hands together on the desk and looked at me pointedly. 'And so do we, Mrs Palmer.' He watched me warily. 'Right. Let's go through this again, shall we?'

Chapter 32

DI Thornton's mobile rang as I was explaining the whole scenario yet again.

He looked at the screen, then said, 'Excuse me a moment, I need to answer this,' before turning off the tape and leaving the room.

I wanted to lean forward and rest my head on the desk and sleep and pretend this wasn't happening, couldn't be happening. It was like I'd been plucked into a parallel universe. I was exhausted from lack of sleep, an overdose of adrenaline and pure terror about what would happen to me. I wondered again where Mason was and what was happening to him. Had those men caught up with him too? Or had he retreated into hiding again?

I fought to keep my eyes open as I watched DI Thornton re-enter, sit down and turn the tape back on.

'We've just been given the pathologist's estimated time of death.' He placed his phone on the desk and sat up straighter. 'Where were you between the hours of five pm and ten pm last night?'

For a moment, I couldn't think. My brain froze. Surely they couldn't seriously think I'd murdered Isabelle in such a brutal way. Then the synapses kick-started again, and my whole body seemed to relax with relief, my shoulders slumping slightly as if the weight I'd been carrying finally let go. 'I was at home. With my boss. Cheryl Lampard. She's the head teacher at Haverhill Community Primary School where I work. She came to my house at four and left at just gone midnight.'

'Can you give me her details, please?'

I told him Cheryl's address and phone number.

'Right.' He looked at me as if I was lying. 'And she'll verify this, will she?'

'Of course she will,' I snapped, frustrated now with all this time wasting.

He announced to the tape that the interview was suspended again and left the room.

I did succumb to weariness then, folding my elbows onto the desk and resting my head against them. I closed my eyes, listening to the sound of the clock ticking and my breathing. It seemed like an interminable wait until he came back with DS Harris.

I sat up and rubbed at my eyes, watching their expressions as they sat in front of me. They weren't giving anything away.

'Cheryl Lampard has confirmed your alibi,' DI Thornton said with what sounded like disappointment.

'I told you she would because it's true. I didn't kill Isabelle. I just went to talk to her.'

'Cheryl did mention something else interesting.' He raised an eyebrow, as if waiting for me to ask what. I didn't, so he carried on. 'She said you thought you were being harassed by a parent of one of your pupils.'

'Angela, yes. I thought she was the one who sent the photo first of all.' I explained how she'd done something similar to another parent.

'But then you changed your story and said she hadn't in fact harassed you at all,' he said.

'Yes, but … that's because I thought it was her who sent me the photo at first. Only now I know that's not true. Now I know it was Mason.'

He nodded but didn't look like he believed anything I said. 'So. Let's turn our attention to the two men you say abducted you.' He paused. 'One of them told you he had a gun and then bundled you in a vehicle.'

'He *did* have a gun. I've told you this already, several times.' I rubbed at my forehead. What would it take for them to believe me? 'It had a silencer on it.'

'Yes, quite. And these men drove you at gunpoint to a remote location in Epping Forest, whereby a deer ran out in the road, causing a diversion which allowed you to spray paint in the gunman's face and attack him before escaping.' There was something in the tone of his voice I couldn't work out but sounded a lot like boredom.

'That's right.' I touched my fingertips again to the sore lump on my head.

'Well, that's the strange thing.' DI Thornton leaned forward, scrutinising my face. 'In my vast experience, kidnapping or abduction is very rare. In my twenty years on the job, I've only ever known of people being abducted because of criminal or drug connections. We've checked you out, and you seem to be a law-abiding primary school teacher, so why would someone want to abduct you? And why wouldn't you come straight to the police if they had?'

I blinked rapidly, my forehead pinching into an angry frown. 'You haven't listened to a word I've said. They kidnapped me because they wanted to know where my husband is hiding.'

'But he's *dead*, Nicole,' DS Harris said, her tone more sympathetic than her boss's. 'Why would they be trying to find someone who's deceased?'

Before I could deny this again, DI Thornton said, 'Regarding the phone call you found on Mason's phone bill after his flight had taken off, I spoke to our technical team about it.'

'Yes?'

'They said it's possible, in certain circumstances, to get a mobile phone signal from a cell tower even at 25,000 feet. In areas where cell phone networks must cover large areas with low population density, which sounds very similar to the bush land you describe the plane crashed in, the transmitters are set up to send a very powerful signal. Since the plane your husband was on travelled at eight thousand feet, he must've been using it on board.'

I shook my head. 'I know he wasn't on the plane.'

DI Thornton studied me carefully. 'Have you been receiving any mental health treatment recently?'

I gasped. 'Of course not. I'm telling the truth. I'm not mad.'

'You see, here's what I think … I think the death of your husband has naturally had a very profound effect on you. I think the stress has made you … confused about things, shall we say. Particularly as there's been no body to repatriate and say your goodbyes to. There's been no proper closure for you. Even your friend Cheryl is worried about you.'

'I'm not confused! My husband isn't dead.' I slapped my hand on the desk. 'Somehow, and I don't know how or what happened, somehow, he survived the crash, or he didn't get on the plane at all. The photo and the card were from him.' I leaned forward, trying to make them understand something I didn't even understand myself. 'And then two men kidnapped me just as I was supposed to meet Mason, and I managed to get away. Then I went to talk to Isabelle, but she'd already been killed. Don't you see? Why aren't you out there trying to find the man who kidnapped me? He must be the one who killed Isabelle.'

'Do you drink much, Mrs Palmer?' DI Thornton asked.

I shrugged with irritation. 'About the same as most people, I suppose.'

'Had you been drinking when you hit your head? Maybe you fell over and banged it?'

'No,' I cried. 'I've told you what happened.'

'As I was saying,' he carried on. 'I think you've been consumed with grief. You've now suffered from some kind of accident.' He pointed at my head. 'Which has further compounded your confusion about events.' He paused. 'We've discovered Isabelle's house was ransacked, most likely by the killer looking for money. After considering the evidence so far, we believe it to be a case that she disturbed whoever broke in and they killed her, so we don't need to question you any further at this time.' His voice was a mix of patronizing pity, talking slowly and clearly in a tone he probably reserved for people with mental health issues.

'It wasn't a burglar,' I mumbled.

DI Thornton held his hand up to silence me. 'I really do think it would be in your best interests to see a doctor. It's not surprising, given the sad circumstances surrounding your husband's death, that you are distraught and upset and confused. And a possible concussion will not be helping matters.' I clenched my fist and opened my mouth to argue, but DI Thornton stood up and said, 'Interview terminated.' He switched off the recording equipment and said to me, 'You're free to leave, Mrs Palmer. I would suggest you speak to someone before things get out of hand.'

Chapter 33

DS Harris watched Nicole's back retreating through the front doors of the police station. 'What do you make of that?' she asked DI Thornton standing next to her.

'I've seen some crackpots in my time, and she's either a pure fantasist or on the edge of a breakdown.'

But Becky wasn't so sure. She'd dealt with mentally ill people numerous times on the job. People who genuinely believed the tales they told about men living in their radiators who only came out at night or with paranoid delusions that aliens had replaced their blood with washing up liquid. It was also surprising the amount of people who came in reporting crimes that had never actually happened, especially when they'd been drinking. But Nicole Palmer's story was *so* outlandish that maybe there was some truth to it. 'If she's not, then she could be in danger. If she really was abducted and managed to get away, they could try again.'

DI Thornton rolled his eyes. 'She thinks her husband's alive! She's nuts.' He turned on his heels. 'We've got a murderer to catch. We've got no time or resources to deal with the crazies.' He started off towards the stairs, heading to where the incident room for Isabelle Moore's murder was busy being set up.

She stood and watched Nicole walk down the steps outside. Nicole paused, looked back, and there was a terrified look in her eyes that jolted through her.

'Are you coming?' DI Thornton said impatiently from behind her.

'Yes.' She waited until Nicole disappeared into the dark night before following him.

Chapter 34

Mason wiped away the tears. He was a surgeon, for God's sake. He worked around problems methodically. He was used to making split second emergency decisions. He needed to pull himself together. So, he tucked away the pity and terror for his wife and tried to think around the problem.

But it was no use. He had no idea how he could find out where they'd taken her. An anguished sob rose in his chest and forced its way through his mouth as he faced reality.

Hours had passed since Nicole had been taken and she was likely dead by now. Probably tortured beforehand to find out how much she knew and if she would give away his location. He knew how Moussa Damba operated, and he, or whoever was working for him, would show no mercy. All this time Mason thought he'd been protecting her and he'd failed.

The world spun around him as he pictured the pain she would've suffered before she was murdered. All to keep their dark secrets.

The only thing spurring him on for the last ten months was the thought that eventually he and Nicole would be together again. And now … now there was nothing left.

He got to his feet, wiped the tears away and rushed downstairs. He opened the front door an inch, his gaze sweeping up and down the street. No one was about. No suspicious vehicles seemed to be waiting outside for him.

He left the house and jogged away. Got in his car and drove, hardly seeing the roads and vehicles, narrowly missing an oncoming bus as he pulled out in front of it, the tears blurring his vision.

It started raining heavily, making it harder to see, even though the wipers were on full blast. But maybe he didn't want to see anymore. Maybe it would be karma if he crashed and died too. He had nothing to live for now anyway. His whole life had been ruined. He'd handled this all wrong and deserved to feel the scythe of grief ripping him to shreds. He wanted to curl into a ball and admit defeat. Be alone with his pain. But there was no time for that. Now he could no longer protect Nicole, it was finally time to tell the authorities what was going on.

He drove towards the nearest police station as a song came on the car radio that reminded him of Nicole. "Patience" by Damian Marley. His wife's face swam before his eyes. He saw himself holding her hand, lifting it in front of his face and stroking her delicate wrist. He always said she had doll's hands. He pictured the way she twirled a lock of hair whenever she was reading. How her bottom lip jutted out when she was concentrating. Her whipping up a moussaka in the kitchen, her signature meal, telling him, *it's the cinnamon that's the secret*, whenever he mentioned how good it was. The grace of her long neck. How she snuggled into him after they made love. The way she tucked the duvet underneath one arm before she fell asleep. How she always sneezed three times in quick succession. She had that rare quality of listening to people, even if it was because she'd rather they talked than reveal too much of herself. How she was fiercely protective of the people she did let get close to her, like an ancient warrior watching over her tribe. And a million other every-day quirks and traits that had kept him captivated through the years.

A memory punched him hard in the chest: Nicole and him sitting at their dining room table, talking about their future, about how she wanted to have two children because of her experiences of being an only child. Then his mind turned to the years of fertility treatment that had pushed them away from each other. They'd seemed like two strangers living in the same house, and instead of fighting for her, he'd turned his back and taken the new job in Africa. He'd needed excitement. A challenge. Needed to stop looking at his wife and seeing the desolate look in her eyes because she couldn't conceive. He'd been selfish. And so, so stupid. He'd led those men to her. He'd put her in danger. Practically killed her himself.

His heart exploded with grief.

If only he hadn't taken that job with Health International. If only he'd made more of an effort to reunite them from the gaping chasm that had opened up after the fertility treatment, instead of pushing further away by taking the job with Health International.

If only.

The song finished, and the news came on. He was so lost in thought that he didn't hear what the reporter was saying at first, until the words "Bolliger" and "multi-billion-pound merger deal" penetrated his stricken mind. He slammed the brakes on and pulled to the kerb, causing the car behind to blare his horn at him, but he barely noticed. He was too intent on listening to the details being announced and the smug voice of Julian Bolliger as they released a soundbite from an interview with him.

A hot flame of anger ignited inside Mason, his hands gripping the steering wheel as if they were closed around Bolliger's throat.

Julian Bolliger who'd caused all this. Julian Bolliger who was so consumed with greed he was prepared to murder indiscriminately.

Mason stared through the windscreen, blazing with pure hatred as a new plan formed in his head. He would go to the authorities, but not yet.

First, he was going to hit Bolliger where it hurt him the most.

Chapter 35

I stood outside the police station, feeling completely and utterly alone. The detectives obviously didn't believe what I'd told them, so they wouldn't help me. Those men who kidnapped me must've known I'd spoken to Isabelle, so had killed her trying to get information or because of something she knew and had hidden. Were they also watching my friends and family? My dad? Cheryl? Aiden? Mason's parents were both dead, so they were out of the equation. Dad was in Thailand. Aiden was at a travel conference. I couldn't go to Cheryl's house – it would put her and her daughter in danger. So where could I go now?

I wanted to succumb to the exhaustion but knew I shouldn't. If they wanted to kill me, then I had to have some kind of leverage, and if I knew what this was all about, if I could find evidence of some kind, then I could use it, present it to the police. They'd have to listen to me then and investigate everything. Then they'd protect me and find Mason. Until then, there was only one place I could think to go for help.

I walked the short distance from the police station towards the taxi rank at the train station. It had started to rain while I'd been cooped up, a spring storm that hadn't cooled the sticky heat from the air. I wiped the droplets out of my eyes as I slid in the first taxi waiting, relieved there was no queue. I gave the driver the address and stared through the window, watching the beads of rain sliding down the glass like tears.

I was lost in thoughts ricocheting around my head as I chewed on my lower lip, oblivious to the passing scenery, until the driver announced we'd reached our destination. After paying the fare, I had ten pounds left.

I got out of the cab on unsteady legs and walked up to the electric gates and high wall that surrounded the property.

Uncle Charlie was my dad's older brother. I saw him sporadically these days, the last time being at Mason's memorial service. Just before I was born, Mum and Charlie had had a falling out over his "lifestyle choices" as she'd called them. He was a criminal, basically. A well-respected figure in the Essex underworld, even though he was supposed to have retired now. If you'd listened to my mum, she'd say Charlie was a "wrongun". A lowlife gangster who she'd wanted nothing to do with in case it tarnished her reputation.

When I was growing up, she had forbidden my dad from taking me to see Charlie, but I remember Dad sneaking me with him to visit his brother, and I always thought Charlie was a loveable rogue. A friendly, larger-than-life character and a fun storyteller whose eyes always twinkled with charm. When my parents met, Charlie was already serving three years in prison for robbery. Inside Wandsworth Prison, Charlie made friends with the mastermind behind the infamous Securitor Depot robbery, which he "allegedly" pulled off in 1983. Although police were convinced of Charlie's involvement, they could never prove anything, and he certainly never admitted it to me, although I suspect he'd told Dad. I think my mum's main hatred of Charlie stemmed from the fact that even though Charlie offered Dad money over the years, my dad would never take a handout from him, despite Mum's nagging him to so she could buy the finer things in life. But, of course, she would never have admitted to being a total hypocrite like that.

I wasn't sure how I felt about what Charlie had apparently done. On the one hand, he'd stolen a lot of money that didn't belong to him. He'd also threatened the staff with guns, although no one was injured or shot. On the other, the banks who owned the depot were some of the biggest crooks on earth, so maybe it was a kind of karma, and Charlie did give away a lot of money to charity. Whether it was to redeem himself or he had a Robin Hood complex, I was never sure.

Either way, his moral code might be questionable, but I knew he wouldn't turn me away, and he was exactly the kind of person I needed on my side. He would be more equipped to deal with the type of people who were chasing me than I was alone.

I pressed the intercom button on the wall outside his house and looked up at a CCTV camera, my head throbbing. I placed a hand on the brick to steady myself as the horrifying events of the day washed over me again.

There was no response. It was now the early hours of the morning, so I prayed he was just in bed and not out. I pressed again, whispering, '*Please* be here.'

'Nicole?' His voice, hoarse from years of cigarettes, spoke through the intercom.

'Yes, it's me. Can I come in?'

'Yeah, 'course, love.'

The metal electric gates began rolling back, and I walked up the driveway towards the imposing large mansion and porch with white pillars.

He swung open the door, his eyebrows raised with surprise. Despite the hour, he was still fully dressed in jeans and a Fred Perry top. His jet-black hair was greying at the temples now and messed up, as if he'd fallen asleep on the sofa. 'What are you doing here at this time? Is there something wrong with your dad?'

But the only answer I could give him was to burst into tears.

'Hey, hey. Come on in.' Charlie wrapped me in his big arms and pulled me to his chest. I buried my head into his shoulder and just let all the emotions out while he stroked my hair. I'd never just turned up on his doorstep like this, so he knew it was serious, yet he didn't ask any questions initially.

When I could finally speak again, I said, 'I'm in trouble. I need your help.' I pulled back, and his electric blue eyes stared into mine.

'Whatever's wrong, you know I'll always help you, love. Come on. Let's get you a drink. You look like you could do with one.' He shut the door.

I followed him down a hallway with polished wood floors into the large modern kitchen-cum-dining room that opened up into a conservatory. I slumped down on a sofa by the French doors overlooking a large garden lined with mature leylandii before my legs gave way. Wiping my eyes with the back of my hand, I watched him pour two generous slugs of Scotch into crystal cut tumblers.

He held one out and sat next to me, his worried expression full of questions. 'What's going on?'

'I'm sorry.' I took a sip of the strong amber liquid and waited until the burn in my throat had disappeared. 'I didn't know where else to go or what to do.'

'You don't need to apologise.' He patted my arm affectionately. 'I'm just glad you feel like you can turn to me if there's a problem.' He took a sip of his own drink and watched me over the rim.

In between a fresh bout of tears, I explained everything. The photo, the note, going to meet Mason, being kidnapped, Isabelle's murder, the police.

When I got to the end of the story, he didn't call me crazy or tell me I needed help, like DI Thornton, he just stared at the floor, deep in thought for a few moments, letting everything sink in.

'I know it sounds surreal and crazy. But I know Mason is still alive. I think the plane was tampered with. Brought down on purpose somehow because he found out about something happening in Africa. Something that must be really bad if people are being murdered because of it.' I downed the last of my drink.

'I don't know about you, but I need another one of these.' He held up his empty glass.

I nodded and he took mine, refilled them, sat back down.

'There's a lot of corrupt shit goes on in Africa – blood diamonds, gold, poaching. When you've got those kinds of natural resources, it's rife. Then again, all governments are corrupt. Maybe Africa is just more honest about its corruption. What do you know about Narumbe?'

'Not much. Health International got involved out there because of massacres going on with rebels who want to overthrow the government. Villages were being destroyed, people murdered. But I need to go there and find out.'

He shook his head. 'That would be madness, love. If there's a civil war going on, it would be far too dangerous.'

'It can't be any more dangerous than here. People are already trying to kill me. Someone out there must know what this is about. I talked to Mason's colleague, another doctor called Jean-Luc, but he says he doesn't know anything. Their local contact, Adama, isn't answering his phone, but I need to find him. He was the last person Mason called on his phone, so I'm sure he knows something about what happened to him and where Mason is. I think Isabelle was murdered because she knew something. And someone called me from a bar out there and warned me about Moussa Damba. I think he's involved and the government is covering up what really happened to Mason out there.'

'If the government is involved, you've got no chance of finding out anything. And if you end up talking to the wrong person, they'll take you out too.'

'But I've got to try. Either the meeting today was some kind of set up to get to me. Or those men managed to capture Mason too. Or he got away and could be anywhere by now. Unless he emails me, he's got no way to contact me again now, so the only way to find my husband is to find out what's going on and who's responsible before I get killed. I need answers. And I think the only way to get them is to go to Africa where this all started.' I took a huge swallow of Scotch. 'They were probably monitoring my calls and emails. They'll be monitoring my bank accounts, too, so I need to borrow some money to book a flight to Narumbe.' I let my head flop back against the sofa and closed my eyes.

'Christ, love, you're knackered. You look like you're about to pass out. Why don't you get some sleep and let me think about this? No one knows you're here for now. And if they do come, I'll be ready. Let's talk about it in the morning, eh?'

I rested my head on his shoulder and felt my lids closing involuntarily, now I was safe, the exhaustion tugged me down into blackness.

Chapter 36

There were no lights on at Nicole's house when the new stolen car Blade was in did a drive by. Frankie had got it from Blade's lockup before picking him up from the Pit. It was a grey Ford Focus, boring as hell, like driving a hair dryer, but it blended into all the other Mr and Mrs Average cars out there.

The cul-de-sac was quiet. No one around. Blade looked at his phone app again. According to the cameras, there'd been no sign of Mason since he'd left the master bedroom, but Frankie hadn't had time to put cameras everywhere. He could still be in the house. Or he could've missed him leaving.

Frankie drove in a loop and out of the cul-de-sac, heading onto the long, curving street that joined it, and parked further down. They got out and fast-walked back towards the house.

Blade could barely contain his anger. He'd had a shit day. Nothing had gone to plan. And if he didn't find Mason and Nicole, he was fucked.

When they reached the Palmers' driveway, they looked around. All the neighbours were tucked up safely in their houses.

The moon was covered by clouds, and the dark shadows of the night masked their approach up the path. As they neared the front door, Blade whispered, 'You go round the back and wait. I'm not letting the bastard get away if he comes out that way.'

Frankie nodded and crouch-ran up the side of the house, disappearing from view before jumping over the wooden gate.

Blade pulled his Walther PPK from his waistband at the small of his back and gripped it in hand as he stepped towards the front door.

He was about to pick the lock when he realised that the door hadn't been shut properly. He pushed it open with his left hand, his right aiming the gun into the hallway, letting his eyes adjust to the blackness. He stood still and listened.

No sounds.

He cleared the lounge, the kitchen-diner, the downstairs toilet, his footsteps silent on the soft carpet beneath his feet. He paused at the bottom of the stairs, his gun trained upwards, then he climbed slowly.

The stairs opened up into a hallway that branched left and right. He melted his back against the wall at the top step and poked his head quickly around the corner to his right.

No one.

To the left.

No one.

He turned right, towards the master bedroom. The door was closed. Slowly, he twisted the handle and then flung the door open, taking a quick inventory of the room. The double bed in the centre. The built-in wardrobes along the wall opposite. The en suite door left open at the far end.

He strode towards the bed and crouched down, looking underneath, his anger reaching new heights. He crossed the room and poked his head around the en suite door. Clear glass shower cubicle, bath and toilet. Mason wasn't there.

He stopped. Listened. Glanced at the fitted wardrobe doors along one wall. Then he crept towards one, aiming the gun steady at it. He pulled open the first door with his left hand. Pointed the gun inside. Then the next one. And the next.

All were empty.

He kicked at the set of drawers next to the en suite doorway. 'Where the fuck are they?'

Chapter 37

It was just gone midnight when DS Becky Harris got back to the station after conducting house-to-house enquiries in Isabelle Moore's street with her colleague DC Ronnie Pickering. Isabelle's house was set back from the road and private – no one had seen a thing. She'd spoken to Isabelle's PA, Jenny, on the phone, the woman who'd called the police originally because Isabelle had failed to turn up for work and wasn't answering her phone, which was very out of character, and had resulted in a police community support officer attending to do a welfare check. As well as being Jenny's boss, Isabelle was also good friends with her in a social capacity, and she could think of no reason why someone would want Isabelle dead.

The house had been ransacked. The contents of Isabelle's handbag in the kitchen had been tipped onto the counter. Her purse was still there, a debit and credit card still inside, although the money was missing. And they hadn't found her mobile phone or laptop anywhere. Other valuables in the house, including some expensive jewellery, were still in situ. There was also evidence of a violent sexual assault, and Isabelle had been stabbed multiple times, but the pathologist said most wounds were superficial slash cuts. Even though they would've been excruciatingly painful, they weren't enough to kill her. The final wound that ended her life was a stab to the eye which penetrated her brain. If it was a burglary, where the offender had been disturbed by the owner, maybe Becky would've expected to see Isabelle being beaten or roughed up a bit. She'd seen it before, particularly with elderly home owners who'd stumbled across burglars, but this was different. This looked as if Isabelle had been tortured, with only a few specific items stolen.

So far, the SOCOs hadn't found any significant fingerprints, other than Nicole's prints found on the umbrella which she'd told Becky she'd used for protection and was obviously not the murder weapon anyway. Neither had SOCO found any other forensic evidence that could lead them to the offender. There was no sign of forced entry. She suspected Isabelle's killer had already been inside the house, lying in wait. But why? Who would want to target her in such a way?

From the background checks, Becky had found that Isabelle Moore had been the director of Health International for fifteen years, and it was a well-known charity that provided medical aid to poverty-stricken and war-torn areas without a whiff of any scandal. She'd already put in a request to Vodafone for Isabelle's mobile phone data, but that would most likely take a while to come back. Ditto for her financial records. Maybe Isabelle had been siphoning off money from the company accounts, and someone was trying to teach her a lesson. Charities could be easy pickings for a certain type of unscrupulous character, although there was nothing about Isabelle to indicate she was untrustworthy.

She sat back in her chair and put her feet on the desk, thinking back to Nicole Palmer's bizarre story again. Becky had researched Health International and found they'd gone into Narumbe eighteen months ago because a group of rebels had spread out through the country with an aim to overthrow the government. There were scant details that she could find on the internet, because it seemed the government controlled the media out there and weren't releasing any negative information. What little she could find said that no one knew who the leader of the rebels was. She'd pulled up the few articles she could find on Mason Palmer's plane crash, which had indeed said that he and three other people on board were killed.

But now his wife claimed he was really alive and someone had tried to abduct her.

Becky couldn't get the image of Nicole's very real terror etched on her face out of her head. Nicole had been very detailed and articulate in her account of what had happened to her. Isabelle's murder and Nicole's story were connected. Somehow. Mason had worked for the same organisation as Isabelle, and her torture and murder and the possible abduction of Nicole smacked of organised crime, even though neither Isabelle nor Nicole appeared to have links to anything like that. Not that Becky had had any experience of organised crime in her six years in CID.

When she'd joined the department as a DC, she'd thought it was going to be a lot more exciting and interesting than it had turned out to be. She'd quickly slotted in to doing the role of analysing documents and desk work, most of the time dealing with repetitively boring paperwork and telephone enquiries. Even though she'd been good at her job, she'd craved something more. If she was honest with herself, and not wanting to disrespect the victims of crime she had dealt with, she'd been getting bored out of her brains with it. So, when her previous boss and mentor DS Warren Carter had left and she'd been promoted to fill his shoes, she'd hoped now – finally – she'd get the chance to be the one out on the streets, in the thick of things, dealing with the more interesting side of solving crimes. She had an intuition this case was going to be something very different, and a frisson of excitement rippled through her for the first time in years.

She picked up the phone and dialled the number for Cambridgeshire Constabulary who covered the area of Jesus Green where Nicole said she'd been abducted from. If Nicole had been telling the truth, the incident could've been caught on CCTV cameras.

Chapter 38

Julian Bolliger's mobile phone rang. He picked it up, seeing Blade's name flash on the screen. 'I trust everything is in order?'

'Actually, boss, we've had a few setbacks,' Blade said.

'Setbacks?' Julian snapped. 'What kind of setbacks?'

'One of my associates messed up. They followed Nicole Palmer and abducted her, but when they were taking her to the abandoned warehouse I was going to meet them at, she managed to get away from him.'

Julian sat down at his ergonomic chair in front of his imposing mahogany desk. 'So find her!'

'I'm trying. She's abandoned her car and hasn't returned to her house. She's in hiding somewhere. And …'

'And what? Spit it out.'

'Mason Palmer is *definitely* alive. I saw him on the cameras planted in the Palmer house. But by the time I got there, he'd gone.'

'I trust you know where he is now?' His voice was cold, and it wasn't really a question. There was a pause on the other end, and Julian knew what was coming.

'Unfortunately not.'

Julian leaped from his chair. 'What the hell am I paying you for? I was assured that you could handle this job quickly! That's why you're getting an extortionate amount for it.'

'I can and I will. I'll find them.'

'We didn't find him for ten months,' Julian snapped.

'That's because you thought he was dead. There was no reason to look for him then. I'll get them both, don't worry.'

'This cannot leak before the merger is signed, do you hear me? Find them and make them disappear for good this time.' Julian jabbed a finger to end the call, picked up his crystal decanter of brandy, given to him by the Queen of the United Kingdom as a gift in return for keeping her in the Bolliger treats she loved, and threw it against the wall.

If Blade fucked this up, Julian would see to it that he was a dead man.

Chapter 39

Blade paced the lounge in the safe house he'd rented for three months in the name of a made-up company. The landlord was a lowlife who was trying to fly under the taxman's radar and so hadn't asked too many questions in return for the cash paid up front. But the place was a shit hole. A one-bedroomed flat no bigger than a shoebox, built in the 90s, on an estate in Dagenham within four equally bland blocks. The location was good, though, because he was central, with good motorway and train links. Plus, the neighbours were mostly young, single workers or couples who kept themselves to themselves.

Frankie typed away on his laptop at the small desk in the corner of the room, hacking into all the databases he could find to search for traces of Nicole or Mason Palmer. Frankie might be an annoying little arsehole, who was more interested in fashion than women, but he was a first-class hacker, a new breed of techno-mercenary. Frankie was going through a waxed-eyebrowed, man-bun stage, with an accompanying long bushy Taliban beard. Blade eyed the beard, wondering what kind of shit was stuck inside it. He knew Frankie was gay, but as long as he didn't make a move on Blade and got results, he could dress like an effeminate twat if he wanted. After all, Ronnie Kray, one of Blade's greatest heroes, was that way inclined, and it didn't stop him doing his job.

'Is there any digital sign of them?' Blade stopped pacing.

'No. Nicole's car hasn't moved. She hasn't used her debit or credit cards yet.'

'I've got a man watching her friend Cheryl's house, but I don't think she would've gone there. After listening to the last conversation Nicole had with her at the house, she didn't reveal anything.

What about other friends and family? Maybe she's hiding out with one of them.'

'I've just got her dad's address.' Frankie wrote it down on a piece of paper and was about to hand it over when Blade snatched it out of his hand.

'I'll go and check it out. Keep digging.'

Blade set up the sat nav in the Ford Focus and drove away. The roads were quiet at this time in the early hours of the morning, so he made good time, arriving an hour later at a semi-detached house. He parked up in the next street and strode back to the property, glancing up and down before pausing outside the front door. He pressed his ear to the wood but heard nothing from inside.

After removing his lock picks from his pocket, he got to work. Two minutes later he opened the door, slipped inside.

He stood for a moment, his eyes adjusting to the darkness, his ears alert for sounds, but all he heard was the humming of a fridge somewhere. There was no alarm system beeping at him.

He walked down the hallway, the rubber soles of his boots not making a sound, his gun with the attached suppressor outstretched in his hand. There was no one in the kitchen, the first room he came to. No one in the lounge.

He softly padded upstairs into a narrow hallway with three doors, all closed.

He moved towards the door on his right and opened it silently. Bathroom. Empty. The next door had to be a bedroom.

Again, he pressed the handle down, and the door opened with no sound. There was a set of built-in wardrobes on the wall to his right. He walked further into the room, expecting to see a sleeping figure in the bed, but it was empty and hadn't been slept in.

He gritted his teeth, retracing his steps until he was at the third door. When he stepped inside the bedroom, he again found it devoid of people.

'Fuck's sake!' he hissed, stomping back downstairs. Where the hell was Nicole's dad? Had he taken Nicole somewhere and hidden her?

He glanced around the tidy lounge. There was a bookcase in one corner with ornaments and photos perched on it. A solitary newspaper folded on the coffee table. Not much to go on.

In the kitchen, he found the usual detritus of kitchen life but not much else, until he glanced at a piece of paper attached to the fridge by a magnet. A printout of an email.

He grabbed it and read a travel itinerary. Nicole's dad had buggered off to Thailand the day before.

He curled the piece of paper into a ball, threw it on the floor and let himself out.

Chapter 40

Despite everything that had happened, I did manage to succumb to sleep, but it was restless. I dreamed that I was in my school playground. It was night time and no one was around, but I could hear Mason calling my name. I spun around, frantically trying to work out where he was. Then I walked towards the front door of the school building, trying to get inside, but the door was locked. I tugged on it, but it wouldn't budge. I tried punching in the code, but every time I did, it just beeped at me and wouldn't open. And then zombies appeared inside the building, staring at me through the glass, their skin in tatters, their faces half mangled, blood pouring down their bodies.

I screamed and tried to run, but I couldn't move. When I looked down at my feet, they'd turned to bloody stumps. The zombies tried to open the door to reach me, and when that didn't work, they started banging on the glass. Spider web cracks splintered on the doors, and then one of them managed to smash a bony hand through. It grabbed at my arm, long nails tearing through my flesh.

I woke suddenly, sweating and afraid, panting hard. For a few moments, I wasn't sure if I was still dreaming. It took a while for my eyes to register the room and realise where I was, but my heart didn't stop thudding for a good few minutes.

I flopped my head back on the pillow as all the events of the last few days came flooding back in a terrifying rush. Isabelle's murder. The abduction. The weapon pointed at me. The fight with the gunman. Running for my life. How close I'd come to death.

There were people out there trying to kill me, and I had no idea why. Was it madness to go to Africa? To the very heart of where I was convinced this thing had started? Where even the government couldn't be trusted to tell the truth. I was petrified but I had no choice – I had to find Mason, and I was convinced Adama held the key. I'd lost Mason once, I couldn't lose him again. The answers, I was sure, lay in a sun-baked continent thousands of miles away.

I dressed quickly in the same clothes as last night, groaning as I did so. My whole body felt bruised and tender from the fight in the van. My ribs screamed at me, and my forehead still throbbed. I tried to ignore all the pain and turned my mind to organisation instead. I couldn't go home and get some clothes and my passport, in case they were watching. Would Charlie be able to do it for me? They wouldn't be watching for him, but what if they were waiting inside?

When I walked down the stairs, I was hit by the smell of fresh coffee. I paused in the kitchen doorway and surveyed the spread on the oak table in the centre of the room. Piles of toast on a plate. Butter. Jam. A cafetière. Jug of milk.

Charlie sat in front of it all with his back to me, reading the screen on his laptop. 'Help yourself to breakfast,' he said, without turning around.

I came up behind him, and he held his hand up, reaching for mine. I slid it into his calloused palm, and he squeezed, his eyes never leaving the screen. 'What are you doing?'

He released my hand, and I sat next to him.

'Research.' He twisted around to face me, then stood up and walked to the French doors of the conservatory. Opened them, stepped outside onto the patio and pulled a packet of cigarettes and lighter from his pocket before lighting one.

'And what did you find?' I stepped closer to the doorway.

'Do you want to eat first?' He took a hard drag and blew out the smoke away from me towards the garden.

I shook my head. 'Later.'

'Apparently, Narumbe has no precious metal mines, no records of ivory or rhino horn poaching, no diamonds, no oil.'

'So, what are they protecting? Because it must be something important. Something worth a lot of money.'

Charlie shrugged. 'Most of their revenue comes from cocoa plantations. That's their only official export. Not exactly worth all this trouble, is it? But I think it's most likely to do with drugs. You were warned not to trust Moussa Damba. He's the head of the secret police. Mason must've discovered Damba was involved in some government corruption out there to export drugs. It looks like the Colombian and Mexican drug cartels are moving into West Africa now. Seems like it could become the new epicentre of drug trafficking. If Mason found out about it and was going to expose it, they'd want him dead.' Charlie took another hit of his cigarette and coughed. 'I should give these bastards up.'

'So, what exactly did Mason find out? I mean, he was a doctor in a remote clinic. He was hardly likely to come into contact with many government officials and learn any dirty secrets about drug trafficking.'

Charlie tapped ash into a heavy glass ashtray on top of a wrought iron patio table set and said, 'There's not much chatter coming out of the country about the war going on out there. Seems like they're keeping a tight lid on things. But Mason would've been treating people whose villages and homes had been massacred. Maybe one of them told Mason something somebody didn't want him to know. Or maybe he saw something he wasn't supposed to. Maybe the whole war out there is really about drugs turf.'

I closed my eyes and rubbed at my forehead, my fingertips brushing the tender lump. A picture of Mason shimmered between my eyelids.

'And if you go out there, you're risking your life. You could either get caught up in a crossfire with rebels or be targeted by the government or cartels. It would be crazy.' He stubbed out his cigarette in the ashtray and came back inside.

I opened my eyes. 'I don't have a choice. I need answers, and this is the only way to get them and find Mason.'

Charlie shook his head and looked at me as if I'd just told him the world was flat.

'You should understand why I have to do this. You're the biggest risk taker I know.' I paused. 'Will you come with me?'

He looked pointedly at me. 'What do you think I could do to help?'

I bit my lip, looked away. Looked back at him. 'Well, you know about protecting yourself, don't you?'

Charlie snorted. 'You've been listening to too much bollocks about me from your mum.' He leaned in closer. 'Look, I've never hurt anyone who didn't deserve it. I never did anyone innocent. I do have *some* morals, despite what your mum used to say about me.'

'I'm not saying that. I just … well, you know how to look after yourself.'

'Yeah, on *my* turf, with *my* crew, on a job I've researched back to front and inside out. Besides, I gave all that up years ago. In case you ain't noticed, I'm not exactly in my prime anymore.' He glanced down at his expanding waistline, then back to me. 'I know nothing about West Africa, other than if you're mixing with Colombian or Mexican drug cartels, they ain't exactly Mary Poppins. Throw in a load of government corruption into the mix, and we could just disappear for good. We'd be unarmed without knowing who to trust. To put it bluntly, it's the most fucking insane thing I've heard, love.'

I looked out the windows at the garden and the swimming pool beyond, thinking. It *was* insane. But … I was going anyway. With or without Charlie's help.

'Okay. I understand. Thanks for letting me stay the night.' I walked towards the door.

Charlie intercepted me, taking hold of my arm. 'Hey, hang on. Where do you think you're going?'

'I'm going home to get my passport.'

He rolled his eyes. 'That's the *last* thing you should be doing. These people are professionals. They'll be monitoring everything you do. And as soon as you arrive in Narumbe, your passport will raise red flags. And you know you can't use your bank cards, they'll be monitoring those too. Shit!' He sighed, shaking his head. 'You'll get yourself killed before you even get on the plane.'

'I have to do this.' I pulled my arm out of his grip, tears springing into my eyes. 'I have to find my husband. And this is the only thing I can think of.'

'Look, love, I hate to say this, but you don't even know he's alive. You said yourself the meeting could've been a set up by those thugs to get to you.'

Tears sprang into my eyes. 'I *know* he's alive.'

'Know? Or hope? They're two very different things. And if he is alive and the meet was genuinely organised by Mason, why go to Africa when he's most likely still in England? Why not wait here for him to make contact again?'

'Because I can't just sit around waiting, doing nothing. And because he doesn't know where I am now to contact me anyway. And those men might've kidnapped him too. If that's the case, I've got no way of finding out who they are and where they've taken him unless I get answers.'

Charlie thought about that for a moment, his eyes narrowed. I'd never been scared of him, despite the rumours, but the darkness I saw then behind his eyes would no doubt have given anyone who crossed him cause for concern. He blew out a frustrated breath. Threw his hands in the air. 'I can't let you go on your own. If you're determined to do this, then we at least need some preparation. I'll get hold of some false passports for us. But we'll have to get in and out of the country quickly. As soon as you start asking people questions, someone's going to leak the information to Damba … or the cartels … or whoever the hell is involved, and two white people are going to stand out like a whore at a kid's tea party. We'll need to get hold of a local contact, too. Someone who knows what's what and can sort everything out. Someone we can trust.'

I gave him a grateful smile, relieved I didn't have to do it on my own. 'Thank you.'

'I know a guy who might be able to help us. He was a merc in the Rhodesian war. Retired now, but he knows Africa better than me.'

'A mercenary?'

'One man's mercenary is another man's protector. Let me give him a call. See if he knows someone out there we can use.' He nodded towards the toast. 'Eat something while I get things organised.' He swiped up his mobile phone from the breakfast bar and walked out of the room.

I heard his muffled voice in the lounge as I half-heartedly picked up a piece of toast and spread it with jam before forcing myself to take a bite. Although my stomach contracted with hunger, there was a lump in my throat that made it hard to swallow. By the time I'd forced down a whole slice, Charlie was back in the room. 'What did he say?'

'He's going to ask around. He'll get back to us soon. In the meantime, we're going to take a trip. Organise these passports and book a couple of flights at a travel agent with cash.'

I nodded, wondering how much of what my mum had told me about his past was true. And then thinking I hoped it all was.

Chapter 41

DS Harris yawned as she entered the empty incident room at eight a.m. She'd only left seven hours before and had carried out her own research at home until the early hours. She'd slipped into bed around three am, much to her husband's annoyance. After resuming their usual row that he never saw her anymore since her promotion, she'd slept on the sofa, getting barely any sleep, though she was still buzzing with the new challenge as she sat at her desk.

Her husband didn't get it. This was everything she'd been working towards, a step up the career ladder, recognition for her efforts, responsibility. Her first murder case as a DS. Something juicy to sink her teeth into and prove what she could really do, given the chance. Why couldn't he be happy for her?

She knocked the sour thoughts about her husband out of her head and opened up her email, hoping the CCTV operator she'd spoken to the night before had found something. And there it was. She clicked on the message and read through it before opening the attached footage. A camera had caught a plain white van parked at the side of Victoria Avenue in Cambridge. She chewed on her lip as nothing much happened, except several cars going past it, a few parents entering Jesus Green with toddlers in tow.

Then she watched as Nicole appeared from the park entrance on the right-hand side of the frame with a tall, thickset man walking close beside her. He had a black leather jacket and jeans on, even though it had been a sweltering day, a cap pulled down low and sunglasses, making it hard to see his face from the camera angle.

Nicole moved stiffly, her wide-eyed gaze fixed on the ground looking unnatural. Her lips moved as she spoke. The man said something in return and leaned against her, pressing her against the side panel of the van. He put his arm around the back of her neck, his face close to hers, but Becky couldn't see if they were talking. Then he opened the sliding side door of the van, put a hand on Nicole's back as she climbed inside. The man looked up and down the road briefly before getting in behind her. Then the vehicle sped off.

Becky did a PNC check for the vehicle registration number, but it came up with no reports lost or stolen. The vehicle on camera matched the make and model registered. It was owned by a man called Peter Ebrooke at an address in Wareham, Dorset. Either Nicole's abductors were stupid, or it was a false or cloned plate.

She pulled up the video again and watched a second time. The man's face was obscured for most of it, but there was a good full frontal shot when he'd turned his head to look up the road. She paused the video. Zoomed in and stared at his face. He had dark eyebrows showing above his sunglasses and a slightly crooked nose. He was around six-feet tall, stocky build. Other than that, he was pretty non-descript. No visible tattoos she could see, no scars on his face. She zoomed in on the driver of the van, but the sun had caused a reflection on the windscreen so there was no clear view.

Still staring at the screen, she picked up her phone and called the control centre for the Automatic Number Plate Recognition cameras. Nicole had said she'd managed to escape near Epping Forest, so where was the vehicle now?

A few minutes later, she had her answer. The last trace of it was getting off the M25 junction at Epping at two thirty-four pm yesterday. It hadn't been spotted since. There was now an alert set up for the van, so if it was picked up by camera again, they'd let her know, though she suspected it would've already been dumped.

She went back to her emails and saw one had also come through from Isabelle's mobile phone provider. She brought that up and checked through recent calls to and from her number. It would take a while to establish all of them, but one number popped up from the day before Isabelle was killed. Nicole had called her and spoken for three and a half minutes, just like she'd said. Becky knew now Nicole was telling the truth about the abduction. She was telling the truth about speaking to Isabelle.

Her knee jigged up and down as she waited for DI Thornton to arrive, staring at the crime scene photos of Isabelle's tortured body now pinned to a noticeboard at one end of the room, anger igniting through her. What did Isabelle and Nicole have or know that those men wanted? Nicole had said they were trying to find out where Mason was, but Becky wasn't convinced Mason Palmer could be alive. The Narumbean government arranging for a plane crash to kill him and Mason escaping before it went down? That part sounded too far-fetched. Those men wanted something, though, that was for sure. And they were prepared to kidnap and murder for it.

As soon as she spotted DI Thornton walking through the door with his briefcase, she jumped out of her seat and picked up her laptop.

'Guv, I've got something here you need to see.' She followed him into his office.

He put his briefcase down and took his suit jacket off, hanging it on a wall hook. 'Give me a chance to get through the door.'

'This is important,' she said breathlessly.

He sat at his desk. 'Okay. What is it?'

'Nicole was telling the truth about being abducted.' She set the laptop on his desk and pressed "Play".

He watched the video with a frown forming. When he finished, he sat back in his chair, looked up at her. 'Who told you to dig into this?' His cheeks flushed red, a sure sign he was about to give her a bollocking.

She swallowed. 'No one, guv. But I was convinced her story was connected to Isabelle's murder. Isabelle's mobile phone records show Nicole called her recently. Isabelle's PA confirms Nicole also met with Isabelle at the Health International Office. The timing seems too coincidental not to be related somehow. I think Nicole really was trying to find out something about her husband's death and this guy wanted to stop her.' She pointed at the screen.

DI Thornton watched her carefully for a moment. 'This doesn't look like an abduction to me. It looks like she knows the man. Like they could be in a relationship, even. And she gets in the van voluntarily. There's no violence involved. He doesn't look as if he's threatening her. I think she's made the whole thing up. I mean, surely you don't believe all this crap about her husband being alive?'

'It sounds weird, for sure. I don't think he's alive, but I think Nicole believes he is. I also think these people are professionals. Although the footage looks a bit ambiguous, I admit ... she said he threatened her with a gun in his pocket so she'd get in the vehicle.'

'I know what she said, but I'm not convinced Nicole Palmer is in any way reliable.'

'She said she thought he was taking her somewhere to ask questions, and no doubt if she hadn't managed to escape, she'd have ended up like Isabelle did. This screams of organised crime, don't you think?'

He pressed his palms together, index fingers extended beneath his chin, staring at the laptop screen. 'Not to me it doesn't. And neither Isabelle nor Nicole raise any kinds of flags like that.'

'But you said it yourself, the only kidnappings or abductions you've known of were to do with gangs or drugs.'

'Except this doesn't even look like an abduction to me. It's footage of Nicole getting in a van, that's all. We've got enough work to do, dealing with real crimes without inventing things that haven't happened.'

She voiced an idea that had been taking shape in her head. 'I did some research last night about Narumbe and surrounding West African countries. It looks like there's an explosion of

Mexican and Colombian drug cartels moving into the area. What if Mason Palmer was smuggling drugs, using his position as medical personnel to protect him? Maybe he got on the wrong side of one of the cartels, or he ripped them off somehow and stole the drugs, so they had him killed out there. Maybe Isabelle was in on it. And maybe they think Nicole knows where Mason's stash was? That would make sense then.'

He scrunched his face up looking at her. 'Look, if this *was* some kind of serious or organised crime gang involved, I'd expect to see Isabelle shot execution-style, but she was stabbed and raped, which doesn't fit with that scenario.'

'Unless they were teaching her a lesson. Or using her as an example to others not to talk about what's going on. She was stabbed repeatedly, like it was torture. And Nicole's abduction would definitely fit.'

'No, it wouldn't, because I don't believe her story, especially after seeing that footage which doesn't prove anything.' He closed her laptop lid with a sense of finality on the subject.

But Becky wasn't giving up just yet. 'Don't you think it's interesting that Isabelle's phone and laptop are the only things that appear to be missing? Maybe there's something on them relating to all this that someone doesn't want found? If her killer was robbing the place, why not take her expensive jewellery and purse as well?

He sat back in her chair and folded his arms. 'I checked out recent murders in the county and found one in Watford with a very similar MO two weeks ago. A woman disturbed a burglar, and she was brutally raped and stabbed repeatedly. Very small items were taken, which were easy to sell on, including her laptop, her mobile phone and the cash from her purse. The offender left semen at the scene, but there's been no match to the DNA database. I'm convinced our killer is the same guy.'

She felt a frustrated flush creeping up her neck. 'What if it's not, though? Nicole Palmer is alleging a serious crime. Surely, we can't ignore that. The man she got in the van with could be Isabelle's killer. And if he tried to abduct her once, he'll try again.'

'God, you don't give up do you.' He threw his hands in the air. 'Okay, I'll humour you. Go and phone Nicole Palmer and confirm she's safe and well. That will put your mind at rest, and we can get on with the real work of connecting this case to the Watford one and catching this guy.'

Humour me? She bristled at his patronising tone but said thanks anyway, picked up her laptop, cursing the powers that be who'd transferred DI Thornton to their department. When he'd arrived and given his introduction speech to them, he'd said solving crimes was a joint effort and he was always open to listening to his team. But the reality was he only liked to hear the sound of his own voice. He seemed to be a career copper, with one eye on the promotion ladder and one on a quick clear up rate to add to his notches on said ladder. But she'd met officers like that before – those who missed the most important little details because they were trying too hard to get their cases closed prematurely, instead of asking the right questions. Yes, she knew there were always holes in any investigation, but Nicole's abduction wasn't just a hole, it was a whopping great abyss, and DI Thornton couldn't even seem to see it.

She stopped by DC Colin Etheridge's desk. Another new addition to the team following a shake up of CID after the departure of DS Carter and the big boss Detective Superintendent Greene, Colin had been brought in to carry out the analysing work she'd spent years doing, and he seemed to be pretty good at his job so far. He was on the phone so she perched on the edge of his desk and waited impatiently.

When he hung up, she said, 'I'm going to email you some CCTV footage.' She explained what it showed. 'I want to find out who the guy with Nicole Palmer is.'

'Okay, cool,' he said enthusiastically.

Give it a few years of drudgery and he wouldn't be so enthusiastic, she thought.

'Also, send it down to the Cambridgeshire Constabulary's local intelligence officer and see if they know who he is. And circulate a still of his face to all forces. I suspect the van was using a cloned plate but can you put in a call to Dorset CID and get them to pay this Peter Ebrooke a visit?'

'Yes, sarge, will do.'

'And can you do some more digging into the backgrounds of the Palmers?'

'Absolutely. Leave it all with me.'

'Great, thanks.' She stood up with a smile. It felt good to be the one giving the orders for a change.

She strode to her desk and dug out Nicole's numbers from a folder and called her mobile. There was no answer, and she wasn't picking up her land line, either. She slipped her jacket on and walked over to DC Ronnie Pickering's desk. He was busy bent over some paperwork, snacking on raw almonds.

'You can leave that, Ronnie. We're taking a trip to see Nicole Palmer.'

He looked up at her a little disappointed. Ronnie had a few strange traits, and one of them was that he seemed to actually enjoy mind-numbingly boring paperwork. 'Are we? But I'm going through Isabelle Moore's financial records.'

She explained her line of thinking.

'But the boss doesn't think the two incidents are related … isn't this more important?' He nodded to the paperwork in front of him. 'We might be able to find a link to the Watford victim.'

That was another thing about Ronnie. He accepted the party line of the Brass every time and went along with it. But DS Carter had always taught her to question even the most obvious. She didn't believe anything unless she could verify it as a fact for herself.

She smiled sweetly at him. 'I don't believe they are connected. There's more to this than a burglar who was disturbed. Or a sadistic rapist-murderer.'

He groaned a little. 'You're like DS Carter reincarnated.'

'He's not *dead!*' She elbowed him. 'Come on, chop chop.'

He followed her down the stairs as she filled him in on her thoughts.

When they pushed their way through the door out into the car park, he said, 'Seriously? International drug smuggling and organised crime?' He stopped for a moment and looked at her in awe.

'I think so. I just have to prove it now. I'll drive.'

'Are you sure?' He swallowed nervously. 'Your driving's quite dangerous.'

'And you drive like a tortoise. I'd like to get there some time today.' She passed her buff-coloured folder of information over to him and slid behind the wheel.

Chapter 42

Blade wanted to sleep, but he couldn't. Not until he found out where the Palmers were. After he'd visited Nicole's dad's house, he'd been to Aiden Palmer's, but he wasn't there either. Frankie was busy trying to find an address for Nicole's uncle, who was apparently some retired old gangster who'd been implicated in a raid at a cash depot in the eighties but had managed to evade arrest. Charlie Briggs wasn't listed on the voter's register anywhere, and he didn't appear to own a property.

'I can't do this with you watching over my shoulder.' Frankie stopped typing on his laptop and glared at Blade, who was staring at the screen, munching on a sandwich.

Blade was about to tell him to hurry up about it when his phone signalled an alert on the surveillance camera app. He put the sandwich down on a plate and pulled his phone from his pocket, opened up the app and clicked on the latest link.

On screen, he watched a woman enter the frame in Nicole's kitchen and look around with another guy following behind.

Police, they had to be.

He tapped the volume marker to switch it to audible and listened to their conversation, watching with growing anger as they searched the house, calling for Nicole.

'Shit.' Blade clenched his fists. 'The police know something, and they're looking for Nicole too. Whatever you're doing, do it faster. We need to find her before they do.'

Chapter 43

Detectives Becky Harris and Ronnie Pickering pulled up on the driveway of Nicole's detached house in a small cul-de-sac that led off a close.

'Her vehicle's not here.' She got out of the car.

'Maybe she's gone shopping.'

She snorted. 'What, the day after someone tries to kidnap her?'

Ronnie shrugged. 'DI Thornton doesn't think that's what happened.'

She approached the front door and rang the bell. 'Nicole? It's DS Harris. Are you here?'

No response. She rang the bell again before moving to the front window on the left-hand side of the door, looking inside it to the kitchen. Nothing seemed disturbed and there was no sign of Nicole, but she didn't like the bad feeling she was getting.

She knocked on the door, and it swung inwards, revealing a hallway, a utility room in front of her, and a doorway next to that leading to the lounge. 'Nicole? Are you here?' She listened for a moment, but there was just eerie silence. 'It's the police.'

She stepped over the threshold, looked in the lounge then went across the hall into the large kitchen/breakfast room that overlooked the back garden with Ronnie following behind her.

'Let's check upstairs.' She climbed the stairs to a square-shaped hallway. Ronnie turned left at the top and she went right. She pushed open a doorway to the master bedroom and looked around. The wardrobe doors were open wide. 'Hello?' She stepped towards the en suite door. Poking her head around, she took in a shower and bath, toiletries on a shelf above the sink. No Nicole.

She walked back to the hallway where Ronnie was emerging from another room. He shook his head at her.

'I don't like this.' She pulled her mobile phone from her pocket and dialled Nicole's mobile number again. It went straight to voicemail. She dialled Nicole's place of work and asked to speak to her.

'I'm afraid Nicole's off on leave at the moment,' the secretary said.

'Can I speak to Cheryl Lampard, then?

'Yes, hold on a moment.'

There was a beep and a pause and then a voice that said, 'Cheryl Lampard speaking, how can I help?'

'It's DS Harris here from Hertfordshire Constabulary. You spoke to my colleague, DI Thornton, last night. I'm trying to find Nicole Palmer. Do you have any idea where she is?'

'I don't know. After he called me asking if I was with her two nights ago, I got worried. I've been trying to phone her, but she's not answering. It just goes to voicemail. I was wondering whether I should call her dad and see if he's heard from her when you rang.'

She heard real concern in Cheryl's voice. DI Thornton hadn't told Cheryl much when he'd spoken to her wanting confirmation of the alibi Nicole had given, simply that Nicole had been helping them with their enquires on an investigation. Then, of course, Cheryl had mentioned the harassment Nicole had spoken to her about, which her boss had latched onto as evidence that she was crazy.

'You mentioned to DI Thornton that Nicole thought she was being harassed by a child's parent. Can you tell me what happened with that?'

'Well, it was strange. Nicole said that Angela had sent her a photo of Mason in the post to upset her. Then she backtracked and said it wasn't Angela at all.'

DS Harris pursed her lips. Nicole had said the same in the interview last night. But Nicole now believed Mason had sent it to her. The question was, if it wasn't Angela who'd done it, and it wasn't Mason, because he surely couldn't be alive, then who had really sent it and why? 'Apart from Angela, had Nicole had any other problems recently with anyone?'

'No, not that I know of.' Cheryl paused. 'I don't think she really dealt with the grief of Mason's death properly and it just seems to have hit her really hard all of a sudden. She *is* all right, though, isn't she?'

'I'm sure she's fine,' Becky said, totally unconvinced. 'Does she have any friends or family she might be with?'

'Her mum passed away, but her dad's still alive. I've got his details on file as next of kin. Hang on a moment.'

Becky pulled a notebook from her pocket. 'You got a pen, Ronnie?'

Ronnie retrieved one from the inside pocket of his suit jacket and handed it to her.

Cheryl came back on the line. 'Right, here we are. Daniel Briggs.' She relayed an address, mobile and landline phone number. 'There's also a brother-in-law. His name's Aiden Palmer, but I don't have contact details for him. He owns Palmer's Travel Agency in Haverhill, though. And she has an uncle called Charlie who lives in Essex somewhere, but I don't have any contact details for him.'

'Okay. How about friends?'

'I think I'm her closest friend. And she didn't mention going to stay with anyone, but I did suggest she go away somewhere for a break. Hopefully she took up my suggestion. Aiden might've booked her something.'

'Yes, maybe. Thanks for your help.' She hung up and told Ronnie what Cheryl had said.

Ronnie's gaze rested over her shoulder, on the open wardrobe doors in the master bedroom. 'She probably did just decide on a last-minute holiday somewhere. Looks like she might've been rummaging in her wardrobes for clothes.'

'And she left her front door insecure? I don't think she's on holiday. She was telling the truth about being abducted, and we let her down. If she fled, it's because she was in danger and we didn't take it seriously, or the men who took her found her again.' She dialled the incident room, it was picked up by DC Etheridge. She asked him to find out who Nicole's mobile phone provider was and see if they could trace her location. When she finished, she called the landline for Nicole's dad, but there was no answer. She then tried the mobile, but it was switched off.

'Let's have a good look around and see if there's any clue as to what happened here. You start with the bedrooms. I'll go downstairs,' she said.

She started in the kitchen/breakfast room, rifling through a pile of papers on the worktop, opening drawers and checking contents but finding nothing helpful. Her gaze drifted around the room as she chewed on her lower lip, taking in the fridge, the shelves, the cupboards. Then her eyes drifted upwards and stopped moving suddenly. She did a double take of the white lighting unit above, squinting at something that looked weird, out of place.

She took a chair from the table in the centre of the room and stood on it. When she was eye level with the unit, she stared at it again. The lights were a contemporary design: a slim white plinth attached to the ceiling with several round glass lamps hanging down on silver wire. On the edge of the plinth there was something small and round, barely the size of a one pence piece. White, so it blended in with the glossy coating on the fixture. She edged her fingernail behind the top of it and peeled it away.

With it in between her forefinger and thumb, she stared at the little lens and shook her head. It was a wireless surveillance camera, most likely feeding off the WIFI. Almost undetectable. Certainly if you weren't looking for it, it would be hard to spot.

Someone had been watching Nicole Palmer.

Chapter 44

I stared at the passport photo of the new me: Justine Taylor. The fake was so good, I couldn't tell it from a real one, but then I wasn't an expert in this world. Charlie was, so I had to take his word for it that the document would pass muster with the UK border control. Once outside the UK, I didn't think the Narumbean immigration officers would look too hard at it, but we had to make it out of the country first.

We shuffled through the queue that led to passport control at Heathrow Airport, my mind wandering all over the place. I was more scared than I'd ever been in my life.

Charlie gently touched my shoulder to move me forwards. I'd been so lost in worry I hadn't realised there was a huge gap in front of me.

'It's going to be okay,' he said reassuringly.

But I wasn't convinced. Everything I thought I knew about my life had come crashing down around me in a matter of days. I was sure my husband was alive but as far away from me as before. And people wanted me dead.

There were a couple of people ahead of me in the queue now. I glanced at Charlie over my shoulder, trying to kick away the fear at being discovered a criminal by trying to leave the country with forged documents. I'd suggested doing this leg with our real passports, but Charlie said they'd most likely have eyes monitoring my movements. To be on the safe side, he'd booked the flights in cash at a travel agent, instead of using his credit card. And he'd left his mobile phone turned off at his house, taking a pay-as-you-go mobile with him instead.

I stepped up to the glass-fronted booth and presented the passport to the officer, offering him a wobbly smile. I was always one of those people who went through customs on the way back from holiday feeling guilty, even though I hadn't done anything wrong. If I looked half as nervous as I felt now, he'd arrest me on the spot. The muscles of my stomach quivered as I held my breath.

He looked up at me with a stern face, then down at the passport. Back to me, scrutinising me carefully.

My chest tightened.

And then he handed it back without a smile, and I walked through the turnstile to the other side, almost giddy with relief. I waited for Charlie, who trudged through a minute later.

'Told you they were good,' Charlie whispered in my ear, taking hold of my elbow and steering me to a quiet spot with some empty seats.

I put my rucksack on the floor next to Charlie's as I sat. We were travelling light. The plan was to get in and out as quickly as possible. Hopefully we would get out alive.

Charlie glanced at his watch. We had another hour until the flight to Paris left. At Paris, we'd change planes for our flight to Galao. Then another light aircraft flight was booked to take us down to Lagossa, where Charlie's contact had found a local man who was trustworthy to take us out to the health centre.

'You okay?' Charlie squeezed my hand.

'Never been better,' I quipped, my stomach roiling.

Chapter 45

DS Harris walked up the path of a tired-looking 1940s semi-detached house with Ronnie trailing behind. They'd already been to Palmer's Travel Agent and spoken to a member of staff who told them Aiden Palmer was away at a conference. After speaking to him on his mobile phone, she'd found out that Nicole wasn't with him, he hadn't booked her a holiday, and he hadn't heard from her since she'd left the police station, although he was worried about her being depressed following a recent conversation when she'd spoken to him at his office. She hoped they'd have more luck as she knocked on Daniel Briggs's door, but there was no reply.

She shifted from foot to foot then knocked again, waited. 'Damn.' She pulled out her mobile phone and called the landline, listening to it ringing inside. Next, she tried the mobile number for Daniel, but it went straight to voicemail. 'Let's try the neighbours.'

They knocked on the door of the attached semi, which was answered by a grey-haired woman wearing glasses.

'Hi, I'm Detective Sergeant Harris.' She held up her warrant card. 'I'm trying to get hold of your neighbour.' She pointed to Daniel's door. 'Do you have any idea where he might be?'

'I hope it's not urgent, because he's gone to Thailand for two weeks with his gardening club.'

'Right. When did he go?'

'Yesterday morning about seven o'clock. His flight was at ten-thirty.'

Which meant Nicole couldn't be with him if he'd already left by then.

'Have you seen his daughter Nicole? It's possible she could be staying in the house.'

'No. No one's been here since he left. The walls are really thin, and you can hear everything.' She leaned forward conspiratorially. 'I would've heard if someone was staying there. I've got a key, though. I'm watering his plants. Do you want to take a look?'

'Yes, thanks. That would be helpful.'

'Righty o. One second and I'll get it.' The woman stepped back inside for a moment before reappearing with a key.

Becky and Ronnie followed her inside Daniel's house and had a look around. It smelled a little stale but was neat and tidy. There was no evidence Nicole had been there, nor that anything untoward had occurred.

'I think she's just gone on holiday for a break,' Ronnie said as they got back in their car parked on the street outside. 'Cheryl said she tried to get her to go away. That's the most likely explanation.'

Becky sighed with frustration. Was she really making more out of this in an attempt to prove she knew what she was doing? Was DI Thornton right and Nicole was just mentally unstable – her story a figment of her imagination? She thought back to the CCTV footage. Yes, maybe it was a bit ambiguous, and it looked like Nicole had got in the van with someone she knew, but it didn't sit right with her. She wasn't giving up yet. She sensed Nicole was in danger. She'd never forgive herself if anything happened to her.

She dialled DC Etheridge in the office and asked him if he'd had any luck tracing Nicole's uncle.

'Some. You'll never guess who he is.'

'Who?'

'Do you remember the Securitor Cash Depot robbery in 1983?'

'No. I was only five.' She laughed. 'It was the UK's biggest cash processor depot, owned by two of the leading banks. Five masked men raided the place dressed as police officers. They had handguns and shotguns and tied up the employees before leaving them locked in the vault after they'd robbed the place. The Flying Squad were convinced Charlie Briggs was one of the gang involved, along with several well-known members of the Essex underworld. They also suspected they had an insider working for them. Charlie was arrested, along with some of his known associates. Their houses were searched, and they were put under surveillance for a while. But there was never any forensic evidence to prove his or anyone else's involvement in it, and they never recovered the thirty-two million pounds that was stolen. Rumour has it he retired after that.'

'Well, that's a bloody nice nest egg to retire on.'

'Apparently, there was a huge reward offered by the banks for information, but no one ever came forward with anything that could lead to the gang's arrest.'

'Someone in the criminal underworld must've known exactly who was involved. Strange that no one grassed on them. Maybe there is honour amongst thieves after all.'

'Last we heard, he lived somewhere in Essex, but he's not listed on the voter's register, and Land Registry don't have him down as owning any property.'

'I bet he tucked all his money and property away in shell companies hidden in offshore havens.'

'That's what I thought, so I spoke to the force intelligence officer at Essex Police to see if they have any intel on his whereabouts. Seems Charlie keeps a low profile. He moved house a few years ago, and they're not aware of where he went, but they're going to do some digging.'

'Okay, thanks.'

'Dorset CID made enquiries with Mr Ebrooke, the registered owner of the van, but his vehicle was at a mechanic's shop all day when the footage was taken, getting an engine problem fixed, so they must've cloned the index plate.'

'Thought so.'

'Also, Nicole's mobile phone provider has got back to us. Her phone's switched off, but they've given us data for the last known location it was signalling from, which was in the centre of Cambridge – around the time she says she was abducted.'

Again, it fit with the story Nicole had told them; that the man who'd abducted her had dropped her phone in the van after she'd been taken.

'According to CCTV, her car is still at the park and ride station just outside Cambridge.'

'Okay, thanks.' She hung up.

'Where to now?' Ronnie asked.

'Back to the station, I suppose.'

She drove in silence, trying to ignore Ronnie wittering on about nothing as she went over every little thing Nicole had said in the interview, again and again. When they arrived, she walked straight into DI Thornton's office to give him an update.

'I told you to call her, not run around looking for her,' he said.

'I don't think Nicole's simply gone away. Her car is still at the park and ride, and maybe she suspected that whoever kidnapped her was monitoring her vehicle so she left it there. I bet you'll find some kind of tracker on it, like the surveillance at her house. Which would be how they followed her when she said she was going to meet her husband.'

DI Thornton gave me an exasperated sigh. 'The video camera you found at her house could've been put there by Nicole herself in case she had a break in. Those wireless things are cheap and easy to set up. They're all the rage these days for home security. And she couldn't have been meeting up with her husband – he's *dead*.'

'What if Mason Palmer is really alive?'

'Of course he's not.'

'Who sent Nicole the photo and message, then? He could've got off the plane before it went down, like Nicole said.'

'And what, he's been hiding for ten months and then suddenly contacts his wife now, out of the blue?' He snorted.

She agreed it sounded implausible, but still … she couldn't let the idea go. 'Maybe we should contact Interpol or the National Crime Agency. They may be aware of who Nicole's kidnapper is.

If he's a professional, he could be on their radar. Something going on in Africa must've set off this chain of events. They may be aware of any drug cartels operating out of there with links to the Palmers and Isabelle.'

'Interpol?' He looked at her like she'd just suggested he had eaten a turd sandwich. 'I've already given you enough leeway with this, and we've wasted far too much time on it. Nicole has most likely gone on holiday, like her friend Cheryl suggested. Maybe she's gone to Thailand to meet her Dad. Let's leave it at that for now.' He picked up a sheet of paper from his in tray and made a big show of studying it. She got the hint she was dismissed and walked out.

She bypassed her desk and headed for the stairs, stomping down them in her rush to get outside to the car park. She sat in her car and rang the number for the National Crime Agency, who had responsibility for dealing with serious and organised crime in the UK and housed Interpol liaison. She might be making the biggest mistake of her short-lived career as a DS by going against her new boss's instructions, but her old mentor had taught her that rules were meant to be broken.

Chapter 46

Charlie nudged me awake just before we landed at Galao airport. I rubbed at my face to chase away the remaining sleep and ran a wet wipe over it.

'You all right?' he asked.

I just nodded because I didn't trust myself to speak. Butterflies resumed their dance of flight in my stomach. I wasn't expecting to find Mason out here, but I hoped I'd at least find answers which would take me one step closer to knowing what had happened to him and where he might've gone.

I had the same attack of nerves as we queued up at passport control, trying to concentrate on not looking guilty or suspicious, but the guard barely glanced at my passport photo before calling Charlie to the counter. He smiled at the guard assuredly with the practise of someone who's used to lying.

We didn't have to wait for any luggage so we headed outside and made our way to the taxi rank. The stifling heat hit me as soon as we stepped onto the pavement. The line of cabs was a mish-mash of old vehicles with *TAXI* hand-painted on the side. That didn't inspire me with confidence, but we were only travelling a few miles down the road to the smaller airport where we'd catch the light aircraft to Lagossa.

The driver at the front of the line seemed oblivious to the heat, dressed in jeans and a Manchester United football shirt. The loose short-sleeved linen shirt and cargo trousers I'd bought yesterday were already sticking to me like a second skin.

He stepped forward and said, 'Welcome to Narumbe. I got good taxi. Take you where you need to go.'

Charlie told him our destination.

He looked disappointed at the short fare. 'Where you flying to?'

'Lagossa,' I said.

'You doctors?' he asked when we got inside the car. 'They the only people goin' out there now. The rebels make it too dangerous for people.'

'Not as worthy as that, I'm afraid. We're administrators, overseeing the health centre down there,' Charlie said. That would be our cover story if anyone asked. We worked for Health International and were doing an inventory mission to see if the centre needed further supplies.

'What areas have the rebels taken control of?' Charlie asked as we slid in the back seat.

'The middle of the country, but they moving further north now. People bein' killed. Villages burnt to the ground. Bad men. Very bad men.'

'Do you know who's in control of them?' I asked.

He glanced in the rear-view mirror and caught my gaze. He looked scared. Then he glanced quickly back to the road, ignoring the question. 'It not good to ask too many things.'

When we arrived at the small building for light aircraft departures, the cheery look was back on the driver's face as he jumped out of the taxi and opened my door.

Charlie paid him and added a generous tip. He looked down at it in his hand and grinned.

'Thank you, mah man. You be careful down there. The rebels … they workin' for the inside.' He tapped his nose secretively, and before we could ask any more, he jumped in the cab and drove off, tyres squealing down the sun-bleached tarmac road.

Charlie and I looked at each other.

'A coup of some kind?' I asked.

'Wouldn't surprise me. Jealousy, rivalry, tribal or religious differences, Africa's notorious for coups. It's no different to the West, really, except we just have the illusion of choice in our politicians. Your mum used to call *me* a crook, but they're the worst lying criminals ever.'

We stepped inside, into the slightly cooler air, courtesy of several ceiling fans. A woman with braided hair wearing a navy uniform checked us in for our flight and pointed to a small fridge where we could get bottles of water and juice.

There were rattan chairs inside that had seen better days and were fraying around the edges and a door that led outside to a small patio. We grabbed a few of bottles of water each. Charlie said he needed to smoke, so we headed outside to wait.

Half an hour later, we were the only two passengers on an aircraft built for six. I wondered if this was the same kind of plane Mason was supposed to have been on when he'd apparently died. A jolt of terror hit me in the chest at what these people were capable of. I tried to ignore it and stared out of the window for the one-and-a-half-hour flight, clutching the armrest as I watched the capital disappear beneath me and open up into smaller settlements and villages, interspersed with barren areas. At the half-way point in our journey, the villages disappeared for a while, replaced by thick, seemingly endless bush. I was pretty sure this was the area where Mason's plane went down, and I pressed my forehead against the glass for a better look.

Eventually, the bush petered out into sporadic areas, and I could see the remains of torched villages, blackened and burnt, materials scattered on the ground. I questioned the sanity of my decision to come out here. It was dangerous, possibly deadly.

I shook the thought away as the horrible sights were replaced by lush green trees of the cocoa plantations.

Thirty minutes later, we landed in the last place Mason had been seen alive.

Chapter 47

Adjoua shuffled her paperwork together on the plastic desk, then stepped towards the glass doors overlooking the runway to watch the light aircraft arriving. She wished she could get on it and fly away somewhere else. They used to get plenty of tourists here. The only people who came these days were doctors and aid workers. She sighed to herself as she spotted the two passengers disembark, still dreaming of escape. The trouble was, she needed money to get away. She was lucky to still have her job, but she was scared about her future. She had a little saved up but not enough to start a new life.

So, it was money she was thinking of when she first saw the white woman look around in bewilderment at the desolate runway cut out from the middle of the bush.

Adjoua gasped. Was it her?

She squinted against the sunshine and watched the woman heading towards her, smiling as she opened the door for them, studying her carefully to be sure. 'Welcome to Lagossa.'

'Thanks,' the older man with her replied, looking around. 'No passport control?'

'No. I check the passports.' There were no guards. The only flights came in from the capital and passports were already checked there. No point in having extra personnel waiting for the few flights per day.

The man handed her his passport. She studied the name, Dean Townsend. Handed it back, then took the woman's. The name read Justine Taylor. She looked at the photograph. Looked at the woman. In the other photograph Adjoua had been shown, she'd looked a little different, but Adjoua was certain it was her.

Adjoua kept the smile in place as she handed it back, then fixed her gaze on them as they walked through the building towards the exit. She rushed towards her locker, pulled out her mobile phone and dialled, then strode towards the exit doors, still watching.

When the man answered the phone, she whispered, 'I think I've just seen Mr Palmer's wife.'

Chapter 48

A white Toyota Land Cruiser was parked outside the airport. A black man whose age was hard to tell leaned against the passenger doors, arms folded, watching our approach.

'Is that our contact?' I whispered to Charlie.

'One way to find out.' He smiled at the man. 'You're Yakouba, right?'

The man laughed. 'Nah, man. Yakouba's my brother. I'm Siaka.'

Charlie nodded, satisfied the code he'd arranged via his contact had worked.

Siaka opened the rear passenger doors, and we got in. He jumped into the driver's seat and twisted around to face us, as if he was waiting for something.

Charlie undid the button on the pocket of his cargo trousers and pulled out a brown envelope filled with US dollars. 'That's half of what I agreed. You look after us and you get the other half when you drop us back at the airport.' He handed it over.

Siaka opened the envelope and looked inside, smiling. 'Yeah, man. Wherever you need to go, I look after you.'

'We're going to the medical centre outside of town,' I said.

He started the engine and drove off down the potholed track with thick bush either side of us. 'Yeah, you checking the centre, right?'

'That's right,' Charlie said.

'You need to be careful down here. The rebels are gettin' closer. Plenty people from the villages found their way down here to get help. Those men dem cuttin' and killin'.'

'Did you get a gun for me? We need some kind of protection while we're here.'

He shook his head. 'No guns. De rebels got dem all.'

'What about a knife?' Charlie asked.

Siaka shrugged. 'You be okay. You with me.' He reached down into the front passenger footwell and picked up a machete, before slicing it through the air theatrically.

My eyes widened as I stared at it. It looked sharp enough to slice your head clean off.

I felt Charlie squeeze my hand as he said, 'Well, hopefully, there won't be any trouble.'

We drove for around thirty minutes, bumping on the rugged red-dirt road, making hard work of the miles. I clutched onto the door handle as we jerked about in the back seat. Dust flew through the open window. Bamboo whipped at the sides of the vehicle as we drove along its edge. Then we came to the small town of Lagossa itself, driving along a strip of road with little shanty-style shops either side, and kiosks erected from a mixture of material – bamboo, palm leaves, wooden pallets and corrugated metal. They were selling food, what looked like roasted peanuts and some kind of dried fish hung on hooks. There was an old-fashioned gas station. A concrete building that housed a supermarket painted bright red. Men milling around, talking. Women carrying heavy loads on their heads with babies strapped to their backs.

At the end of town was an older building that had a sign outside saying, "Metro Bar and Hotel". I kept my gaze on it as we drove by, wondering if the same person who'd warned me about Moussa Damba was inside.

After that came more bush, and finally there was a sign for Health International Medical Centre on our left. Next to it was a well-rutted road that led off the main one, and Siaka drove up it. After a couple of miles, it opened into a clearing with two huge white tents, surrounded by smaller tents. Outside the small tents were a couple of guards dressed casually, with rifles slung over their shoulders, sitting cross-legged on the ground, chatting.

'Dis is it,' Siaka announced.

As we got out of the car, I felt the desolation and destruction of the place permeate my bones.

One of the guards spoke to Siaka in a language I didn't understand, and Siaka replied in the same tongue. The guard nodded and pointed towards one of the tents.

'You wait for us right here, yes?' Charlie asked Siaka.

'Sure, man. The doctor is in the big tent there.' Siaka pointed in the same direction the guard had. Then he slid his mobile phone from his pocket, leaned against the car, crossed one leg casually over the other and said, 'I just play game on phone 'til you come back.'

'He doesn't exactly inspire me with confidence,' Charlie whispered to me before a middle-aged man slid through the flaps of the larger tent with a plastic packet of medicine in his hand. He was dressed in short-sleeved blue scrubs, his blond hair covered with a plastic surgeon's cap.

He noticed us and said, 'Please wait a minute and I'll be with you,' before disappearing into another tent and coming back out empty-handed. 'You are injured?' His eyes scanned us in a practised appraisal.

'No. We're …' I paused. Now that I was here, I wasn't sure what to say. The police hadn't believed anything I'd said, and I was pretty sure this man wouldn't either. 'You're Jean-Luc, aren't you?'

He nodded and then squinted at me. 'Nicole?'

I nodded. We'd never met, but I guessed Mason had shown him a photo of me.

'What are you doing here?' he asked, surprised.

'I was hoping to speak to Adama and some of Mason's colleagues about …' I stopped abruptly, still hesitant to ask the questions I really needed answers to. Isabelle was dead. Mason was missing. I'd barely survived being kidnapped. It was time to be honest now and that meant sharing what I knew. 'This is going to sound like a strange story.'

He tilted his head, studied me casually, looking like he'd had numerous strange stories told to him throughout his career and I couldn't beat anything he'd already heard. 'Maybe you should tell me your strange story over some coffee? I think you've had a long journey, no?'

'Thanks.'

He nodded decisively then pointed at the large tent behind him. 'This is the medical ward we've set up.' He pointed at a slightly smaller one. 'Operating theatre and treatment rooms.' As we walked past some smaller tents, he said, 'Staff quarters.' He led us around in a circle behind the ward tent to one which had the entry flaps rolled back, exposing tables and chairs inside, a couple of fridges, and an elderly black woman sitting at one table washing dishes in a blue plastic bowl.

Jean-Luc pressed a hand to the woman's shoulder lightly. 'We have some guests, Mariam. Is there any chance of coffee?'

'Yes, Doctor.' Mariam stood and walked behind a makeshift wooden counter towards a small gas burner. She took a battered metal saucepan from a shelf and filled it from a large bottle of water, using a pump attached to the lid.

'Please, have a seat.' Jean-Luc sat at one of the tables.

I wiped away the sweat on my brow and sat opposite him with Charlie to my right. 'What did you hear about my husband's accident?'

His gaze drifted between me and Charlie before settling back on me. 'Just that he died in the plane crash. It's very tragic.'

'Well, the thing is, I don't think he was on the plane. I think he survived.'

He raised his eyebrows, shocked. 'Why would you think that?'

'It's a long story.'

'O-kay,' he said hesitantly.

'We think he discovered something that was going on out here,' Charlie added. 'He must've seen or heard something. Something that was important enough to some people who were prepared to kill him over it. Isabelle Moore has now also been murdered.'

'Isabelle?' His eyes widened. 'She's dead?'

'You hadn't heard?' I asked.

'No. It takes a while for things to get filtered out here. That's just awful.' He paused. 'Did you know Adama, our local man who deals with our logistics and supplies? He has gone missing.'

'I've been trying to contact him,' I said, thinking it was now likely something bad had happened to him.

'I wasn't too worried. The phones here play up sometimes. But I hope to God he's okay.' He pressed his lips together. 'Do you think we're in danger here? I mean, in danger from something other than the rebels?'

'I really don't know,' I said. 'But it would help if you don't tell anyone we're here.'

'The only people who seem to be in danger are those who know something about whatever it is Mason discovered,' Charlie added.

'I'm not sure how I can help you because I have absolutely no knowledge of anything like that.'

'Is it possible to speak to any other staff you have here?'

The woman making coffee appeared then and placed three mugs on the table with a bowl of sugar.

'Thank you.' I looked up at her.

She gave me a sad smile that revealed several missing teeth.

'Sorry, there's no milk. We've run out of some supplies. Adama usually handles things like that but …' Jean-Luc shook his head. 'Isabelle is dead and Adama is missing … this is terrible. I need to speak to head office in London and find out what to do about this.'

'Are you aware of any trafficking of illegal drugs going on out here?' Charlie asked.

Jean-Luc pressed his lips together and shook his head with surprise. 'I barely get time to leave the centre. And when I do, it'll be for a quick trip into the only bar in town and back. We're out in the middle of nowhere here.' He shrugged. 'But I haven't heard or seen anything like that going on.' He picked up his mug again. 'We have three nurses here and two guards. And Dr Olsen, who arrived as a replacement after Mason was …' He paused, seemingly not knowing whether to say dead or not. 'She's on R and R at the moment, but she didn't know Mason anyway, although you can gladly ask the other staff your questions. But I really think someone would've mentioned it before if they knew anything like that.'

I smiled my thanks at him and took a sip of the bitter coffee.

'What do you know about the rebels' demands?' Charlie asked.

Jean-Luc sucked in a breath. 'The local guards talk to us about it. They say they think the head of the secret police is behind what's going on.'

'Moussa Damba?' I asked.

'Yes. They say he wants to take over from the president. The rebels are stampeding their way through the country, decimating villages. The people who turn up here for treatment are those who don't oppose a new regime change. Any adults who are against it are annihilated so they can't fight back and their children are kidnapped. The women …' He looked at us with sadness. 'Most of the women arriving have been raped. Few people are getting through now, though. The trouble is escalating.'

'The children … are they kidnapped to become soldiers?' I asked.

'I would guess so. Child soldiers are not uncommon in Africa.'

A young woman dressed in identical scrubs rushed into the tent and said, 'Sorry, Dr Martin, but we need you in the ward. Sita is haemorrhaging.'

Jean-Luc slammed his mug on the table and said, 'Sorry, emergency,' before he rushed out following the nurse.

'What a godforsaken place,' Charlie muttered. 'Come on, let's talk to the other staff and then get the hell out of here.' He took a final swig of coffee and stood.

As I got up to follow him out, Mariam strolled into our paths and held her hand up to us.

'Wait. I can help you,' she whispered.

Chapter 49

Blade drove down the quiet country lane past Charlie Briggs's house, but he couldn't see much from the road. The house was on the edge of a small Essex village, surrounded by high walls topped with metal spikes. The electric gates were closed. There was an intercom system by the gate and a CCTV camera. The guy obviously liked his privacy and security. Not surprising, Blade thought, wondering if Charlie had a home safe with any of the money he'd blagged from the Securitor robbery. Frankie hadn't managed to find out where Charlie lived. It had been Blade who'd discovered Charlie's address from a contact of a contact who was more than happy to dish the dirt on the old timer for a bit of spare cash. So much for modern technology. Sometimes, good old grassing in the criminal underworld did the trick instead.

He carried on, passing the next property, which was half a mile away, doing a recce of the area, then he turned around and double-backed. The target house was surrounded by chest-high wheat fields that would help mask Blade's approach from the rear. Perfect.

Further down the lane, he found a track etched out of mud by heavy-duty tractor wheels and drove his nicked 4x4 down it, parking well away from the road. He got out of the vehicle and surveyed Charlie's place in the distance, but it was hidden from this angle by hideously high leylandii. All was quiet, apart from the sounds of birds.

He set off walking, a rucksack over his shoulder, his Walther PPK tucked against the small of his back, his stiletto knife in a sheath in the leg pocket of his combat trousers, his breathing steady. His mouth watered at the anticipation of a kill, sure now that Nicole would be hiding out with her uncle. No doubt an old-school armed robber like Charlie would be tooled up, but the guy was in his late fifties now and retired. He'd be out of practice and out of shape. Blade would be quicker than him. He'd do Charlie first then have time to spend with Nicole before searching the house for valuables. A little unexpected bonus to tide him over.

He stood in front of the trees that surrounded the rear and side of the property. He fucking hated leylandii. It was thick and rough and almost impenetrable. Almost, but not quite. Not with a bit of determination.

He chose an area with a slight gap between the trees and parted some of the thick foliage with gloved hands, gradually pushing his way through to the other side until he came to another ten-foot brick wall.

'Shit.' Blade stared at the moss-covered brick looming above him. He had rope in his rucksack, but there were no spikes on the top of this wall, and the leylandii was cut into a boxy hedge, so there was nothing for the rope to hold on to sufficiently. He'd have to go in through the front of the property instead with more risk of being seen.

He gave the wall a kick with his steel-toe capped boot as a parting shot and retraced his steps, his anger mounting.

He walked past the 4x4, back down the track and onto the country lane. He stopped in front of Charlie's front wall, listened, looking up and down the road. He hadn't heard or seen a car since he'd arrived, but he didn't want to be spotted scaling the wall. He could wait until dark with less chance of being seen, but he didn't have time, so he looped the end of the rope into a lasso and tossed it up towards the spikes. It caught hold of two, and he tugged it tight, then climbed up. When he got to the top, he pressed each hand either side of a spike and swung his legs over. He picked off the rope and then jumped down, landing with a roll of his body.

Now he was completely exposed on an expanse of lawn. To his left was a swimming pool with a terrace around it. At one side was a pergola with a tiled roof, a wrought iron table and chairs underneath it, along with a gas BBQ. At the other was a summer house. Dead ahead of him was a half metre border wall that separated the lawn from the house.

He kept low, crouch-running towards it, eyes on the side of the house and conservatory. He dived behind the wall and stayed there for a minute.

Then he edged his head upwards. The place was silent. No windows or doors were open, even though the day was already hitting the late twenties. He had a good view through the conservatory into the kitchen from here, but no one was inside.

He watched and waited for ten minutes, but there was no movement coming from the house. Above the French doors that led in from the conservatory was an alarm box, flashing a blue light. There was a CCTV camera next to it.

Was anyone inside? Only one way to draw them out.

There were some loose shingle stones near the wall so he edged towards them, keeping covered, then picked one up and threw it at the French doors. It bounced off with a *crack*, landing on the terrace.

He watched the house, but there was still no sign of anyone. He picked up another stone and hurled that at the door. Again, it bounced off the glass, but no one appeared to check it out. Was Charlie watching from the CCTV cameras?

His gaze surveyed the expanse of the side of the house once more before he took a risk and ran towards it, gun in hand, ready to shoot, but no one came and nothing happened.

Convinced no one was inside, or that they were hiding, Blade edged around the house, looking in windows and doors. Still saw no sign of life. When he got to the front of the house, he spotted a second alarm box flashing above the porch as well as another camera. Blade could pick locks, but alarms were not his strong point, and this guy had more than one. He could ring Frankie to try and hack into the alarm systems, but that would take time he didn't have. If Charlie was here, he would've spotted Blade by now and made his presence known, surely.

He edged away from the house, towards a detached double garage with wooden doors and a Yale lock. He got out his lock pickers and, a minute later, opened the door. Inside was a black Range Rover Sport. He took a photo of the registration plate. He'd get Frankie to find out whose name this was registered in, because so far Frankie hadn't found any property or vehicles in Charlie's name.

He was shutting the doors again when he heard the rumble of a car engine behind the front gates.

'Well, well, well, here they are now,' Blade whispered to himself and slunk around to the back of the garage.

He held the pistol tight in his grip and grinned.

Chapter 50

As Charlie and I approached the woman behind the kitchen counter, her gaze wasn't on us but kept steady on the open flaps of the tent, watching for someone or something.

'What do you know?' I asked gently.

She looked at us then, and I noticed for the first time she had a nasty scar running from beneath her right ear to her chin. It was still an angry raised red, as if it was fairly recent.

'Adama was my friend. He was good man. Very good man. He try to help people all the time. He got me this job.'

I nodded encouragingly.

'Now he is dead. They kill him.'

'Oh, God.' My hands cupped my mouth.

'Who did it?' Charlie asked.

Her eyes welled up. She blinked rapidly. 'You know what is going on here?' But before I could answer, she wiped her eyes with the back of her hand and shook her head. 'No, course not. People don't really know. Someone came before. A journalist from France. He was asking questions, and then he disappeared. They killed him too. Anyone who asks questions is in danger. Our President … he started off a good man. But then he don't care no more. He drive round in a big car, live in big house, get rich, but the people they poor. The people unhappy, you know?'

'Is this about drugs?' Charlie asked.

She squinted up at us. 'This is about the cacao.'

'Cacao?' I frowned, waiting for the word to sink in. 'You mean, *cocaine?*'

'No. *Cacao.* It is what you call cocoa.'

'What?' I asked incredulously.

'Yes. The only industry here is the cocoa bean, and the government controls it all. They set the price of the beans they give the farmers very low. Then they sell the beans to the foreign companies. The big chocolate people. The President, he get greedy, and he want to make more money, so he reduce the price he give to the farmers for beans and put up their taxes. Then he charge more to the chocolate people to buy them.' She pursed her lips, looking between Charlie and me to make sure we got it.

'So, Mason found out about what … government corruption here?' Charlie asked.

'More than that. The farmers all poor, they barely make enough money from the cacao. But when the government tax them more and reduce the price to buy from them, now the farmer make *no* profit, so they need to do something 'bout it, but they don't know what. But there is man in secret police, he have all the answers for them.'

'Moussa Damba?' I asked.

'Yes. He think he is God, but he is a devil. Adama tell me Damba work out way to change everything so it's better for him and he can get the people on his side.' Her gaze drifted to the tent flap and then back to us. 'Damba start his own rebel army and supply the weapons with money from one of the big chocolate companies. Damba tell the rebels if they overthrow the President, he take over and he make things better for the people. He give the farmer more profit and put money into the country. But the rebels, they get too crazy. They start burning people villages. They burned mine.' Tears welled up in her eyes. 'They kill my husband.' Her head dropped to her chest, her shoulders heaving up and down as she struggled to contain her tears. 'They try to kill me.' She touched the scar on her jaw. 'I just manage to escape, but now they take everything away from me.'

I reached out a hand and placed it on her shoulder, casting a sad glance at Charlie.

'They …' She sniffed and looked up again with watery eyes. 'They kill the men who fight back so they can't stop Damba taking over. The children, they kidnap and take to cocoa farms to work. And they are not allowed to leave. They keep them there as slaves.'

I sucked in a horrified breath.

'So, the farmer happy now, because he get free labour from children slaves and make more profit. And he think he will make more when Damba come to power and put up prices he pay them and cut their taxes. The rebels happy because they getting money and food and power from Damba. But everything get worse for the other people who are even poorer now and have lost their families.'

'How did Mason get involved in this?' I asked, rubbing her shoulder, my heart clenching with sadness for her.

'Adama and Mason was good friends. You don't know who to trust here. Damba and his secret police have eyes everywhere. But Adama, he trust your husband. He know Mason was good man.' She reached out and clenched my hand with surprising strength. 'Adama tell him what is happening, and Mason want to help. Adama took him to some of the plantations to show him the child slaves. Your husband film everything on his video camera. Adama also have friends in government who make secret recordings of Moussa Damba and the chocolate people talking. Adama wanted Mason to take it back to England. Do something 'bout it. Tell the world what is happening and try to help us.'

The air was stiflingly hot in the tent, but I shivered as if someone had poured a bucket of icy water over me.

'And Damba discovered what they were doing?' Charlie asked.

'Yes.'

'Which plantations did they go to?' I asked. 'Do you have any names?'

'There are many here. But the last one he went to was the Royale Plantation.'

I took a deep breath. 'Mason didn't get on that plane, did he?'

'No. At airport, Damba take Mason's equipment, but Mason get away. Adama think they mess with the plane. Make it go down or maybe not put enough fuel in. People ask questions if a white doctor go missing, they asked when the journalist disappeared, and Damba didn't want that to happen again. If a plane go down instead, it is accident and people not ask questions.'

I pressed a hand to my heart.

'Mason got off the plane and hide because he suspicious. He call Adama and tell him what happen. There is old track that go round the border into Mali – no guards there – so Adama smuggle him across. Adama get false passport for him so they can't trace him. Damba, he tell Mason at airport if he tells anything, they will kill you.'

I felt my knees buckle beneath me as I pictured everything, her words answering so many questions that had raced through my mind. I leaned against the counter for support.

Charlie gave me a look to say, *are you okay?*

I took a deep breath and nodded. 'That's why Mason waited so long before contacting me? He was hiding for ten months to make sure they weren't watching me to see if he'd told me anything before he was supposed to have been killed? To make sure it was safe to get in touch again?'

'He was hiding because they didn't have enough evidence against Damba then,' she said. 'But now Adama is dead, Moussa Damba must have found everything he had and destroyed it.'

'What I don't understand is if they thought it was finally all right to let Nicole know Mason was safe, what changed?' Charlie asked. 'Somehow, Damba's men knew Mason was still alive.'

'Because they finally found the plane,' she said.

Chapter 51

Becky stared out of the window as they drove down the country lane towards what they thought was Charlie Briggs's house. The force intelligence officer in Essex had finally come through with a suspected address for him, which had been bought by an offshore company called Plex Enterprises. DC Etheridge was having trouble trying to find out more details, but offshore companies were notoriously difficult to get information on.

They passed rolling fields of wheat until the sat nav announced their destination at a property surrounded by high walls topped with spikes, just outside a quiet, small village.

Ronnie pulled up in front of the gates. 'Let's hope Nicole is here safe and well, and I can get back to some real work.'

She gave him a look. 'This is *real* work.'

'You know what I meant. I actually quite like paperwork. Going through Isabelle's business accounts is very therapeutic. There's something about numbers that's relaxing.'

'You must have a really weird social life.' She grinned at him. 'Rather you than me. I've had six years of paperwork. That therapy didn't work on me.'

Ronnie shrugged. 'And anyway, we're not even certain this is Charlie's house.'

She got out of the car and pressed the intercom system on the wall next to a letter box.

Ronnie watched her through the car window.

When there was no response, she pressed it again, looking over her shoulder at Ronnie with a worried expression.

She tried the metal gates, but they were electric and unmoveable. Ronnie got out of the car as she stepped backwards, looking up at the ten-foot wall.

'What do you reckon? Can you give me a leg up that far?' she asked.

'Not unless you're Spider Woman.'

'What about if you stand on the roof of the car and then hoist me up?'

He looked at the car. Looked at her. 'Maybe. But are you sure we should be doing this?'

'We're doing a welfare check. And I've got a feeling in my gut this is the right place. Don't just stand there. Move the car alongside the wall and let's give it a go.'

She watched Ronnie manoeuvre the car so it was in position, and then he got out.

They stood side by side, staring up at the spikes.

'How are you going to get out again from the inside?' he asked.

She opened the boot of the car, pulled out a tow rope. 'I'll use this. Come on, then, let's do it.'

Ronnie climbed onto the roof of the car, holding out a hand to help her up. 'Those spikes look nasty.' He grimaced. 'I wouldn't fancy getting impaled on one of those. You could be disembowelled.'

'Thanks for that cheery graphic thought. Anyway, I like a challenge.' She turned to him. 'And it's better than sitting on my arse in a stuffy office going through boring statements. This is the most excitement I've had since … well, a frigging long time.'

'You shouldn't go in there alone. He's got a record. He probably hates the police. You should do a risk assessment.'

She rolled her eyes. 'I've got my CS spray. That'll do nicely as a risk assessment.' She patted her trouser pocket then looped the rope loosely around her neck. 'Right. I'm ready.'

He bent his knees, grabbed both of her calves and hoisted her upwards.

Her fingers clutched onto the top two long spikes.

Ronnie's arms shook. 'Hurry up. I'm wobbling all over the place.'

'Are you trying to say I'm fat?' She laughed, pulling herself upwards with her arms, pleased that all the work she'd been doing in the gym had paid off. She shuffled her knees up, the toes of her boots scraping against the wall, carefully lifting one leg over and placing it between a spike, before lifting the other one in the same way so she was bent over like a crab. 'Do *not* look at my arse.'

'I'd never do that!' He sounded astounded, as if she'd just suggested he'd murdered a puppy. He was always straight-laced and politically correct, never joining in with the banter in the office.

'Why, what's wrong with my arse?' she teased him.

'Um … well, nothing. But you're my boss. I don't, you know … it's inappropriate.'

She chuckled fondly at his discomfort, lifting her neck out of the rope and tying a loop around one spike, letting it dangle down the other side. 'I'm going over now.' She swung herself around so she was hanging on the opposite side of the wall, still holding onto the spikes, her shoulder sockets stretching. Then she dropped down, bending her knees on impact.

She turned to look at a large house and dusted her palms together, whistling at the opulence of the place. 'Who says crime doesn't pay?' She called out to Ronnie before walking towards the imposing white mansion with thick pillars and a porch at the front. Okay, so it was a bit too much of a typical Costa-del-crimey, gangster type villa for her tastes, but it still would've cost a packet. She wondered just how much Charlie Briggs had secretly stashed away after the robbery.

To the right of the house was a big detached garage. To the left, she could see the edge of a swimming pool where the garden wrapped around the property. Her gaze scanned the house windows as she approached. When she got to the front door, she rapped the cheesy brass knocker in the shape of a lion, glancing around while she waited.

She put her ear to the door but heard no sounds from within, so she rapped the knocker again, before calling out Charlie's and Nicole's names. No response.

She stepped back and looked up at the house. The curtains were open in every window. There was no letter box to peek through.

She wandered around the house, past a swimming pool on her left and a conservatory-cum-kitchen on her right next to a lounge and a study, then she checked the summer house, but that was locked and as she peered in the glass doors noted it was just full of outdoor furniture. She carried on until she'd done a full loop of the house, trying door handles and windows to see if they were insecure, but the house appeared locked up and empty with no signs of disturbance.

She pulled her phone out and called DI Thornton, giving him an update. He hadn't been enthusiastic about her still looking for Nicole, to put it mildly, and had given her this one last chance to find her, but that was probably because he knew she wouldn't shut up about it, and all he wanted was a quiet life.

'There's no sign of anyone or any break-in. I'm wondering whether to smash a window. If the people who kidnapped Nicole have found her again, she and her uncle could be in there dead or injured for all we know.'

'We've got no cause to effect an entry when we're not even sure it's the right house, and we need to cover our arses here. I can just imagine the complaints we'll get if the property doesn't even belong to him. And I'm still not convinced she was kidnapped.'

She puffed out a frustrated sigh, wandering over to the garage and opening the doors. 'I'm pretty sure this is the right place.'

'Pretty sure isn't good enough. We need to be one-hundred per cent certain.'

'There's a Range Rover here, but I found no vehicles listed to Plex Enterprises, nor any mobile phones. Could you do a PNC check on this one, please?'

'Yes, I suppose so.' He sighed. She gave him the index plate number, and he said, 'Hang on,' before putting her on hold.

She carried on staring at the Range Rover while she waited.

'The vehicle's registered to a company called Southern Holdings,' he said when he came back on the line.

'I bet he's got half a dozen off shore companies with things registered in their names. How about getting DC Etheridge to check out any mobile phones registered to this new company?'

'No, I'm not taking him off Isabelle Moore's enquiries for that.'

She walked back to the house and peered up at the alarm box above the door. 'Okay, well, there are two alarm systems here. It might be quicker to contact the companies and see if you can get hold of any mobile phone contact details they have for this address, guv. One's called Secure Alarms, and the other is Genesis Security.'

'The alarm company won't divulge contact details without a warrant, and we have no reason to get one. Now that's the end of your jolly out.'

'Yes, but, what if–'

'What if nothing.'

'But guv, the house feels empty but … I'm really concerned about Nicole's welfare now.'

'Leave a note there for the owner to contact you and then get back to the station as soon as possible.'

'Okay.' She hung up and pulled a face at the phone before stepping back and looking up at the upstairs windows.

She walked away to the far end of the house, just about to do another loop, when she thought she heard a noise. It was only slight, a muffled scraping sound. She stopped dead in her tracks and strained her ears, listening. It hadn't come from the house. It sounded like it was near the garage.

She turned around, the rubber soles of her boots quiet on the block-paving, heading for the garage. When she got in front of the double doors, she listened again but heard nothing.

She walked past the doors, around to the other side, keeping close to the brickwork, but there was nothing there apart from thick bushes that butted up to the garage walls.

She stared into the bushes. Maybe it was a cat or mouse inside. Or maybe she'd been mistaken in the first place.

Chapter 52

Even though Blade was hiding behind the garage, he could still hear the female pig's conversation. He recognised her voice as the one who'd gone to Nicole's house and found his camera. He could've just killed her and not batted an eyelid, but he was way off track on this job now and couldn't afford the hassle of dodging a national manhunt for a cop-killer. Time was running out. He was sure the house was empty, but Nicole must've turned to her uncle for help – so where the fuck were they?

He listened in, hoping to hear something useful, but the copper didn't seem to know much about Charlie or the Palmers whereabouts either.

As the conversation wrapped up, he walked slowly and silently away from the back of the garage, towards the summerhouse and hid behind it. She was unlikely to check that area again. Then he waited until she'd fucked off before leaving the same way he'd come in, already making plans to return at a later date when this job was sorted so he could rob the place. He was certain there'd be some kind of safe in there with a huge wad of cash inside, and it would teach them all for giving him the fucking run-around.

Chapter 53

One of the guards entered the tent and interrupted our conversation by asking for coffee. Mariam sniffed and replaced the sadness on her face with a smile, but the trembling in her hands gave her away. She was scared, that much was obvious. Paranoid the guards were secretly working for Moussa Damba?

'Thanks for the drink,' Charlie said to her casually.

'Yes, thank you,' I added, so grateful she'd chosen to trust us. 'It was the best coffee I've had for a long time.'

Charlie took hold of my elbow, steering me outside where the sun burned my eyes, towards the edge of the bush land beside the canteen tent, and whispered to me, 'I don't think we should talk to the other guards. If we do, it would cast suspicion on Mariam, and they could be involved with Damba for all we know. She said he had ears and eyes everywhere.'

'I agree. But I can't believe this is all about cocoa beans,' I whispered back, but my tone was fierce, angry at what the local people were going through, what Mason had gone through. At Isabelle and Adama's murder and the journalist who'd disappeared. 'People are prepared to kill over *cocoa beans*.'

'It's not about the cocoa. Not really. It's about the end product. Think about how much chocolate is consumed all over the world and how much money is involved. That's what the big boys at the top will be protecting. The farmers and rebels and the locals are just pawns being played in a massive game of profit and corruption.'

'Do you think the chocolate companies know that villages are being massacred and children taken as slaves to work the farms?'

'Probably. They'd sure as hell want it covered up if they did, and Damba didn't do all this on his own. He had to have had some powerful help internationally to get to you.'

I stared down at the sun-baked ground. 'Mason must've told Isabelle what was going on out here when he spoke to her on the phone a couple of days before he was due to come home. He must've wanted to discuss with her what to do.'

'So why didn't she do anything about it? Why did she try to hide it from you? If she covered it up, she's as bad as that fucking Damba arsehole.'

'I don't know if it's as simple as that. Health International aren't the kind of NGO that gets involved in political problems. Maybe she thought that if she blew the whistle on what was happening, she'd get her permits revoked and her team would be thrown out. Is it better to help some people fleeing the rebels who desperately need it or get kicked out and help no one?'

The empty Cloudbox account suddenly popped into my head. I'd forgotten all about it until then. I explained it to Charlie and said, 'I think Mason was intending to uploaded his footage onto a cloud before he left here so he had backup evidence, but there were no files on it, so for some reason he never did, and the only copy he had was the one Damba confiscated.'

'I think we should get the hell out of this place. You found the truth. Now it's time to leave.'

I chewed on my lip for a moment until a rustling noise somewhere out in the jungle of palm and bamboo caught my attention. I froze, the first thought in my head was *lion!*

But before we could both run for cover, a black woman appeared, stumbling through the trees into the clearing. It was hard to tell the colour of her clothing because the front of it was soaked in wet blood. Her feet slowly dragging herself along were bare and also bloody. More blood ran from the top of her head, smeared onto the right side of her face.

'Jesus!' Charlie ran towards her and caught her just before her eyes rolled upwards into their sockets and her knees collapsed beneath her.

'We need some help here.' I cried out. 'Help! There's a woman here that's badly injured.'

Charlie picked her up and rushed around towards the front of the ward tent with me following. The guard who'd had coffee in the kitchen tent rounded the corner casually and just watched, as if he'd seen it all before and it was nothing new. Siaka looked up from his position leaning against the Toyota, surprised. Just as Charlie got to the ward, the flaps opened from the inside and Jean-Luc stood there.

Inside, I could see beds completely full of patients, some moaning in pain, some asleep, some with their eyes open staring at nothing.

'Take her to the treatment tent.' He pointed to the tent next door, quickly following behind Charlie.

I stood in the entryway, cupping my hands to my mouth uselessly as I watched Charlie lay the woman down gently on a treatment table covered with white paper.

Mariam approached from behind me and gasped, looking over my shoulder, horrified. 'Poor woman.' She pressed her hands to her cheeks.

'Sallie, I need you out here,' Jean-Luc called loudly as he quickly inspected the woman's head and pulled up her blood-soaked T-shirt to check what wounds she had. There was a deep gash in her stomach that looked like a machete had sliced through her.

I looked at the floor, feeling sick as the nurse who'd interrupted our coffee earlier almost knocked in to me in her rush to get inside the tent. She immediately took stock of the emergency and reached for some scissors in a plastic drawer set before cutting away the T-shirt.

Charlie turned away to protect the woman's modesty and led me outside. 'Poor bloody woman.'

'Her village must've been hit by the rebels.' Tears sprang into my eyes. Seeing the horrific reality of what was happening here made me think of the question Charlie posed earlier. Was it better to help some of the people and ignore the other crimes going on out here than help none at all? I suddenly understood Isabelle's reasons for keeping the truth from me.

'Come on. We need to leave.' Charlie clutched my forearm and led me towards the Land Cruiser.

Siaka watched our approach while animatedly talking with one of the guards.

I dug my heels into the ground and shook my arm away. 'We can't leave. Not yet. Not after seeing first hand what's happened to that poor woman and listening to Mariam. I want to finish what Mason started. It's the only way to expose what's going on and stop them coming after me.'

Charlie let out a noise that sounded like a growl, his eyes hard. 'You're going to get us killed.'

I shook my head stubbornly, looking at Mariam who was close by, watching us with tears in her eyes. 'No. Think about it. I have no idea where Mason is. If he's gone into hiding again, I might never see him. And it seems any evidence he or Adama had has been destroyed by Moussa Damba. But if I can get hold of the same footage Mason took with the child slaves, we can expose what's happening here. People will have to do something then if they're shown evidence – the UN, Interpol, I don't know. But some organisation will have to take action. We need to go to the Royale Plantation and see for ourselves what's going on.'

He snorted. 'I wouldn't be so sure any organisation will come rushing to help.' He narrowed his eyes at me, an angry twitch starting in the corner of his right eye. It was a look that chilled me. A look that I was sure he'd given countless people in his days as a gangster. 'And you're on Damba's turf now. You don't think they're all going to let you just walk into one of the cocoa farms and film what's going on, do you? We have no weapons, either. How are we going to protect ourselves?'

I didn't know how it would work. I didn't have a proper plan. But one thing went in our favour. They didn't know we were here yet. We would have the element of surprise.

Chapter 54

'That poor woman,' I said, getting in the back seat of the Land Cruiser.

Charlie grunted with anger as he slid in next to me and looked out of the window towards the treatment tent.

'Dis is normal here,' Siaka said, shaking his head. 'Told you de rebels gettin' closer.'

Maybe that was true, but I couldn't accept that. I had to do something about it. Exposing the cocoa slavery meant exposing the reason the rebels were doing this to their own people.

'You go to Metro Hotel now for some refreshment? No flight out of here until six pm.' Siaka got behind the wheel.

Charlie turned his head and looked at me, intense anger distorting his features. He was silent for a moment, then he said, 'We wanted to get a feel for the area while we're here. Can you take us to the Royale Plantation?'

'You mad, man?' Siaka shrieked. 'De rebels could be anywhere in the jungle. You get yourself killed. Why you want to see that?'

I attempted to keep my voice as casual as possible. 'We don't have anything like that back home. It would be good to see one before we leave.'

'Dey won't just let you in to look round,' Siaka said.

'We'll just have a walk about and stretch our legs up there, then,' Charlie said, trying to appear casual.

'In the *bush*?' His voice pitched high. 'You got plenty wild animals out there too, ya know.' He shook his head like we were mad. Maybe we were. Then he lifted his hands in a *you're-the-boss* gesture. 'You the one paying for my time, so if that what you want … I can take you to a plantation, but I can't hang around there with the vehicle. If the rebels come, they just shoot me. I'll have to drop you there and you call me when you ready to come back.' He twisted round in the seat and looked at us. '*If* you come back.'

Charlie said, 'That's why we'll need some kind of weapons to protect ourselves, just in case we bump into the rebels.'

'Or a lion.' Siaka shook his head and started the engine. 'I told you. I can't get a gun.'

'You have a machete,' Charlie pointed out.

'It for my own protection.'

'So, take us back to the town we drove through first. We can get a machete or knives there, right?' Charlie said.

Siaka twisted around to face us, raising his eyebrows with disbelief. 'You know how to use a machete? You doctor people. What you be doing with a machete? You probably cut your own hand off.'

'Can you help or not?' Charlie's voice had a hard edge to it.

Siaka snorted, as if he didn't care one way or the other. 'Yeah, yeah. We go town and get you machete. Then I take you cocoa farm.'

We drove silently back to Lagossa, the visions of that injured woman playing through my mind. I pictured Jean-Luc working on her and wondered if she'd live. I thought about everything Mariam had told us and tried to get my head around it. This was all about *cocoa?* It was insane.

Siaka parked outside a hardware shop that was really more like a shack with a corrugated tin roof. 'You stay here. I get you tools.'

'Do you trust him?' I asked Charlie when Siaka was out of earshot. I looked around. We were being watched with interest by a group of five men, standing around a kiosk, chatting with the vendor.

'I trust my contact who organised him, but who knows? If you want to go ahead with your plan, then we don't have much of a choice, do we?'

'You understand why I need to do this?'

'I understand. But you need to understand we could both end up dead.'

'Maybe I should go alone.'

'Don't be ridiculous.'

My head told me to leave. Go to the Metro Bar where someone had warned me off and wait there until six pm when we could catch the flight out and get as far away from here as possible. Doing this could put both our lives at risk. But my heart told me that the people who were trying to kill me wouldn't stop unless they were exposed. I thought of the poor injured woman again. Of Mariam. I had to stop this. I had no choice.

Siaka emerged from the shack with two machetes. He slid in behind the wheel and handed them to us, handles first. The machetes weren't new. They were rusty and dented but looked sharp enough to do some serious damage. They were ridiculously long, and I didn't have a clue how to use one. If the time came to protect ourselves, I probably would end up cutting off my own finger or something.

Charlie tested the weight of the machete in his hand, then placed it flat in the footwell. I set mine down in the same way.

Siaka swung the car around and headed back where we'd come from. Eventually, we passed the track to the medical centre and drove further along the dusty, pot-holed road until we came upon a sign that read Royale Plantation, an arrow pointing right up a well-worn road through the bush, wide enough for a lorry. The ground was compacted into solid red-brown mud.

'We here.' Siaka stopped next to the sign, his head turning left and right as he searched the dense foliage of trees for potential rebels. 'You call me when you ready. I pick you up same place.'

'Okay.' Charlie got out of the car, then leaned back in to pick up the machete, holding it down by his thigh.

I followed suit.

We watched Siaka drive off, a terrible sense of foreboding erupting inside me.

Chapter 55

'This is madness,' Charlie whispered as we walked through the bush, avoiding the main road that ran to the plantation entrance. Occasionally, the palm and bamboo were so thick, he sliced at it with the machete to clear a path.

Mosquitoes honed in on us, and we constantly slapped at any exposed skin.

'We could get bitten by a snake or attacked by a lion or leopard. I bet leopards like this dense area,' Charlie snapped. 'Not to mention end up with malaria or dengue fever. That's if we don't get spotted and shot.'

'For Christ sake!' I shout-whispered. I knew he was trying to protect me, and it was coming out as moaning, but after what I'd discovered today, I was more angry than scared. 'I thought you were supposed to be a hardened criminal. You're a bloody wimp!'

'I never went in anywhere without a proper plan and a team around me. *And* I had a fucking big gun.'

We pushed through the jungle, eyes alert. My whole body was covered in a sheen of sweat, rivers of it running along my hairline and down the small of my back, my hair stuck to it, wrapped around my neck and face like a coiled rope.

Charlie pulled a bottle of water from his backpack and handed it to me. I quickly drained half of it then gave it back, but it did little to quench my parched throat.

'You must get your stubbornness from your mum,' he said a few minutes later as we trudged on.

'Right. Definitely not from you, then?'

'Shush.' He held a hand up in the air and looked dead ahead at a high wire fence that had appeared in the distance.

We approached it as quietly as we could, peering through the diamond-shaped gaps. There was a hand-painted sign that read "KEEP OUT", with another written in a foreign language beneath it, and the fence made a buzzing sound.

'It's electric,' he said.

'To keep animals out or the slaves in?' I looked at him with a growing sense of dread.

Chapter 56

The same man who'd taken the call from Adjoua at the airport had been trying to find Mrs Palmer and her friend. He'd arrived at the airport too late; they'd already disappeared. When his mobile phone rang, he was just approaching Lagossa, driving up the main street, looking for them.

He answered it quickly and recognised the voice straight away.

'His wife was here,' the voice spoke quietly, telling him what had happened.

'Do you know where they went?' he said.

'I overheard them speak of going to the Royale Plantation.'

'Thank you.' He hung up and pressed down on the accelerator.

Chapter 57

We stared through the fence into the dense plantation and saw nothing but trees bursting with cocoa pods.

'Let's go this way,' Charlie pointed to the left. 'The other way will lead to the plantation's entrance, and there will probably be guards there.'

We set off walking along the perimeter, the machete heavy in my hand. I'd never wielded so much as a penknife before. If the time came when I had to use it, I wasn't convinced I could do so effectively. And if anything happened to us, it would be my fault. Charlie was right – we should've gone to the hotel bar and formed a proper plan. At least tried to get hold of a gun for protection. Not that I'd ever held a gun before either, let alone fired one, but these people had already proved they'd stop at nothing to keep their horrific secrets.

My stomach ached with anxiety as we trudged on, one eye on the bush for rebels or animals and one eye on the plantation.

We eventually spotted a large clearing through the fence and stopped, hiding behind a banana tree. It was a deserted camp, in the centre of which was a fire pit with the remnants of blackened earth. To the right was an open-sided lean-to made of wooden poles with a tin roof, storing drums of chemicals. I didn't know what kind, but I recognised the international skull and crossbones sign for poison and suspected they were some kind of pesticide. Behind the fire were woven racks with cocoa seeds laid out in the sun to dry, the earthy rich sweet smell permeating the air. Off to the left were stacks of bulging hessian sacks piled high and a big shack with a tin roof and no windows. The door was wide open but had a padlock hanging on the outside of the handle and a bolt on it. Inside the gloom, I could make out a mud floor strewn with a few rolled up bits of material or clothing.

'This must be their living area,' Charlie said.

'I wouldn't call this *living*.' A wave of white rage flooded through me. 'Where are they all?'

'Let's carry on this way.'

We walked for a further ten minutes before we heard the rhythmic chop of machetes echoing through the still air.

Charlie froze in front of me and turned to the fence. I stopped behind him.

He pointed into the plantation. And there, between some cocoa trees, sat a group of eight children, cross-legged on the ground around a huge pile of cocoa pods. Holding the pods in one hand, they swung their machetes in an arc through the air to crack into them. Once split open, they scooped out the gooey white seeds inside with their fingers before throwing them into a plastic basket. In the distance, I spotted some other boys amongst the trees, cutting down more pods.

Charlie made a flapping hand gesture, indicating at me to crouch down so we were obscured by foliage. I forced the thoughts of snakes and spiders out of my head and stared at the boys. They were dressed in dirty, raggedy clothes and barefoot. Their ages ranged somewhere between five and fifteen.

I pulled my phone from my pocket and started videoing them, watching their desolate faces through the screen. They had no water with them, and they looked very thin and weak with a deadness in their eyes. A few of the boys had fresh bruises or bloody swellings on their faces. Some had nasty cuts or scars crisscrossing their arms and legs, or open welts with flies busy trying to feast on them. One of the younger boys' arms was shaking with the effort of constantly swinging the heavy machete down to split the pods, his eyes half closing with exhaustion. His tiny, emaciated body made him clumsy, and his eyes closed for a split second, the machete missing the cocoa pod and slicing into his forearm.

I gasped.

His pitiful scream filled the air.

The other boys sat still, looking around frantically as if terrified. One of the older boys ran to the younger one and lifted his injured arm in the air, presumably to stench the blood flow.

A guard dressed in a makeshift army uniform of camouflage trousers, a Chelsea football shirt, camouflage cap and black boots ran out from between the trees behind the boys. He had a big gun in his hands, some kind of automatic weapon, and shouted at them in French. He pointed the gun at the injured boy and his helper.

The other boys flinched and lowered their eyes but carried on working.

The guard shouted some more. The helper rushed back to the outer circle of boys and picked up his machete again, swinging at the cocoa pods. The younger boy had stopped screaming when the guard appeared, his face full of fear and shock and pain, but his mouth was wide open in a silent cry as tears streamed down his dirty face. His lips trembled, and he cowered on the ground.

The guard pulled up the injured boy by his good arm, blood dripped down the wound and onto the fallen leaves on the ground. He shouted some more in French, getting in the boy's face.

The boy said something back as he clutched his arm, doubling over with pain.

The guard yelled in his face and waved his gun at him, motioning for him to get back to work.

My skin prickled with fear. I wanted to climb over the fence and help the boy. Rip the gun away from the bullying guard and get some medical help. I started to rise from my crouched position, but Charlie grabbed my arm. I looked over at him. He shook his head, his eyes fiery, mimed a throat slitting action.

I hesitated for a moment, feeling as powerless as I'd ever felt in my life, my mind quickly turning over. If I revealed we were here and intervened, what would happen? At the very least, we'd be arrested. At the worst, we'd be shot. Neither would help save the boy and the other slaves anyway.

Charlie's nails dug into the flesh on my arm.

It was the hardest decision I'd ever had to make. If we were killed, we couldn't do anything. If we got out of here alive, we could send proper aid. Tears sprang into my eyes as I sat back slowly on my haunches.

Blood streamed from the boy's injury. He looked down at his feet. The guard gestured again with the gun for him to get back to work. I held my breath. Then the boy ran away from the guard, towards the dense plantation's endless sea of green behind.

The guard turned, shot him in the back.

I flinched. The breath I'd been holding exploded out of my lungs, my eyes widening as I watched the boy fly through the air as if weightless, before hitting a cocoa tree trunk and sliding to the ground. His head lifted to the side, blood spread rapidly across the back of his tattered T-shirt. He blinked, dazed, in pain. He tried to speak, his lips moving with a terrible rasping sound as blood bubbled out of his mouth. Then his head dropped to the ground, his life oozing away as his blood pooled out into the earth around him.

The guard turned around to the other boys and shouted viciously at them. I couldn't speak French, but body language translates all dialects, and I was sure he was telling them to get back to work or they'd suffer the same fate.

The boys quickly averted their eyes from the dead boy and frantically swung the machetes at the pods.

The guard took hold of the dead boy's arm and dragged him away in the direction he'd come from like he was just a piece of garbage.

Chapter 58

Moussa Damba was out of the loop. He'd heard nothing from Zurich about Nicole and Mason's whereabouts. If Julian Bolliger deigned him too inconsequential, he could think again. Moussa could make things very hard for him when he got the green light that the merger had been signed, and Moussa could prepare to finally overthrow the president.

He was the one in control. Now and always. *He* controlled the cocoa plantations, and *he* would control the distribution centres. *He* would set the cocoa bean price, and the chocolate companies would have to accept it. The deals they'd been getting for years were what made it possible for them to make their billions in profit off the back of Moussa and his country. So, his friends in Zurich needed to be careful, if they knew what was good for them. He didn't play second fiddle to anyone.

He ground out his cigar in the ashtray on his office desk, thought about calling Bolliger for an update, but that would make him look needy and not in control. He couldn't have that. Then his phone rang.

The caller stated his name and started talking …

'A white woman and man arrived in Lagossa this morning. They say they administrators for Health International, but I get a weird vibe from them. They ask a lot of questions.'

'Do you know their names?' Moussa's body instantly became alert. It had to be the Palmers, he thought. But why would they come back here? It didn't make any sense. Unless they were trying to get to him. He almost cackled to himself. They were so stupid; they had no idea how it worked in Narumbe.

'No, I don't know.'

'Where are they now?'

'That the strange thing. They want to go to a cocoa farm and see what it like. I took them to the Royale Plantation. You find them there.'

Moussa gritted his teeth. So, the Palmers wanted to come back and film more of the footage he'd confiscated. That had to be the reason they were here.

'I'll make sure you're suitably rewarded.' Moussa hung up, then scrolled through his mobile phone, looking for the name of the plantation owner. If the Palmers were there, Moussa's rebels guarding the slaves would find them and kill them.

Then *he'd* be the one in control again. The one to tell Bolliger that he'd dealt with the problem once and for all.

Chapter 59

Blade drank from a bottle of water as he lounged on the sofa, waiting for Frankie to come up with something he could work with. He would much rather be drinking a beer, but he had to stay in control until the job was done.

Frankie had hacked into the two alarm companies that operated at Charlie's house and come up with contact details in the name of Southern Holdings. The mobile phone number listed for them had been switched off, although its last GPS location came from Charlie's house.

'Hey, this is interesting.' Frankie looked over at Blade.

'What?' Blade shot off the sofa. He rounded the desk and looked at the laptop screen over Frankie's shoulder.

'I started searching airline databases from ten months ago. Mason Palmer had to have left Narumbe somehow if he wasn't on the plane that crashed.'

'And what am I looking at?' Blade narrowed his eyes at a page on the screen with a list of names he didn't recognise, not even trying to disguise his impatience. 'We don't have time for a big fucking fanfare. Just get to the point.'

'I was working on a hunch he must've crossed the border into Cote D'Ivoire or Mali and made it out from there. A flight left the capital of Mali at ten-fifteen pm the next evening to Paris.' He pointed to the screen at the name Nicholas Porter. Then clicked on another tab and the screen changed to show a British passport. 'I checked the Charles de Galle passport control systems. They scan passports now. This is a copy of it.'

Blade let out a slow laugh. Nicholas Porter was Mason Palmer. 'So, what happened to him?'

'He caught a flight to Barcelona shortly after and then disappeared from the system until four days ago, when he arrived at Heathrow.' Frankie gave Blade a smug smile and ran his hands over his perfectly-arranged man-bun.

'And he hasn't left the UK?'

'Nope.'

'Wipe that stupid grin off your face. You still don't know where he is, do you?'

Frankie frowned. 'It's only a matter of time. People can't stay hidden forever.'

Chapter 60

'Did you get all that on film?' Charlie whispered.

'Yes.' My heart clanged beneath my ribs as if trying to climb out of my chest. My hands and legs shook. 'I can't believe what we just saw. That poor boy. *Boys.*'

'The guard must be one of the rebels working for Moussa Damba to protect the slave-master's interests. There will be others in there. We need to get out before they spot us. You've got enough footage to use against them.'

I chewed on my lip, torn again. Part of me wanted to stay, to help rescue those slaves, even though I didn't have a clue how we could with no tools to cut through the wire and no contacts here to help smuggle them out now Adama was dead. Another part of me wanted to get more footage. Even though what we had was damning, would it be enough for the UN or Interpol or some other agency to come in and investigate what was going on out here? But Charlie was right, it wasn't safe for us, and we needed to pass this on to the relevant authorities and get them to act. Surely the footage must be enough for that.

'Come on, we need to go now,' Charlie snapped.

'Okay.' I shoved my phone in my pocket and tried to suppress the impotent rage I felt.

We started walking fast down the incline of jungle that would eventually take us back to the main road. I was drenched in sweat, still trembling from what I'd witnessed.

Charlie came around me and took the lead again, pushing up the pace, slicing through the dense greenery with his machete when needed.

Mosquitoes buzzed in my ears and stuck to my skin, ravaging on my blood as I constantly slapped at them.

Suddenly, the ground covered by palm fronds dipped, and I missed my footing, twisting over on my ankle.

A cry involuntarily escaped my lips and I toppled over, clutching my leg as I sprawled on the ground.

Charlie stopped and retraced his steps to me. 'Are you okay?'

The pain blossomed in my ankle, but I moved it tentatively, gritting my teeth to block it out. 'Yeah. I just twisted it.'

He leaned forward and took my arm, hauling me up. 'We need to get a move on. Can you walk?'

I rested my foot on the ground and tested my weight. It hurt a little but was bearable. 'Yes, let's go.' I hobbled as fast as I could beside him while he gripped my hand.

A loud crashing sound erupted in the dense jungle somewhere to our left. The noise of the foliage being disturbed by something big and heavy.

Charlie let go of me and raised his machete in the air, his head turning in the direction of sound.

'Is it a leopard?' I asked, fear taking an iron grip on me.

But then the reason for the noise became apparent. It wasn't a leopard.

It was much, *much* worse.

Chapter 61

DS Harris sat at her desk, staring at the notice board that dominated the room, looking at the photos SOCO had taken of Isabelle Moore. They'd found some damning evidence in Isabelle's mouth. She'd managed to bite her killer, and there was a small sliver of skin found in between her teeth. Unfortunately, there were no DNA matches from the skin to anyone in the national databases, nor did it match the DNA from the semen taken at the Watford rape and murder. DI Thornton's theory that they were connected had flown out of the window, and they were no further forward with finding the offender.

Nicole's mobile phone was still switched off. Becky had spoken to the contacts she'd built up over the last few years with mobile phone companies, asking them unofficially to see if they could trace a mobile phone number for Southern Holdings or Plex Enterprises. O2 had found one for Southern Holdings, but it was switched off, and the last location it had been transmitting a signal from was in the area of Charlie's house. Were Nicole and Charlie inside, wounded … dead?

If DS Carter was still here, she knew what he would've done. Broken in to the house to find out and fuck the boss's reservations. But she'd already gone behind DI Thornton's back contacting the NCA/Interpol, and she was reluctant to test his boundaries further.

She turned back to her computer screen, frustrated, and her landline extension rang on her desk. She picked it up and answered.

'Hi. It's DS Leadbetter from Interpol Manchester.'

She sat upright in her desk. 'Oh, hi, thanks for getting back to me. Have you found something?'

'Yes, I have, actually. The CCTV footage you sent over of the man who abducted Nicole Palmer, I have a name for you.'

'Really?' She reached for a pen, suddenly wide awake.

'Yeah. I'm on secondment here from the Eastern Region Regional Organised Crime Unit, and I recognised him pretty much straight away. His name's Sean Fowler, although he's had multiple aliases over the years – Dean Bridges, Lee Fuller, John Brown, Steve Price, and the nickname Blade.'

'Blade?'

'Due to his sick penchant for using a knife. He was a wannabe soldier when he was a kid but got his application to join the army rejected when he was sixteen because they thought he was mentally unstable. Then he embarked on his criminal life as a small-time drug dealer, before getting involved with the London-based Hopper Gang, a couple of brothers whose main activity was smuggling drugs and prostitution. But he's a real psychopath, and as he worked his way up the ranks, he indulged his violent side by becoming an enforcer for them. Now it seems he's branched out, and he's a hired assassin for the UK criminal underworld.'

Becky's eyes widened. She'd had a feeling the case was going to be different but this was huge.

'He's suspected of multiple murders in the UK and a series of contract killings in Spain, bumping off various drug rivals of the Hopper gang, but we've never been able to prove anything. He's careful and clever. Whenever he's been nicked for something, any witnesses we've had have either refused to testify or disappeared. He's been off the grid for a year or so. There have been a few possible sightings of him in various countries, but nothing confirmed.'

She sat back, stunned. 'Maybe he's not so clever this time. Whoever killed and tortured Isabelle Moore left a piece of his skin in her mouth, and I'm pretty certain it belongs to Sean Fowler.'

'Let's hope you can catch him, then. I've circulated a new notice my end, which is an alert to all Interpol member countries, with the intel you've given me about the Moore murder and Palmer abduction. We need to get this bastard behind bars, once and for all.'

'I'm working on it. Sorry, can you give me those aliases again?' She scribbled down the names and underlined Sean Fowler five times. 'So, if he's a hired merc, he could be working for anyone.'

'Anyone who pays well.'

'Do you know anything about drug cartels operating in Narumbe? Mason Palmer's death must've started all this, and I think Isabelle was involved in it through her work, so the link has to be something that happened out there. And this is something big, if they're using assassins to murder people. It's more than likely that Sean Fowler has already kidnapped Nicole Palmer again; there's no trace of her anywhere. Time is ticking. She may already be dead.'

'Narumbe isn't a member country of Interpol, so I can't tell you a lot about it. However, the neighbouring countries, Cote D'Ivoire and Mali, are, so I know there are a number of Mexican and Colombian drug cartels moving into the West African countries. I can try and get you a contact number for police in Narumbe.'

'Thanks.' She tapped her biro on her pad, grinning, as he confirmed the theory she'd built up. This had to be about some kind of drug smuggling operation.

She thanked DS Leadbetter and hung up, her mind reeling with the new information as she went over everything she already knew. Nicole Palmer had said Moussa Damba liaised with her after her husband's plane crash. And someone called her from a bar in Narumbe when she started asking questions about Mason's death, warning her not to trust him. Was Damba involved in it all as a corrupt government official? Was Mason Palmer murdered – the plane tampered with somehow – either because he knew something important or witnessed something? Did Moussa Damba want him eliminated so he arranged for the plane crash?

He would be in a position to do that and cover it up, make it look like an accident.

It seemed likely to her that Sean Fowler AKA Blade killed Isabelle because he thought she knew something. The phone records showed Mason had called Isabelle shortly before he was due home for his last R and R, so maybe they'd talked about whatever he'd discovered and what to do about it. What DS Harris couldn't work out was who had sent the photo and messages that Nicole thought came from Mason. It seemed unlikely Fowler tried to lure Nicole out to Jesus Green by pretending that he was Mason Palmer who was still alive, so he could kidnap her and kill her. Because … why? After all this time, ten months after Mason's death, when she didn't seem to know anything? And why not just come after her in her own home? Why all the elaborate sending of notes and photos?

She frowned. That part didn't make sense. Fowler was a professional killer. He wouldn't want to lure her into a public place when he could do it quickly and easily in private and eliminate all risks of being seen or her escaping. And if he hadn't sent them, who had? She mulled that over. There was far more to this mystery than she was grasping. And she could only think of one person who would've done it.

She walked out of the office and headed to the ladies for a quick toilet break before stopping at the canteen to get a bar of chocolate. Becky couldn't go a day without her sweet treat, and the stash she usually kept in her office drawer had run out. All the while thoughts swirled around her head, trying to make the jigsaw pieces fit into place and coming up with the one bizarre possibility that she couldn't shake off.

She stuffed the chocolate bar down en route back to the incident room. When she walked back inside, DI Thornton spotted her through the glass window of his office, leaped out of his seat, stormed towards her. His face was a mottled shade of red, which she didn't think boded well, especially when he barked, 'In my office. Now!'

'What's happened?' she asked.

He sat at his desk. 'I've just had a DS Leadbetter from Interpol on the phone. He was trying to get hold of you but got put through to me when you didn't answer. Apparently, he had a contact number for police in Narumbe he was going to pass on to you.'

Oops, DS Harris thought. 'Well, I was actually coming to talk to you about it. I've had some thoughts on–'

He jerked his hand up to cut her off. 'I strictly remember telling you not to speak to them, so who the hell authorised that?'

'Um … no one, sir.' She bit her lip before carrying on. 'But we really could be onto some big drug cartel working out of Narumbe with possible government connections. It's–'

'I was warned that DS Carter might've left behind a legacy of unorthodox ideas and failing to adhere to instructions, and you seem to be following the same path. You need to nip it in the bud if you want people to take you seriously as a DS.'

'But, guv, you'll definitely want to hear this. Especially now you know for certain that Isabelle's murder isn't related to the Watford one.'

'I've already heard it all, from DS Leadbetter. Sean Fowler, international assassin with previous links to a drug gang in the UK, was the man with Nicole Palmer. If the info hadn't been so good, I'd be disciplining you for insubordination right now,' he said in a furious tone.

She opened her mouth to speak, but he cut her off again.

'In light of what they've said, I think it's most likely that the Palmers were involved in an international drug cartel operating out of Narumbe, smuggling it into the UK.'

She stared at him, open-mouthed, as he took the credit for being the one to work out the drug angle.

'Here's what I think happened … Mason Palmer was murdered because of his involvement in a drug smuggling ring. As a doctor working for an NGO, it would be the perfect cover. Maybe he wanted out of it, or maybe he'd pissed off the wrong person in the cartel, or stole from them, so they arranged for the plane crash that killed him.' He smiled cunningly, warming to his theme.

She raised her eyebrows, distinctly remembering saying something virtually identical in a previous conversation with him, but he'd poo-poohed her idea. However, while she'd voiced this theory initially, her thinking had since changed, and she didn't believe Mason was guilty of any involvement. She now believed he'd inadvertently been caught up in it.

'But we're never going to prove that, and anyway, it's out of our jurisdiction,' he carried on. 'We need to concentrate on our own clear up rates. I think Nicole was involved in it all too, and Isabelle found out what they'd been doing and was going to blow the whistle. That's why Nicole had been in contact with her recently. To tell her to back off. When that didn't work, she got her accomplice, Sean Fowler, to murder Isabelle. Fowler must've been the Palmer's contact, distributing any drugs coming into the UK. Then Nicole concocted a story about being abducted to take the heat off her.'

'But that doesn't make any sense. Why would Nicole return to Isabelle's body the night after she was murdered if she was involved?'

'Maybe she went back there because she realised Fowler had missed some incriminating evidence against them when he searched Isabelle's house. Like her prints being found on the umbrella she'd touched, and she went back to retrieve it.'

'The cab driver we spoke to who dropped her off said Nicole asked him to wait there for her. That's hardly the actions of someone guilty. If she was doing something criminal, she wouldn't have wanted him hanging around. And why would Nicole tell us all about her husband really being alive if she was trying to hide his involvement? I think Fowler did abduct Nicole Palmer.' Becky wanted Thornton to admit he was wrong, because she was still very scared for Nicole's safety. 'We should've done more to find her after what she said when we interviewed her.'

'I don't think she's in danger. On the contrary, I think she's very dangerous. She's not the victim here – she's up to her neck in it all.'

'Look, sir, it's more likely that Mason was the one who arranged to meet her at Jesus Green, but Fowler followed her and snatched her because he was looking for Mason. This is to do with drugs, I'm sure, but I don't think Mason or Nicole are involved in it at all. I think Mason witnessed or found out something going on in Narumbe about the cartel, and they wanted to shut him up. He spoke to Isabelle to discuss what to do before he flew home, but then they tried to kill him in the plane crash.'

DI Thornton rolled his eyes. 'I don't think so.'

'But that would fit with the scenario of what's been happening. They thought he was on the plane, but he got off before it left the runway, hence the phone call he made after the plane took off. Then Mason finds out what's happened to it and realises he needs to make it *look* like he's dead, so he goes into hiding because he knows they'll be after him. Then when ten months pass and he thinks it's safe, he contacts his wife again. But the government or Moussa Damba realise, *somehow*, that Mason's not dead and get Fowler to go after Nicole to find out where he is, but she escapes. They also torture Isabelle to find out Mason's whereabouts, because they think she knows something and then kill her. This all started when Nicole began asking questions about her husband's death which someone wants to hide.'

'I disagree. I know this is your first big case as DS, and you're very enthusiastic about it, but I have far more experience in this than you, and we're going to follow the evidence rather than your outlandish theories,' he said with an edge of sarcasm. 'Our priority is to catch Sean Fowler and Nicole Palmer.' He stood up. 'I'm going to organise a press conference releasing Fowler's details saying he's wanted for questioning for Isabelle's rape and murder. I want you to circulate Fowler and Nicole's info with other forces and Border Control and concentrate on tracking them both down.

Also, get DC Etheridge and DC Pickering to delve into the Palmer's backgrounds and personal records.'

She hesitated, wanting to try and change his mind.

'Do you have a problem with that, DS Harris?'

Reluctantly, she said, 'No, sir.' Even if they were on different pages and seemed to be solving different pieces of the same puzzle, hopefully the endgame would be the same – finding Nicole and Mason safe and well and arresting Fowler.

She turned on her heels and headed back to her desk, where she promptly picked up the phone and called DS Leadbetter back. Because the other thing was, if her theory was right, and Mason Palmer *wasn't* actually killed in that plane crash, he'd have needed a false passport to get out of Narumbe and get to Barcelona where the photo he sent Nicole was taken. She needed to get hold of some contact details for police in Cote D'Ivoire and Mali, the neighbouring countries, where he might've been smuggled to. It was a long shot, though, and she wasn't sure if it would bear any fruit, but she had to try.

Chapter 62

Three guards dressed in the same makeshift army uniform emerged through the thick bush, pointing guns at us. I didn't know what kind of gun, but they were big and scary and could easily snuff out our lives as quickly as they'd done with that poor boy.

One of them shouted something in French, indicating with the muzzle of his gun that we should put our hands up.

Charlie dropped his machete on the ground before lifting his arms in the air. 'We're fucked,' he said to me.

I raised my hands, following suit, the machete slipping from my grasp as I trembled. The testosterone was practically oozing out of their pores as they looked us up and down, their faces snarling with anger.

'No need to shoot,' Charlie addressed them. 'We were just out for a walk and got lost. If you can tell us where the main road is, we'll go.'

The guards looked at each other and spoke in rapid French.

'Do you speak English?' Charlie asked.

My pulse roared in my ears, my breath hissed in and out uncontrollably. We were going to die, and there was nothing we could do to stop it. I pictured our dead bodies splayed out on the dusty earth, riddled with bullets, never to be found.

'You come with us,' the guard on the right shouted, the whites of his eyes flashing at us.

'Look, we'll just go,' I said, my voice cracking with fear, trying to control the tremor inside. 'Sorry, we didn't know this was private land. We weren't doing anything.'

'You no speak. You come with us,' he snapped, before turning around to lead the way.

The two others started to circle behind us.

I looked at Charlie. He looked at me. Our hopeless expressions mirrored each other. My whole body sagged with a mixture of fear and helplessness. There was no way out of this. I kept replaying the boy being shot in the back. Certain that's what was about to happen to us.

One of the guards dug the end of his gun into my spine pushing me forward.

Charlie reached for my hand and held it tight as we trudged through the jungle. 'We don't understand what's going on. We're not doing anything wrong. We just got lost,' Charlie tried again.

The man behind him shouted, 'Shut up, motherfucker.' Then laughed.

The man in front had just began joining in on the laughter when his head exploded.

I couldn't tell where the shot came from. I just watched as he hovered, as if suspended in air by invisible puppet strings, before slouching to the ground.

Charlie pulled me down while the other two guards crouched, their gazes and guns moving in a circle, trying to pinpoint the shooter.

As Charlie and I lay flat, I heard the sound of a second shot. The guard behind me was hit in the head. He toppled over from his crouched position, fell on his face.

The third guard grabbed hold of my arm and yanked me towards him, pulling me upright, using me as a human shield. One of his arms was tight around my neck, the other outstretched with the gun.

His heavy breath panted in my ear as he swung the gun around in an arc, but there was no sign of the shooter.

I struggled beneath his grip, but his arm tightened against my throat, crushing it, making it almost impossible to take in enough oxygen.

I clawed at his arm with my fingernails but it was no use – his grip was like iron. And then, as the guard swivelled his head in the hopes of seeing the shooter, Charlie launched at him.

The three of us toppled to the ground. The guard let go of me, and I rolled away. Charlie straddled the guard, his knees pressing on his arms so he couldn't lift up the gun.

Charlie punched him hard in the face two times. He was quick, but the guard was younger and fitter and managed to twist his gun hand out from underneath Charlie's knee.

As he swung it up towards Charlie's torso, Charlie punched him so hard, the back of his head bounced off the earth. But that didn't seem to slow the guard down, and with an almighty cry, he wrestled himself out from under Charlie, and in a split second, their positions were reversed, the guard now on top.

Charlie struggled beneath him, but he wasn't quick enough. The guard pressed the barrel of the rifle under Charlie's chin, and Charlie stopped rigid, waiting for the inevitable bullet that would end his life.

That's when a third shot rang out, hitting the guard's head, spraying blood and brain matter over the nearby palm leaves beside Charlie.

I clutched my hands over my head, stayed still, my pulse roaring in my ears.

Footsteps crunched through the bush, and a man appeared with the same make of gun the guards used.

'Come on. We must go now,' he ordered.

Chapter 63

Mason sat on the bed in the cheap hotel room he'd checked into close to Heathrow airport. He was typing frantically on his laptop.

He still had the footage he and Adama had taken on numerous occasions at the plantations. He'd downloaded it all to Cloudbox the day before he was due home, for security backup. When Mason had arrived in Barcelona, he'd set up another cloud account under his new false identity and stored it there. But while the video footage of the child slaves had been horrific, they didn't have enough evidence to prove Moussa Damba or Julian Bolliger's involvement in everything, so he'd had to wait it out. He couldn't risk Damba or Bolliger being tipped off about what he and Adama were up to.

While Adama and his friends were gathering more incriminating evidence Mason had been waiting. Eventually, ten months after his "death", Adama's network of contacts had successfully bugged Moussa Damba's phones and emailed it all to him. Now they had everything they needed to expose Moussa's involvement with the rebels and Julian Bolliger's big role in it all.

His plan had always been to get Nicole to safety before he went to Interpol with the evidence. But he couldn't risk doing it before then, in case there was a leak. Bolliger had powerful friends in high places and a lot of money to throw around. And as he'd proved time and time again, he would stop at nothing to silence Mason.

But now he was finally going to show the world the atrocities that were happening and, in doing so, exact his own revenge on the people who'd stolen his life and the lives of so many others.

The evidence he had was in hundreds of separate audio and video files, which wasn't a problem if he was simply handing it over to the authorities who would trawl through it all systematically. But since he'd found out about the merger happening, he needed to do something different with it, and he could already see in his mind how his idea would transpose. He was going to hit them somewhere that would ensure the maximum coverage for their heinous crimes and attract the most amount of global attention.

In two days' time, Bolliger was signing a merger with Galleaux at the famous international chocolate exhibition in Zurich. Whilst Bolliger was the biggest chocolate manufacturer in the world, Galleaux was the biggest processer, producing millions of tonnes of cocoa a year and turning it into cocoa powder, cocoa butter and solids. The merger would make them the most powerful corporation in the industry with the biggest market share of profit.

Mason practised with the video editing software again until he was confident he could do what he needed.

He just hoped he could pull off what he was planning.

Chapter 64

'Who are you?' I asked the man as we raced through the jungle.

'Adama sent me,' he said over his shoulder, expertly flipping back palm fronds.

I looked at Charlie, who was wiping the blood off his face with his shirtsleeves, worried we were walking into another trap. 'Adama is dead.'

'He still working from beyond the grave. Come on. No time for talking now. Keep moving. Others come.'

I didn't know if we could trust this man, but he'd just saved our lives. He had a gun, and he was our only hope.

Despite being fit, the heat and humidity sapped my energy. Charlie and I were both panting, but the man with us was barely out of breath or breaking a sweat.

'I need to give up the bloody fags,' Charlie said, a hand pressed to his heaving chest.

Muffled shouting sounded in the distance as we pushed ourselves forward as quietly and quickly as possible.

Eventually, we came to the road.

'My vehicle up there.' He pointed further along.

'I don't see it,' Charlie said suspiciously.

'It hidden.'

We moved parallel to the road, and eventually, the man stopped next to a copse of low trees. He tore off palm leaves and bamboo stacked over and against a green Land Rover that had been expertly arranged to look like foliage and blend in with the background. Charlie and I helped until it was completely uncovered.

He opened the driver's door and jumped in, putting his rifle in the footwell of the passenger seat. 'Let's go.'

Charlie and I got in the back, and he bounced over a rut at the side of the road and onto the pot-holed track in the opposite direction of Lagossa town, his tyres spraying mud into the air.

'Where are we going?' Charlie asked, twisting in his seat to look behind him out of the rear windscreen.

I turned, too, checking if anyone was following, but the road was empty.

'They know you here. They have eyes and ears everywhere.'

Charlie growled. 'Siaka must've told them.' He unbuttoned his blood-soaked shirt before shoving it in his hold-all then pulled on a new one.

'You can't go back to airport. They will wait for you there. I take you across border to Mali.'

I turned back around and met the driver's gaze in the rear-view mirror. He was young, probably only early twenties, with a haunted look in his eyes.

'Same way your husband got out,' he said.

'Adama got him out of the country, didn't he?' I asked.

'Yeah. This is what we do. We have network. We try to smuggle the slave boys out of the plantation. We take them to orphanage in Mali.'

'And then what happens to them?' Charlie asked.

'We hope they find new life in the end. At least they free and safe there. And maybe when the war is over, they can find their families again.'

'Do you know where Mason is? Are you in contact with him?' I asked, my gaze frantically searching his as he looked in the mirror again.

'No. I don't know. It was only Adama who in contact with him. But he definitely left Africa.'

I closed my eyelids, disappointment tearing my heart in two.

'How far is it to the border?' Charlie asked.

'Twenty mile. But we go through back road and avoid the guards who are owned by Damba.'

The Land Rover bounced over a big rut in the road, jerking me out of my seat, my right shoulder banging against the metal. I held on tight to the door handle and alternated my direction of gaze between the rear window and the front. But no one followed, and we saw no other cars or people on our journey.

So far, so good.

'I don't know how to thank you for coming to help us,' I said.

'Yes. We owe you our lives,' Charlie said, digging his hand into the leg pocket of his cargo trousers, pulling out the same kind of envelope he'd given to Siaka, what would've been his second payment for taking us back to the airport. Charlie held it out through the gap in the back seats to him. 'This is for you. It's all I have on me.'

'What's that?' the driver glanced down.

'Money. You've earned it.'

The driver shook his head. 'I don't want your money. This is not why I do this.'

Charlie, who'd been motivated to commit huge crimes for money, looked at the back of driver's head with an expression of disbelief. 'Why the hell would you put yourself at risk for people you've never even met?'

The driver was quiet for a long moment. 'When we get across border, I will show you why.'

Chapter 65

'What do you mean they escaped?' Moussa Damba's anger exploded as he stood at the guarded entry gate to the Royale Plantation and stared at the owner.

The owner looked down at the ground, trying to avoid Moussa's wrath.

Two of the rebels guarding the gate shifted from foot to foot, their AK-47s hanging from straps on their shoulders.

'I don't know how they got away, but three of your men are dead,' the owner said, still afraid to look up.

Moussa paced the dusty ground, his bespoke Italian leather loafers being covered in a thin layer of red soil. He turned to Chief Inspector Sumano, who stood behind him. 'They must've had help. When I find out *who,* they will die a painful death.' He paced some more, thinking. Then he whipped his phone from his pocket and called Siaka, who answered on the second ring. 'Are they with you?' he shouted.

'No, sir. I thought you had them by now. They were s'posed to ring me to pick them up, but when they no call, I thought you got them.'

'Urgh!' Damba growled and hung up. Next, he called the Metro Hotel. He spoke to the owner, but no one had seen them. 'Someone is hiding them!' He paced some more, hands clasped behind his back.

Then his anger deflated a little, and he smiled to himself. 'There is only one flight out of here at six and they will be on it. We will intercept them there.' He looked at his watch. It was almost four pm. He turned to the plantation owner and slapped him hard across the face. 'I'll return to deal with you later.'

As he walked back to the black, shiny SUV, he glanced down at his shoes, his anger igniting again at seeing the dirt on them. His dog of a maid, Fanta, would have to work twice as hard tonight to clean them. It would serve her right for screaming so much last night. He hated it when they screamed. It put him off his stroke.

When Moussa arrived at Lagossa airport, he strode inside, straight to the check-in desk. That snooty little Adjoua must've seen them arrive and not informed him. When he took over as President, he'd see to it she was sent to the cocoa plantations to work as a slave. That would teach her for thinking she was above everyone.

'Earlier today two people arrived on a plane from Galao,' he snapped.

She blinked rapidly under his glare. 'Y … yes, sir.'

'But you did not inform me.'

'Um … I did not know they were important.'

He glared at her. 'They will not be leaving again. And neither will you.' He gave her a nasty sneer then nodded to Sumano, who took her roughly by the arm and marched her along the corridor behind her desk.

'No! What's going on? I haven't done anything wrong.' She struggled to get away from Sumano's grip.

Moussa watched her curves wiggling in her tight uniform. Before the day was out, when the Palmers were captured and killed, he'd have some fun with her.

After Sumano pushed her inside a store room and locked the door, standing outside it with his hands clasped behind him, Moussa strode across the floor of the building into the same office he'd taken Mason Palmer to on the day he was supposed to die. The other officer, Sergeant Diawara, rushed to keep up with him.

Moussa sat at the desk, opened the bottom drawer and pulled out a bottle of brandy. 'Get me a clean glass.' He barked at Diawara, who rushed off to obey. When he returned, Damba filled it and took a gulp. He licked his lips and felt the burning liquid soothe him.

'What do you want me to do?' Diawara asked.

'Mason Palmer knows what Sumano and I look like, so I will stay in here and Sumano will keep out of sight. You must change out of your uniform into civilian clothes and wait in the seating area until you see them. Then bring them to me.'

Diawara nodded and left.

Moussa looked at his watch again. It wouldn't be long before the Palmers would finally be obliterated.

Chapter 66

The Land Rover made slow progress down the bad roads, but eventually, we approached the outskirts of a town mostly filled with houses made of mud with corrugated iron roofs. In the distance, there was a bustling market place and a group of buses parked up haphazardly with crowds of people milling around. Horns blared and goats ran around.

'The border is on other side of the bus station,' the driver, who'd told us his name was Issa, said. 'The guards too lazy to patrol in this heat. They sit in little office drinking coffee all day. We go off road now.' He swerved away from the rutted main road, and we drove past chickens dust-bathing and a side street of small shanty kiosks selling roasted peanuts, cigarettes, and cell phone cards, and along what seemed like a well-used path cut out through high vegetation that appeared endless.

It felt like I was on a roller coaster ride as the Land Rover bounced up and down, the tyres kicking up dust like a herd of stampeding elephants, obstructing our view.

We drove in brooding silence, Charlie and I clutching the door handles, lost in our own thoughts, until Issa said, 'We in Mali now,' although I had no idea how he could tell. The area was just vegetation and soil with nothing to distinguish it.

I breathed an inner sigh of relief that we'd got away from Narumbe. My stomach muscles clenched tight. I told myself it was to keep me steady as the Land Rover bumped along at full speed on the uneven surface, but I knew it was purely because my nerves were shot to pieces. In just four days since this had begun, my life had been torn apart. I'd had a message from a ghost, was a witness to the murder of a child and the enslavement of others, I'd found Isabelle's dead body, I'd been kidnapped and attacked and threatened with a gun, and I was on the run. What the hell was going to happen next? I just hoped Mason was still alive when we got back home and started sharing the footage, but I was becoming increasingly more worried for Mason's safety because he still hadn't emailed me. I tried to push the thought away. I didn't want to go there.

I slid my hand into the pocket of my trousers, reaching for my phone to reassure me that soon this would be over.

But it wasn't there.

I tried the other pocket. Not there, either.

Then I tried my back pockets. 'Shit!'

'What?' Charlie asked.

'My phone. I put it in my pocket, but it's not here.' I scooted forward on the seat and frantically searched around behind me and in the foot well, in case it had fallen out in the Land Rover with all the bumping around.

'Are you sure?' Charlie bent down and searched his side and under the front seat.

My fingertips scrabbled under Issa's chair. I slapped a palm to my forehead, my face twisted with disbelief. We'd risked our lives for that footage. It was the only way to bring Mason back to me and to expose what was going on. 'It must've fallen out when we were rushing away from the plantation. Or when I fell. Oh, God. What are we going to do now?' I collapsed my head in my hands.

Charlie slid his arm around my shoulder and pulled me towards him as tears pricked my eyes. 'We can't go back. We'll be killed.'

'We have to! We have to get more evidence.'

'He right,' Issa said. 'They be looking everywhere for you now. You must get away.'

'How could I be so stupid!' I wailed, pulling away from Charlie and fighting back tears. But before I could say anymore, we rounded a corner of tall grass and spotted two guards standing in the road with rifles slung over their shoulders, smoking as they watched our approach.

'Great,' Charlie said as the guards threw their cigarettes on the ground and stood shoulder to shoulder, pointing their weapons at us.

Issa slammed on the brakes, and we skidded to a stop. He shoved the rifle underneath the passenger seat. 'These not official guards. This illegal checkpoint. But I do not want to antagonise them with gun. They are unpredictable and will have other men hidden nearby. Do not move. Do not go for gun. Do not speak unless they ask you a question.' His voice was strained with concern.

I clutched my sweaty palm on the door handle, fear gnawing in my chest. I'd managed to escape death twice. I didn't think I'd be so lucky a third time.

I glanced around at the thick bush, wondering if there were other men watching us now with weapons trained on us. I looked at Charlie, but he was staring dead ahead at the guards dressed in camouflage uniform, his jaw clenched tight.

Issa wound his window down as one guard approached him, speaking rapidly in a language I didn't know. Issa replied in a placatory tone, shrugging his shoulders.

The second guard walked towards the passenger side, his gun trained on us.

I swallowed hard and held my breath. A bead of sweat trickled down my spine.

Time seemed to stand still as the second guard walked around the back of the Land Rover. I turned my head and saw him peer inside the rear screen before coming around to my open window. He had bloodshot eyes, and I could smell his body odour. He stared at me. I dropped my gaze, avoiding his eye contact.

He shouted something.

I flinched.

He shouted again.

Issa turned around and spoke to him in their language.

The second guard shouted something back, gesturing with the gun for us to get out of the vehicle.

My chest tightened. If we got out, we might never get in again.

'He want you both to get out,' Issa said, the tremble in his voice obvious now.

My eyes widened as I glanced at Charlie. He looked like he was torn between following Issa's instructions and going for the gun under the seat.

'What do they want? A bribe?' Charlie asked.

'Yes, but you need to get out first.'

Both guards stepped back to let us out.

Issa slid off his seat and stepped out onto the track. I followed suit, trying to keep my eyes concentrated on the ground so as not to antagonise them in anyway. Charlie got out of his door on the other side and walked around so he was next to me.

One guard spoke again to Issa while the second stepped closer to me so we were barely inches apart. Fear clutched every part of me. I struggled to breathe.

He put the barrel of his weapon under my chin and lifted it up so I had no choice but to look at him. I panted in and out, trembling. He grinned, looked me up and down slowly, his gaze making my skin itch. Then he shouted something to the other guard and they both laughed.

'Hey! There's no need for any problems,' Charlie said, his eyes flashing with defiance. 'We have money we can give you.'

The second guard turned his weapon on Charlie, digging it into his chest. He got in Charlie's face and shouted something, spittle flying from his mouth.

Charlie's eyes flashed with anger, his right fist clenched, as if he was going to punch the guard. I grabbed his arm and dug my nails into his skin to stop him. There was no point trying to be a hero out here. This wasn't England. They could quite easily kill us and no one would know. And for all we knew, they could have other men hiding nearby, watching, and we'd be ambushed if we started causing trouble. It was better to just give them what they wanted and hopefully we'd get out alive.

Issa's forehead was pinched with worry. He spoke again to the guards, a long stream of words, rapidly getting higher in pitch.

The first guard replied with some hand gestures that could've meant anything

The sweltering heat outside did nothing to chill the icy terror raging through me.

The guard in front of Charlie released the barrel of his gun from his chest and turned it back to me, speaking fast.

'He wants your rings,' Issa said.

I glanced down at my hand. I still wore my gold wedding ring and engagement ring with a square cut amethyst in it. I'd never brought myself to take them off after hearing about Mason's death.

I touched my rings and Mason's face flashed into my head; our wedding day. I saw him sliding the ring on my finger, me looking into his eyes, my mouth aching with the widest smile. I wanted to refuse to hand them over, but we were hardly in a position to. 'Yes … yes, okay. Just, please, let us go.' I tugged at them, my fingers swollen with the heat so it was hard to pull them over my knuckles. I spat on my hand, rubbing the saliva over my ring finger for lubrication and then tugging. When I'd got them off, the guard held out his open palm. I handed them over, feeling sick.

Then there was another exchange between Issa and the first guard, and I watched Issa's shoulders slump slightly, but I couldn't tell if that was good or bad.

The one holding my rings said something to the other guard, who nodded and spoke one word to Issa in a harsh tone.

'Come on,' Issa said to us, 'We can go.'

I clambered back in the Land Rover quickly before they could change their minds. I held my breath and didn't exhale until we'd left them standing there in the distance.

Chapter 67

Dusk was falling when we arrived at a village. My throat and eyes felt scratchy and raw from the dust and heat and the tears I'd silently cried as I replayed in my head over and over again that little boy being killed in front of my own eyes. I thought of the children at my school; loved, secure, fed and warm, and the contrast of those boys on the plantation; stolen, starving, injured, working in such horrific conditions, living in terror, captive in slavery. The world was a horrible place, and I'd been confronted with that horror in such brutal reality. No wonder Mason had become involved in trying to save them with Adama and Issa.

I rubbed at my forehead, fighting the exhaustion threatening to take over me as I stared out of the Land Rover window.

We drove along a muddy road with deep tyre tracks, past small shops that looked like shacks, wares hanging outside, and ramshackle market stalls dotted around selling food. Issa slowed down and drove up another track in between thick banana trees, their leaves slapping at the sides of the vehicle. We emerged in a clearing in front of a large house built of wood with a decked porch. A group of boys ranging from the ages of about five to mid teens were kicking a football to each other, running around and laughing. A man sat on the front step dressed in a T-shirt and jeans, with his arm around a little boy whose right arm was missing from the elbow. The man was wiping tears from the boy's eyes.

'We stop for some food and drink here for a while. Then I take you to capital. To airport.' Issa turned off the engine.

'Thanks,' I said, getting out of the car as the man patted the little boy on the shoulder. He stood up and walked towards us, his arms outstretched, a huge smile on his face.

'Where are we?' Charlie said.

Issa ignored the question, jumped down from the Land Rover and spoke in a foreign language to the man. The man walked over and embraced Issa in a bear hug. When they stepped back, the man looked over, his smile never wavering as he nodded at us.

'Welcome,' the man said. He had a round face and a jolly twinkling in his eyes. 'My name is Oumar. It would be my pleasure to give you some refreshments for your journey. Come, come.' He turned around and walked towards the steps of the deck, touching the little boy on the shoulder as he went past.

'Hello.' I stopped in front of the boy, who looked up at me. He had sunken cheeks which made his eyes look even bigger in his emaciated face.

He blinked, sending tears dribbling down his cheeks.

'Hey, don't cry.' I wiped his tears with my fingertips and crouched down in front of him as Charlie followed Issa and Oumar onto the porch. I glanced at his missing right arm, the end of the stump a messy patch of uneven scar tissue. He was wearing clean shorts and a T-shirt and had scars marking his left arm and legs. There was also an old burn mark on his thigh, and I suddenly knew that this place was the orphanage Issa had spoken of.

'What's your name?' I smiled at him. He just stared at me with his huge eyes. It made my heart melt, because I'd seen the same look of desolation and despair in those boys at the plantation. 'My name's Nicole,' I said. 'Aren't you playing with your friends?' I pointed to the other boys who were still kicking the football while watching us openly with intrigue.

He sunk his head down onto his chest, not looking at me as his lower lip trembled. I wanted to take him in my arms and hold him, but I was afraid that was the wrong thing to do. Afraid I might scare him.

'Nicole,' Charlie called from the porch. He was sitting on a rattan sofa with Oumar. A tray of cold drinks was on a coffee table in front of them. Issa had disappeared inside the house.

'Yes, come.' Oumar smiled, beckoning me with his arm. He held out a glass of cold coconut milk, and I took it gratefully, drinking it down in one big gulp. 'Food is being prepared now. It will not be long.'

'Thank you.' I put the glass down on the tray and sat next to Charlie.

'That is Sekou.' The man pointed to the small boy. 'He came here just two months ago.'

'Are these boys all from cocoa plantations?' I asked.

He nodded. 'I'm afraid so. Trafficking of children and their slavery has been going on a long time here. Long before Moussa Damba dreamed up his rebel army. But Damba has just made it more attractive. The cocoa farmers used to pay 200 euros for a trafficked child slave. Now they can get them for free from the villages the rebels are massacring.'

'Christ.' Charlie stood up and walked to the railings at the edge of the decking, watching the boys playing, his shoulders taut. 'How many children do you have here?'

'Too many.' He sighed sadly. 'You see, there are thousands of cocoa farms in West Africa. The only way it will grow is on small holdings. Some farmers make enough to pay their workers a proper and fair wage, but mostly, it is the opposite and they earn barely enough to survive, let alone pay for employees. They have to deal with high taxation, ongoing conflicts, extremes of poverty, high levels of government corruption, low price they are given for cocoa beans and low yields for their hard work. Farmers are at the mercy of the prices the government set, so of course they turn to slave labour.'

'How do you pay for all this?' Charlie turned around.

'I use my own money. Sometimes, we get a few donations, which consist of mostly food. Feeding growing children is never ending.'

I carried on watching Sekou, all alone, my heart breaking, thinking about what he'd been through. Sensing he was being watched, Sekou turned around. I smiled at him. Slowly, he stood and walked up the steps cautiously toward us until he was standing a metre away, just watching me.

Oumar said something to Sekou I couldn't understand, holding his hand out.

The boy dropped his head to his chest and shook it.

'Sekou is learning English now. I teach them here too. On the plantations, the children don't get such luxuries as school. They are forced to work every day, all year, never getting paid. Harvesting cocoa is very dangerous. They must carry heavy loads. Frequently, they are beaten. They work with dangerous chemicals and pesticides. Some have accidents from the machetes.' He nodded to Sekou's arm. 'His wound became infected, but they did not get him medical help. Instead, one of the rebel guards cut his arm off with a machete. He was kidnapped by the rebels from his village in Narumbe along with his brother. His brother did not make it out alive. He cut his thigh open when working and bled to death.'

'Jesus.' Charlie's face turned into a furious snarl.

I looked at Sekou with tears in my eyes.

'Yes, it is tragic,' Oumar continued. 'Accidents like that are not uncommon for these poor children. Some of them get sick, get bitten by poisonous snakes or spiders, they then die because they don't get treatment. They are disposable. If they try to run, the punishment is severe. They live in filth with no running water, living off corn meal and bananas, sometimes forty, fifty children sleeping in a locked tin hut with no ventilation and no beds.'

I pictured the camp area we'd seen at the plantation and realised what the hut with the padlock had been for.

'Do you know what happens to the beans when they are harvested?' Oumar asked.

I shook my head.

'The beans are fermented and dried, then they get shipped out of the country. Big cocoa processors turn them into cocoa solids and cocoa butter. Then the chocolate companies turn them into every kind of chocolate you can think of.' He pointed to the children still kicking the football but watching us at the same time. 'These boys have no idea what they're growing. None have even tasted chocolate. It is the life of the country but made with blood spilled by the slaves on the plantations.'

'So, what's the answer to solving this?' Charlie asked.

Oumar shrugged. 'In some ways, it is very complex. In other ways, it is simple. What happens here is inextricably linked to the west. Without the cocoa farms, this industry would crumble. But the international food giants know what's going on. The amount of money it would take to eradicate slave labour on the plantations is nothing compared to the obscene worldwide profits they make. But, of course, the big chocolate kings want to exploit our cocoa resources to feed a global market and make sure that how it's grown will never get out.'

He stared into the middle distance. 'The disparity between the rich and poor is great. However, child labour is an economic problem. You solve the poverty problem and you can eradicate slavery.'

'You're a saint,' Charlie said, pulling a pack of cigarettes from his pocket. He took one out, put it in his mouth, then thought better of it, put it back in the packet and shoved it in his pocket again.

Oumar laughed sadly. 'No. I am no saint. I am just one human trying to make a difference. Here, the children learn. They learn and they heal. And we help find their families, so they can be reunited. I do many things. Teacher, cook, cleaner. But it is worth it.'

Charlie leaned his back against the rail. 'Funny, I never thought of school as a luxury. Couldn't wait to leave. This definitely changes your perspective on things, though.'

'Why don't you say hello, Sekou.' Oumar bent his head so he was on Sekou's eye level, tickling him under the chin. 'Do you remember how we practised it?'

The boy shook his head but stepped closer to me. I held out my hand. Tentatively, Sekou reached for it and inched closer. Then he climbed up on my lap and rested his head against my chest.

My heart cracked a little. I wrapped my arms around him and rocked him gently.

'You have made a friend.' Oumar grinned.

The door to the house clattered open, and Issa came out with a tall boy who was maybe thirteen and grinning equally as broadly as Issa.

'Hello,' the boy said in accented English.

Issa clasped his arm around the boy and said, 'This is my brother, Yaya. He works here now.'

Charlie and I said our hellos.

'Very soon, I will bring you vegetable stew and rice,' Yaya said, treating us to an endearing grin. 'I made myself. I want to be a chef.'

'Thank you. It sounds delicious.' I smiled at him.

Issa and Yaya sat crossed-legged in front of us.

'I said I would show you why I do this,' Issa said, tilting his head towards his brother and then sweeping an arm around to the boys playing football. 'Everyone here has a bad story to tell. West Africa has too much poverty. There are many mouths to feed in families, and it is tradition that any child or young person who can leave home to make money must go, while the elders stay at home and tend crops. I have five brothers. Some days, we were so hungry, we ate dirt. Parents and children think they will come back with money in their pockets to make life better, but a lot never come back. Many disappear forever.

'Some children are tricked and sold to slavery. They are lured into going with brokers, who promise them job with pay. The plantation owners pay the broker to buy them. When the children arrive, they think they're going to a proper job, but they are slaves. They never earn out the money that their bosses pay for them and they never allowed to leave.'

I held onto Sekou tighter, fighting the surge of anger sparking through me at what so many children had suffered, were *still* suffering. 'Is that what happened to you and Yaya?'

'I was lucky,' Issa said. 'I got work for a nice man. A farmer on a banana plantation. After I return home one year later, I find out no one ever hear from Yaya. I go to bus stop just over the border in Narumbe, the one you saw. That is prime place for traffickers to get children when they coming from Burkina Faso, Mali, Cote Ivoire or wherever, searching for work. I ask questions, and I hear Yaya been sold to a broker. It took me a long time to find him. And in that time, I meet Adama and his group of friends who are trying to rescue the slaves. He help me get my brother back.' Issa looked at Yaya proudly and said, '*This* is why I do this.'

Chapter 68

Mason woke with a start. He was lying on the bed, the laptop still on his chest. He'd fallen asleep working on it. Had been typing solidly since his arrival and finally succumbed to pure exhaustion.

He set the laptop aside and fixed himself upright on the bed, wondering where he was for a few moments. Then it sank in. The grief of losing Nicole. The anger. Dusk was falling outside. His stomach rumbled loudly. He couldn't remember the last time he'd eaten, but the thought of food made him queasy. He hadn't left the room since he'd got to the hotel, making do with tap water, two sachets of tea and the four packets of biscuits provided. But if he was to go on, he needed refuelling. Needed food.

He rubbed at his swollen eyes, his eyelashes caked together with the remnants of salty tears. He swung his legs over the side of the bed and rested his elbows on his knees, his back hunched over, realising then how stiff his muscles were, his bones had chilled with inaction.

He stumbled into the en suite and splashed water on his face. His clothes were crumpled. He smelled of sour sweat. Looked a mess, but that was the least of his worries.

He ordered room service. Strong coffee, a sandwich, chips. While he waited, he checked through the footage one more time. He'd tweaked and edited and enhanced, turned the hours of film into a documentary.

But there was one more thing he needed to do.

He leaned back against the headrest, picked up the laptop and pulled up the Skyscanner website, searching for a flight to Zurich.

It was now seven-fifteen pm. There was a flight at eight-thirty, but he'd never make it. The next flight at ten was fully booked so he settled on a flight at six am for the following morning, leaving from Heathrow.

After it was booked, he inhaled a deep breath and spoke into the silence. 'This is for all of you.'

Chapter 69

Blade was bored out of his skull. Being holed up in the safe house with Frankie wasn't his idea of fun. All Frankie talked about was hair products and the best tanning shops. Blade needed to be active, but until they could find a trace of the Palmers, he was stuck here, getting increasingly more pissed off.

He lay on the sofa, flicking through a take away menu.

'I've got something!' Frankie barked.

Blade threw the menu on the sofa and swung his legs to the floor. 'What?'

'Mason Palmer, AKA Nicholas Porter, just booked a flight to Zurich at six am tomorrow morning from Heathrow.'

'What about his wife?'

'No sign of a booking for her.'

Blade wondered why the hell Mason would do that. Palmer would be heading right into the lion's den. But he didn't really care *why*. All that mattered was Palmer would be his now. All he had to do was follow him from Zurich airport, or even intercept him when he walked out, and Mason Palmer would be a dead man. Finally. He threw back his head and roared with laughter. After all the running around he'd caused, Palmer was making it so easy for him.

'Book me on the same flight. If you can get me on the seat next to him on the plane, even better.'

Frankie's fingers tapped away at lightning speed. 'Done.'

Maybe Frankie wasn't so useless after all.

Chapter 70

DS Harris sat at her desk opening the wrapper of her sandwich, which amounted to her late lunch and dinner combined. She was getting nowhere in her search for Nicole and Charlie, and the worry for their safety was increasing every hour. Had Sean Fowler already found them? And if he had, she wasn't convinced police would ever locate their bodies. Fowler's face had been plastered all over the news and with the border control agency, along with his aliases, but she wasn't holding out much hope they'd find him any time soon.

She took a bite of dry bread as her mobile phone rang. She chased the stale-tasting sandwich down with a mouthful of cold coffee before answering. When DS Leadbetter announced himself, she threw the sandwich on top of its wrapper and said, 'Hi. I hope you've got some good news for me.'

'Good and bad. The bad news is we haven't got round to trying to check flights from West Africa ten months ago for Mason Palmer yet. It won't be a priority, I'm afraid. But it is your lucky day. You know I mentioned that Sean Fowler has several aliases?'

'Yes.'

'One of them is John Brown.'

'Yes, I remember.'

'He's booked on a flight to Zurich at six am tomorrow morning.'

'Really?' She sat up in her seat, excitement fizzing through her veins. 'That's fantastic. I owe you one. Thanks.'

After they said their goodbyes, she rushed into DI Thornton's office. They needed to come up with a plan. She wasn't going to let this bastard get away.

Chapter 71

Blade stood behind a pillar to the side of the Swissair check-in desk, watching for Mason's arrival. Blade had a baseball cap on, pulled low, his jacket collar pulled up to hide some of his face, rubbing against the few days' worth of stubble that had grown. He kept his head down to avoid the many CCTV cameras getting a clear shot of him.

Because of the X-ray machines at the entrance, Blade couldn't bring a gun or knife into the airport, but he could kill with his bare hands, so that wasn't a problem. The problem was getting Mason somewhere quiet in a confined space with no witnesses.

Mason Palmer didn't even look in his direction as he arrived to join the check-in queue. Blade emerged from behind the pillar and ambled slowly over, joining the queue behind him.

They edged forward until Mason stepped up to the counter and handed his passport to the ground staff. The desk next to Mason became free and Blade did the same, watching out of the corner of his eye as Mason had his hand luggage marked with a baggage label. Then he saw Mason walk away.

Blade took his boarding pass from the woman at the counter and casually followed Mason, keeping a surreptitious distance away and slipping amongst the throngs of people, just one more face in a crowd of thousands. He pulled his phone from his pocket and called Bolliger. 'I know where he is. Won't be long now. I'll call you when it's done.'

'And where is his wife?'

'I don't know. Her uncle is missing, and we think she's with him. Frankie's still working on it. We'll find her soon.'

'You'd better because I will not tolerate mistakes. Do you understand?'

Blade's lip curled up with defiance, but he said, 'Yes.' He put his phone back in his pocket.

Mason was heading towards the security area, but then seemed to change his mind and veered off to the right.

Blade hovered outside WHSmith, pretending to scan the newspaper headlines on display while keeping one eye on Mason, who was walking in the direction of the toilets. Blade was under pressure now. If he had the opportunity to finish Mason off here, then he could quickly get back to finding his bitch of a wife and make sure his reputation for sound work stayed in tact.

Blade nonchalantly strolled away from the shop in the same direction, catching sight of Mason ahead as he turned left, up a narrow side corridor with signs to the men's room. No one was around. If he could get Mason in one of the cubicles, he could have it done and dusted in seconds without anyone seeing. He just hoped there wasn't anyone at the urinals.

Mason pushed the door to the men's room open, completely oblivious.

Blade grinned to himself, hot on his heels.

And then he felt a shadowy presence either side of him, a split second before two armed police officers came around in front and pointed their MP5s at him.

He froze as two other armed police fell in behind him.

'Armed police! Do not move,' one of them shouted.

And then a runty-looking woman and a tall man, both dressed in suits, walked up and stood next to the police in front.

'Sean Fowler, also known as John Brown, I'm arresting you on suspicion of the murder of Isabelle Moore,' the man said.

Chapter 72

Frankie sat at his laptop in the safe house and took a swig of strong filter coffee. Mason Palmer would be taken care of soon; now if he could only find the wife, his bonus would be impressive. Maybe he'd even get Blade's job. That would teach the arrogant bastard a lesson for fucking up in the first place. If he had to listen to Blade's homophobic digs for much longer, he'd shove his laptop up Blade's arse.

He stroked his bristly beard with one hand, the habit weirdly soothing as he stared at the screen. Even though Charlie Briggs was an old timer, a blagger who'd been on the scene before all this technical surveillance was possible, he seemed to be a careful guy, or maybe he was just paranoid. Fair play to him for pulling off the Securitor job. The coppers had never found the dosh Charlie stole. Frankie hadn't found any trace of it in any bank accounts, either, so the bastard was savvy all right.

Blade had suggested hitting up Charlie's house when this job was over in case some of it was stashed there, or at least some valuables he'd bought with the proceeds, and Frankie was definitely up for it, even if it meant putting up with Blade for a while longer. Frankie had already managed to hack into Charlie's security system and set things up in preparation. All Frankie had to do now was log into them via his phone or laptop and he could override them. He leaned back in his chair and put his hands behind his head, day dreaming about what he'd do with that kind of cash. He'd probably go to South America. Had heard the gay scene was pretty good out there. He could rent out a house on a beach and check out the fit guys in their tight shorts from his deck while sipping a pina colada. He got hard just thinking about it.

He took another sip of coffee and sat upright as an alert pinged on his laptop.

He tapped a few keys and brought up Charlie's credit card details.

'Hel-lo.' Frankie grinned. The transaction had only just gone through his account, but last night, Charlie had made a payment to Air France.

Frankie quickly hacked his way into the accounts of Air France's website, searching for the same reference number as on Charlie's bill and cross matching it to two flights from Mali to Heathrow via Paris in the names of Justine Taylor and Dean Townsend.

'Sneaky little gits. Using fake passports, eh?' He grabbed his mobile and phoned Blade. He'd be at the airport by now checking in, and the Air France flight was due soon. The call went straight to voicemail.

Oh, well. He'd just have to deal with it himself. In the films, the hacker guy was always portrayed as a geeky twat, but Frankie was nothing like that. He had a cunning, evil streak that matched Blade's, though he preferred working with a gun. Fuck getting all that blood and shit on his expensive clothes from messy knife wounds.

He grinned to himself, reaching for the pistol and his jacket.

Chapter 73

As we were leaving the orphanage, Sekou had clung to me tightly, refusing to let go. We were both crying when Oumar had prised him away. Even though I'd only just met the sad little boy, I felt a connection with him that ran deep.

Before we'd got in the Land Rover, Charlie had given all the money he had to Oumar to use for the boys. Oumar had refused it at first, saying he couldn't accept such a generous donation, but Charlie had insisted. My mum always said Charlie had a cold heart, but I'd seen nothing but generosity and kindness from him. It was only when we got to the airport and realised we had no cash that Charlie had to use his credit card in the name of Southern Holdings to book the flights. He was aware there was a slight risk they could've found the company's connection to Charlie and were watching any account transactions. But we'd had no choice by then, and the chances were slim that they'd have figured this out.

During the flight from Mali to Paris, I'd finally succumbed to the exhaustion dragging me under and I slept most of the way. But on the second leg from Paris, I stared out of the window, every horrific thing I'd witnessed in the past days turning over in my mind. I went to touch my wedding and engagement rings, to twist them, a habit I'd got into over the years, but realised they were no longer there.

I closed my eyes and drifted into a memory. I hadn't wanted the fuss of a big wedding. I didn't want all eyes on me. Instead, Aiden got us an amazing deal at Sandals in Antigua, and it had been everything I'd wanted. Intimate, with just Charlie, Dad, Aiden, Cheryl, and us – magical and stress free. The hotel had arranged everything from the music to the cake, to the photographer, so we hadn't had to worry about a thing. It was on a secluded spot on the beach, under a pergola threaded with fragrant frangipani that we both said, 'I do'.

I snapped my eyes open and wondered for the thousandth time where Mason was now. And it hit me then, like a shard of glass stabbing me inside; the real reason Mason hadn't shown up at the meeting place and why he hadn't tried to email me since. The reason I'd been trying so hard to ignore. The same gang who'd kidnapped me at Jesus Green must've spotted him there too. They were following me to get to Mason and they must've succeeded, murdering him. This time, Mason really was dead, just like the boy on the plantation, like the others who'd been massacred out there, like Isabelle and Adama.

I rested my forehead against the window feeling a pain so physical, it was like a blade slashing through my flesh, shredding my heart.

So now what should I do? It all felt pointless anyway. Going to Africa had brought me answers but put me in a worse position because, although I really did know everything that Mason had tried to hide so he could protect me, I'd lost the footage I'd taken and had nothing to bargain with. These bastards wouldn't stop until I was dead too.

I couldn't spend every minute looking over my shoulder, a lifetime of hiding, changing my identity, moving from country to country to lay low. I finally got exactly what Mason had been through over the past ten months.

Charlie held my hand as the plane bumped and shook when the wheels hit the runway at Heathrow.

I felt drained and tired to my bones. 'Mason's dead, isn't he?' I said sadly, too numb and shell-shocked to even cry anymore. 'They must've already killed him.'

He squeezed my hand and sighed. 'It seems most likely, yes.'

'I don't know what to do now. They'll keep trying to find me, won't they?'

He nodded.

'I need to disappear too.'

'Damba and Bolliger need to disappear. They're the ones giving the orders.' A muscle ticked in Charlie's jaw as he clenched it.

'I'm not so sure that would change things. Someone else will just take over.'

'Then we keep fighting back. Look, let's get back to my house. Get some rest. We're both knackered and not thinking straight. After we're rested, we can talk about next steps and make a plan. At least we know exactly what we're dealing with now. That's half the battle. And there's no way I'm letting them get away with everything they've done.'

'So, what are you saying?'

He just grinned in response, and even to me – his niece – it looked pure evil.

Chapter 74

Mason swept his gaze over the people seated at the airport gate for anyone taking too much of an interest in him – the man sitting opposite wearing a suit and reading a newspaper. The younger guy in a hoodie lounging against the wall with ear buds in, fiddling with his phone. The middle-aged couple in matching walking gear staring at the plane on the runway.

An announcement came over the tannoy that his flight was ready to board, drawing his gaze away from the strangers.

He stood and joined the queue. Staff checked passports and boarding cards and the line shuffled forward.

He didn't know why he chose that moment to look out of the gate at the moving walkway in the concourse area. Later, he'd think it was his heart, so in tune with hers, which was calling out a warning to him. But then he thought it was just pure luck. It took a few seconds for his brain to compute what his eyes were telling him.

It can't be her. Can it?

Oh my God.

She's alive!

It was the sight of her uncle Charlie alongside Nicole that confirmed it.

For a moment, Mason stood there, rooted to the spot, staring, unaware of the tutting of passengers in the queue behind as he held up the queue.

His frozen body finally caught up with his racing mind, and he ran out of the gate, through the open doorway, his eyes searching for her blonde hair above a sea of people. He was sure he caught a glimpse of it before she turned left at a sign marked Passport Control. He stepped up his pace and followed.

By the time he got to the passport area, the hordes of people blocked any sign of her. He leaned around the person in front and scanned the multiple booths with border control agents behind glass screens. No Nicole.

Then he remembered that her passport had an electronic chip inside, so he swept his gaze over to where the section of automatic scanning machines operated. There was only a small queue there and a member of staff assisting one elderly woman.

Nicole and Charlie were gone.

Shit!

Every cell in his body vibrated with impatience as the line of people moved agonisingly slowly. He clenched his fists, his muscles taut against his skin with frustration.

Come on! Come on!

Chapter 75

Frankie thought about the logistics of tracking Nicole Palmer from the airport. Her uncle's car was still at his house, so he was pretty confident they'd have to take a cab or be met by a driver. He was also pretty confident they'd return to Charlie's house, and he could've waited there for them, but there was still the little element of doubt that they could be going to another location, so he'd erred on the side of caution and stood outside the arrivals area, his gaze locked on the waves of people pouring through the doorway.

He'd already checked the monitors and seen their plane had landed. Right now, they were probably going through passport control.

He dialled Blade again, but his phone still went straight to voicemail. Maybe he'd already boarded.

To pass the boring time, he thought about South America again. He'd always fancied owning a yacht. Didn't have a clue how to sail one, but he could get crew for that. He thought about sunning himself on the deck, oiled up. Maybe he'd try scuba diving. He'd been promising himself that thrill for years.

His gaze checked out the passengers streaming through the doors. *Fat Woman. Neo Nazi Skinhead. Blue Rinse Brigade. Businessman. Taylor Swift lookalike. Fat Man. Grungey teenager. Nicole Palmer.*

Game on.

Frankie watched Charlie lead Nicole straight past him, towards the revolving doors that led to the taxi area. Then he turned and followed.

There was a queue at the rank, and he stepped in directly behind them.

Nicole and her uncle didn't speak as the queue filtered down. There were five people in front of them.

Four.

Three – all of whom got in the next taxi.

Charlie and Nicole jumped into the vehicle at the front of the queue just as another one swung into the rank behind it. Good timing.

Frankie jumped in and said to the driver, 'Follow that cab.' And then he laughed. He'd heard that line so many times in movies and had always wanted to say it himself.

He pulled out his phone, hacked into Charlie's security system once more and typed away.

Chapter 76

Mason's fake passport didn't include a chip, so he'd had to queue in the guard-controlled booths at Passport Control. Then he'd been interrogated as to why he hadn't got on his flight, citing a family emergency. He'd spent the time waiting in line trying to call Nicole's mobile number again and again, but it was dead, just like it had been before when he'd tried to call her after she was abducted.

He finally rushed outside of the departure door and ran to the taxi rank. There was a short queue. He knew there was no point in trying Nicole's phone again, but he did it anyway. He didn't have Charlie's number so he couldn't try that.

They could be anywhere by now, but it was a reasonable assumption that they would be headed to Charlie's house, which he'd been to several times.

He slid into the back seat of the taxi that pulled up, praying he was right.

Chapter 77

By the time we arrived outside Charlie's house, I was struggling to keep my eyes open, but the overspill of adrenaline from our trip – coupled with the knowledge that Mason must be dead – kept my body in a state of overdrive, bombarded with emotions.

Charlie opened the front door and turned off the first alarm system. I followed him inside the house and put my travel bag by the door. He went to the cupboard underneath the stairs where the CCTV cameras were monitored and keyed in another code to the second alarm system.

'Right. I'll rustle up something to eat and drink, and then I'm going to have a kip for a few hours. I can't sleep on bloody airplanes and I'm knackered,' he said as he walked into the kitchen. 'Sound all right with you?'

'I'm not hungry,' I mumbled.

He turned at the tone of my voice and pulled me into his arms. 'Oh, love. I'm sorry you're in this mess, but we'll fix it, I swear. There's always a way round a problem.'

'Even if we do, Mason will still be dead.' I leaned my head on his shoulder.

'But we'll still save a bunch of kids from a lifetime of slavery. And kill the bastards who ordered Mason's death.' His voice hardened. 'It's about revenge now. And revenge makes grief a whole lot easier to deal with.' He let me go, patted me on the shoulder.

'Are we even safe here? Surely, they would've worked out you're my uncle by now and that we're together.'

'There's no way they can find this place. It's not registered in my name and is pretty much untraceable.' He opened up the fridge, peered inside. 'How about an omelette?' he said, grabbing a carton of eggs and some cheese without waiting for my answer.

I filled the kettle, just to do something, trying to keep busy with a mindless task to stop me thinking about Mason. I'd used denial in the past ten months as a way to cope. I'd pushed myself into work to the point of exhaustion so I could sleep at night and not think about him. I didn't know if I could do it all again.

Chapter 78

Frankie asked the cab driver to pull in about five hundred yards short of Charlie's house. The village was like a ghost town, and as he paced towards his target, he didn't spot another car or person.

He'd already overridden the front gates so they wouldn't make an alert when opened, and he'd fixed the CCTV camera above it so it was just showing previously recorded footage on a loop.

He typed in the code on the entry panel on the wall, and the gates slid open. Then he crouch-ran towards the garage at the side of the house, his hand clutched firmly around his gun. From the cameras inside, he'd seen on his mobile phone that they were in the kitchen at the back of the house, so he didn't think he'd be spotted until it was too late for them.

Chapter 79

As Charlie chopped mushrooms, I pulled mugs from the cupboard and filled a cafetière with spoonfuls of filter coffee.

The kettle clicked off boil, and I reached for the handle. But my hand never got there.

The sound of glass exploding, and an iron patio chair flying through the conservatory window shot my stomach into my chest.

I spun around and saw a guy with a beard step over the shattered glass littering the rug on the chequered tiled floor, pointing a gun at us.

'Drop the knife,' he said to Charlie.

I turned my head and watched Charlie, knife in hand, looking unruffled, as if this was an every-day occurrence. Maybe it had been back in his hay day.

'Whatever they're paying you, I'll pay more,' Charlie said, without missing a beat.

'Drop the knife and make no sudden moves.'

The knife clanged off the tile floor as it landed.

'Kick it away from you,' the gunman ordered.

Charlie held up his hands in a placatory gesture. 'There's no need for all this aggro. Name your price and you can be on your way, a rich man.'

'Kick it,' he repeated.

Charlie kicked the knife. It slid under the sofa by the conservatory.

'Okay.' The gunman smiled. 'Let's talk money. How much are your lives worth to you?'

'I've got a hundred grand here in cash you can have.'

The gunman laughed and stepped closer. 'That little? I know all about you and the Securitor robbery you pulled. You must still be sitting on a fucking fortune.'

'All right, two,' Charlie said calmly, as if he was just working out an ordinary business transaction. I doubted the guy would let us go if and when they did agree on a price for our lives, but I figured Charlie was just buying some time.

While the gunman was distracted with Charlie, I inched my trembling left hand behind me towards the work top.

'Don't insult me.' The gunman snorted.

'Okay, three. Right now. And I want the name of the person you're working for.'

The gunman scrunched his lips up as if he was considering it, stepping closer. 'Three? Make if five and I might consider it.'

My heart hammered loud in my ears as I reached up and tried to get hold of the kettle. If I could flick the lid off, I could throw the boiling water at his face. My fingertips skimmed the red-hot chrome, and my natural reaction was to jerk them away.

The gunman saw me flinch and swung the gun in my direction. 'Tut, tut, tut. What did I say? No sudden moves. Hands where I can see them.' He waggled the gun.

I dropped my arm away from the kettle and held my hands up. The guy's gaze flicked between us. Charlie had no weapons to hand. Throwing a block of cheese at him wasn't going to do much damage.

I tried to swallow, but my throat was thick with fear.

'So, we can agree on five hundred grand, yeah? I give you the money, you give me a name and then you fuck off out of here?' Charlie said.

'Show me where it is.'

'Some of it's in there.' Charlie jerked a thumb towards the fridge. 'Let me get it for you.' He made a move to turn around and reach for the fridge door.

I held my breath, my whole body trembling.

'Not so fast. I'm not that stupid. Where's the rest?'

Charlie stopped moving. 'Upstairs. In a hidden safe.'

'You hide that much cash in the house?' the gunman asked with a sceptical look.

'Funnily enough, I don't trust banks,' Charlie said.

The gunman studied Charlie's face for a moment, unsure if my uncle was being sarcastic or not. 'Okay. You two, step away from the counter.' He pointed in the direction of the oak kitchen table. 'Sit down there and put your hands on your head.'

I cast a sideways glance at Charlie. He moved to the table, put his hands on his head, sat at one end. I followed and sat next to him, hands on my head, my knees trembling together.

The gunman watched us for a second.

Two seconds.

Three seconds.

It felt like a lifetime.

A lifetime that could end very soon.

He walked sideways to the fridge, eyes on us the whole way. 'If it's in there, then we talk about the rest.'

'It's in there,' Charlie replied, his face expressionless.

'Whereabouts?'

'Vegetable basket at the bottom. In a white plastic tub.'

The man inched closer to the fridge. He kept his gaze and gun on us, his free hand reaching for the fridge handle. He grabbed hold of it, swung the door open. He glanced to the bottom of the fridge and the two blue plastic vegetable compartments next to each other.

There was no way we were going to survive this. If there was money in there, he'd only take it and then kill us after he'd got the rest of it. I looked at Charlie. He didn't seem to be able to think of a plan either.

We were going to be killed.

His gaze still on us, the gunman leaned down and took hold of the plastic box on the right.

A vicious wave of sickness washed over me at the thought of dying. My mouth watered. Sweat pricked at my forehead.

And then I saw a ghost.

My eyes widened as Mason appeared at the French doors to the conservatory, fear and panic in his eyes as he took in the situation in front of him, his face pale. My breath lodged in my throat, but I knew if I made any obvious reaction, the gunman would notice. I glanced at the gunman, who had his back to Mason, distracted by pulling out a wedge of bank notes from the Tupperware box.

Mason picked up the heavy cut glass ashtray from the patio table by the door and crept stealthily inside towards the gunman, his footsteps inaudible on the rug.

Stomach acid rose into the back of my throat. I tried to breathe slowly through my nose, trying to fight the nausea.

Mason got closer.

Eight metres.

Seven.

Six.

And then the gunman heard him. He was already turning, his eyes widening with surprise, when Mason raised his hand in the air.

It was close. But Mason was quicker.

As the gunman brought his weapon swinging around towards Mason's chest, Mason swung the heavy glass ashtray to the side of his forehead.

There was a sickening sound of the crack of glass on bone.

The gunman grunted in pain, staggered, dazed. Tried to clutch onto the edge of the worktop, but his fingers missed and he dropped to one knee.

Mason raised his arm to hit him again.

Charlie slid his hand underneath the table and, in a split-second manoeuvre, was holding a gun.

Before Mason could bring the ashtray down on him again, Charlie had blasted a shot through the gunman's chest.

Mason leapt away.

Charlie fired another two bullets in quick succession, hitting the gunman's shoulder and stomach.

The man's eyes bulged. He lost the grip on his gun, and it clattered to the floor. He clutched his chest, tilting over sideways, half sitting, half lying against the kitchen cupboards, a wheezy breath gurgling from his mouth.

Charlie kicked away his gun, towering over him until he took his last breath.

I stared at the scene in front of me, the world seeming frozen for a moment. Maybe I should've been used to people pointing guns at me by now, but it was still a huge shock that my mind was quickly trying to process. Then my brain kick-started, and I leaped out of my seat, rushing towards my husband. I was sure his look of overwhelming relief mixed with surprise mirrored my own swirling emotions.

I ran into his arms, unable to breathe or move or speak. It felt like I was teetering on the edge of a precipice, not wanting to make the wrong move in case I was imagining him here and one false step would send me crashing into a dark reality.

Chapter 80

DS Harris and DI Thornton entered the interview room after giving Sean Fowler time to confer with his expensive lawyer.

Becky slapped her folder on the desk between them and stated who was present as well as the date and time.

DI Thornton said, 'So, what should we call you? Sean Fowler, or should I say John Brown, or any of the string of aliases you've used over the years?'

Blade leaned back in his chair, legs splayed out in a posture of calm arrogance, giving them both evil looks.

'Okay, let's go with Sean,' Becky said, leaning her elbows on the desk. 'We know you brutally murdered Isabelle Moore, so why don't you save us all the time and admit that you killed her?'

'My client isn't admitting to anything,' the lawyer, whose name was Linwood Cuttingbourne, said pompously, crossing one leg over the other and fiddling with his cufflinks. 'And quite honestly, this is a waste of all our time. My client has never heard of an Isabelle Moore. You obviously have him mixed up with another Sean Fowler. It must be quite a common name.'

Blade grinned and pointed to Cuttingbourne. 'Yeah. What he said.'

'I don't think so.' She turned to Cuttingbourne briefly before opening her folder and making a show of reading some documents. 'We know all about your past, Sean. Army reject. Drug dealer. Next up, you worked for the Hopper Gang, as an enforcer and drug smuggler. And now you're a hired assassin, aren't you? That's quite a career choice.'

'That's preposterous.' Cuttingbourne snorted. 'My client has never been convicted of anything.'

'Why did you book a flight to Zurich in the name of John Brown?' DI Thornton asked.

Blade rolled his eyes. 'No comment.'

Cuttingbourne answered for him. 'You can't prove he booked such a flight. Mr Fowler was at the airport waiting for a friend to arrive, minding his own business, when armed police just swooped on him for no reason.'

'But he happened to have a passport in the name of John Brown in his pocket, along with a boarding pass in the same name,' Becky said. 'Pretty weird coincidence, isn't it? Or did you happen to pick up your *friend's* passport by accident?' Her voice oozed sarcasm. She took the passport from the folder and slapped it on the desk between them, showing them the photograph page. Even though Fowler had a beard, glasses, and looked fatter in it, you could still tell it was him. 'A friend who looks identical to you?' She raised her eyebrows.

Cuttingbourne peered at the passport photo, looking a little unnerved, said, 'This man is not my client. He doesn't look anything like the man in this photo.'

'Well, that'll be for a jury to decide, won't it? And when we trace back the digital transaction that paid for the ticket, I'm pretty sure it will come back to you. That, and the fact that we watched him check-in under that name and caught it all on CCTV. So, again, why did you use a false name for this flight? Were you running away, Sean?'

Blade just gave a smirk.

Cuttingbourne glanced briefly at Blade.

'Why did you kill Isabelle?' DI Thornton said.

'No comment.'

'It was because she knew something about Mason Palmer's whereabouts, wasn't it?' she asked.

DI Thornton still didn't agree with her theory that Mason Palmer was alive and innocent, but she'd be damned if she was going to miss this chance to put it to him. DI Thornton looked at her sharply but didn't say anything to admonish her line of questioning. They had to appear to have a united front.

'No comment.'

'Mason Palmer confided in Isabelle about a drug cartel operating in Narumbe, didn't he?' Becky stared at Fowler.

'And what possible relevance does that have to my client?' Cuttingbourne chimed in.

'That's why you killed her, wasn't it?' DI Thornton stepped in before Becky could say anything else. 'She was going to blow the whistle on your operation and you needed her silenced.'

'No comment.' Blade gave them a surly glare.

'What have you done with Nicole Palmer?' she asked.

'No comment.'

'Nicole Palmer escaped from you the first time, after you bundled her into the van. Then what happened? Did you find her and kill her too?'

Blade's jaw tightened, and he narrowed his eyes at her.

'Where's Nicole Palmer?' she asked.

Blade jigged his leg up and down.

'Where is Mason Palmer?' she tried.

That earned her a glare from DI Thornton.

Cuttingbourne leaned towards Blade and whispered something. Blade shrugged nonchalantly.

'You have absolutely no foundation for such bizarre claims. My client has never heard of any of these people. What evidence do you have?' Cuttingbourne asked.

'Well, we have Sean on CCTV for starters, abducting Nicole Palmer.' She smiled sweetly as she slapped the still taken from the camera in Cambridge on the desk.

Blade didn't look at it. She could feel DI Thornton tense next to her, because he still thought Nicole was involved.

'This proves you know Nicole Palmer,' DI Thornton tapped the photo.

Cuttingbourne leaned forward and peered at the image. 'That's not even a good likeness to Mr Fowler.' He tried the same excuse again, waving his hand through the air casually. 'It could be anyone.'

'Who paid you to kill Isabelle Moore?' she said.

He eyed her coldly, like a barracuda. 'No. Fucking. Comment.'

'You know, for a contract killer, you're very sloppy.' She leaned back in the chair and crossed her arms, as if she had all the time in the world.

'My client is an ordinary, law-abiding citizen. And you haven't got a shred of evidence against him, so I demand that you let him go.'

'Really?' Becky raised an eyebrow. 'Isabelle fought back, didn't she? She bit you.' Her gaze strayed to his hands. Fowler wore a long sleeved top and jeans, and she could see no sign of an obvious bite mark, but she knew it was there, somewhere. 'And guess what? A piece of skin was lodged in her teeth. Skin that could only have come from her killer.' She grinned back at Fowler, wanting to punch him. She settled for doing a mental fist pump in the air.

Cuttingbourne frowned and leaned into Blade, whispered something in his ear. Blade watched her with a sneer on his face.

'We're one-hundred per cent confident that the DNA we took from you on arrival will match that skin sample. And I'm sure we'll find a corresponding bite mark somewhere on your body when we get you examined,' DI Thornton said.

Blade didn't reply, but a bead of sweat formed on his forehead.

Cuttingbourne leaned in for a whisper, but Blade ignored it.

'Maybe you need some time to confer with your client as to how his DNA ended up on the body of a woman who was brutally raped and murdered?' DI Thornton stood up and smiled pleasantly at them. 'Interview suspended. DI Thornton and DS Harris leaving the room.' He switched off the recording equipment and strode to the door.

She followed her boss out into the corridor. 'Bloody no comment interviews. I can't–'

'What the hell do you think you're doing?' Thornton pointed to the interview room door. '*I* decide the line of questioning in there. You're making out Nicole and Mason Palmer are innocent in all this, when they're not. I've given you strict instructions of the shape this investigation will take and you just completely bloody ignore me. When this is over, we're going to have a serious meeting about your conduct and you *will* be reprimanded.'

Becky bit her lip and offered an apology she didn't mean, trying to sound as sincere as possible. She was right about everything. She knew it. She just had to prove it before she got kicked out of her new job.

DI Thornton turned and marched away down the corridor.

'What do we do now?' She rushed to keep up with his long strides. 'He's not going to tell us what's happened to Nicole or Charlie … or Mason. And he's not going to admit to killing Isabelle.'

'I've pulled a favour in getting Fowler's DNA test expedited. As soon as SOCO arrive, they'll photograph every inch of him and we'll find the bite mark. But that will take a lot longer for a forensic dentist to examine.'

'The DNA's not going to come back within the twenty-four hours we've got to hold him, though, is it? We might have to apply to keep him for longer.'

'They've promised me a quick turnaround. Fingers crossed we'll soon be in a position to charge him.'

Her mobile phone rang in her pocket. She fished it out, registering Ronnie's name on the display before she answered.

'Sarge, our contact at O2 just called,' Ronnie said with excitement. 'Charlie Briggs's phone has just been turned on.'

An injection of adrenaline rushed through her. 'From which location?'

'His house.'

'Thanks.' She hung up and raised her eyebrows. 'Looks like Charlie Briggs is back at home. Hopefully Nicole's with him.'

'Okay, let's go. I can't wait to hear *her* story. I'll have her locked up in the next cell to Fowler.' He gave Becky a superior look that said he was going to be proved right. 'We'll take that shitbag back down to the cells for a bit, let him stew while we check it out.'

Chapter 81

Julian Bolliger was panicking. He hadn't heard from Blade. He'd already rang him eleven times, but not once was his call returned. He lit a cigar and dialled Blade's number again.

It went straight to voicemail. This time, he was so incensed, he left a message.

'Where the hell are you? I want an update on the Palmer situation, and I want it now! Have you disposed of the problem yet?' he barked out, anger overriding his sense of caution at not mentioning names and deeds over the phone. The merger was happening tomorrow, and he didn't need any surprises coming out of the woodwork before then. 'For Christ's sake, call me back!'

His thumb jabbed the "off" button and he kicked his desk bin, sending it hurtling across the room. Then he sank into his chair, staring at the giant flat screen TV on his wall, where presenters on *Bloomberg* were talking excitedly about the merger of Bolliger and Galleaux; how much money the deal was worth, and how their shares had been going through the roof since the plans had been announced.

He swallowed hard and loosened his shirt collar, a vein throbbing in his temple.

Chapter 82

One of Mason's hands held my back, the other curled around the top of my head as he pressed me against his chest. I breathed in his familiar scent for the first time in ten months, and all the horrors of the past few days faded away.

We stayed frozen to each other like that while Charlie spoke on his mobile phone in the corner of the room, telling one of his contacts he had a package he needed disposing of.

Eventually, I pulled back, stared into Mason's eyes. 'I can't believe you're really here,' I cried, clutching his jacket tight.

'I thought you were dead,' we both said at the same time.

Then, oddly for the situation we happened to be in, I laughed.

His lips curved into a smile, his own laughter sounding different than I remembered, as if he hadn't done it in a long time. Hardly surprising. He wouldn't have had much to laugh about.

My hands cupped his cheeks, and I kissed him, hard and needy and definitely not the romantic reunion I'd planned on before. Our lips pressed together as tears of joy rolled down my cheeks.

'I can't believe … I thought … God, this has been too much, I don't know …' Mason couldn't finish a whole sentence.

Words couldn't express my feelings either. So instead of speaking, I just pulled him tighter and drank in the feel of his body enveloping me, his heart beating against mine, his breath tickling my face, until Charlie spoke from behind us.

'Let's go in the lounge and talk. We'll be more comfortable in there,' he said. 'Someone's coming to help me clear that shit up later.' He nodded towards the dead man casually, as if it was an everyday occurrence for him to kill someone and get rid of the body.

'That was bloody lucky you had a gun under the table,' I said.

'It's not luck. I knew one day someone might come calling. I've got weapons stashed all over the gaff. There's one in the fridge.' He bent down, pulled some crystal glass tumblers from a cupboard. 'I definitely need a drink. I don't know about you.' He glanced at us over his shoulder.

'A drink would be good. Brandy, please, if you've got it.' My nerves were shredded. My hands still shook, although I didn't know if that was fear at almost dying again or joy at seeing Mason.

'Yeah, brandy sounds a damn good idea,' Mason said.

'Go on through.' Charlie nodded his head towards the lounge doorway. 'I'll bring them in.'

We walked inside the lounge. I clutched Mason's hand and pulled him onto the sofa next to me, unable to stop looking at him.

'I can't believe this.' I touched his face. 'I can't believe you're really here. How did you get inside the gates?'

'Just as I was arriving by cab, I saw a young guy slipping in through them. He was obviously one of them, and I managed to sneak in behind him before the gates shut.' He slid his arm around my shoulder and pulled me towards him. 'You have no idea how much I've dreamed of this moment. The last ten months have been hell.' His eyes watered as he tried to contain the tears.

'Were you in Barcelona all that time?'

'No. I travelled around. Took odd jobs to pay my living expenses. And every day I was just waiting and waiting to be able to contact you again. God, it was so hard without you, but I had to make sure it looked like I was actually dead. I don't know how the hell they found out I was still alive.'

'I do,' I said, gripping his knee. I explained how just before I'd received the first photo he'd sent, they found the plane in Narumbe without his body inside.

Mason told me how he'd got on the plane at first, but then saw something – one of Moussa's men giving a shifty nod to the person filling the plane who nodded back. Something about it seemed off to him, suspicious, and he suspected they wouldn't just let him go like that. Mason thought it was a set up and had got off the plane when they weren't looking. He thought they'd be waiting for him in Galao when he arrived and never imagined they'd take down the plane with three innocent people on board.

He clutched my hand tight. 'I saw you. That day we were supposed to meet at Jesus Green. I was watching out of a hotel window across the river and you were early. But then … I saw them take you. By the time I'd got outside, you were gone. I thought they'd killed you.' He touched his fingertips to my face, blinking back tears.

Charlie entered the room with a tray of tumblers filled with brandy. I took one and downed most of it in one go. Mason did the same. Charlie put the tray on the coffee table, picked up his drink and stood in front of the ornate marble fireplace, leaning his elbow on the mantelpiece as he sipped his drink. 'Who are those men working for? Moussa Damba or one of the chocolate companies?'

'Probably Julian Bolliger. He's the owner of Bolliger Chocolate.'

'They're not going to stop looking for you both,' Charlie said. 'We need to get out of here. And we need a plan. I can get in touch with my old contacts, get a crew together and kill the bastards.'

Mason shook his head. 'I'm a doctor. I'm supposed to preserve life, not take it away. I took an oath.'

'An oath won't keep you safe.' Charlie snorted. 'The only way to do that is to eliminate them. It's kill or be killed. They've already proved that. And besides, you didn't mind cracking that guy's skull a minute ago, did you?'

Mason shook his head. 'I was trying to incapacitate him, not kill him. And there have been far too many deaths over this already. I have a better plan. One that doesn't involve any risks or anyone dying. It will *save* lives. If we get all the information out to the public, people will have to sit up and take notice. We can hit them where it hurts the most – their pockets.'

Charlie swore under his breath. 'You're mad.'

'Bolliger is about to sign a merger with Galleaux at a high-profile chocolate exhibition which will make them the most powerful chocolate manufacturer in the industry. I'm going to expose them for what they truly are. I've got footage. Plenty of it.

Plus, audio of secretly taped conversations between Julian Bolliger and Moussa Damba about what they were up to.' Mason swallowed some more brandy.

'Who do you trust to give the footage to?' I asked.

'The crimes were committed in Narumbe, so they'd have jurisdiction, but I couldn't turn it over to the government. Moussa would've quashed it in seconds as he's involved in everything. I was going to hand it over to Interpol. But any investigation would take months, and I want to stop the merger before that. I thought of a way to do it. I–'

He was interrupted by a buzz from the gate intercom.

'Who the hell's that? My guy's not due yet.' Charlie put his brandy glass on the mantel piece and reached for the gun tucked in his waistband at the small of his back.

I looked at Mason. Mason looked at the front window.

Charlie picked up an iPad on the coffee table in front of us and turned it on, typed away. A picture came up on screen from the CCTV cameras outside. 'It's a man and a woman.' He frowned. 'They look like cops.' He turned the iPad round to us.

'I know who they are. They interviewed me after Isabelle was killed.'

Mason's jaw dropped open. 'Isabelle's dead?'

'Yes. I found her. It was awful.'

'Christ, poor woman.' Mason rubbed at his clenched forehead.

'Charlie Briggs? Nicole Palmer? Are you there? We need to talk to you,' DS Harris spoke through the intercom, her voice loud on screen.

'I should answer her. She might be able to help us,' I said.

'Are you mad?' Charlie scowled. 'I've got a fucking dead guy in my kitchen! How's having a copper in here going to help anything? I'm not going back inside for that piece of shit.'

'It was self defence,' I said. 'If we explain what happened … everything that's happening, then–'

'What, with my record?' Charlie snapped. 'I don't trust them. No way am I letting them in here. Even if they do accept it as self-defence, we'll be held at the nick for hours, days even. No. I'm not risking it.'

'So, shut the door,' I said. 'No one will let her in there. She must have contacts with Interpol. We need to tell her everything.'

A muscle worked away in Charlie's jaw as he thought it through. 'Are you really sure you want to involve the police?' The way he spat out the word *police* was filled with hatred. 'There are other ways to handle this. I know people. We can–'

Mason squeezed my hand and looked at Charlie. 'So much of what's happened has been wrong. We need to do this the right way now. And we need them on our side.'

Charlie shook his head. 'Okay. But no one mentions that body in there, right?'

'Right,' Mason and I agreed.

Charlie walked out of the room, and I heard his footsteps going up the hallway towards the kitchen. Heard him shut the kitchen door. Then the sound of his footsteps coming back to open the front door.

I looked out of the window as the electric gates opened again, and DS Harris and DI Thornton walked up the driveway. Charlie brought them into the lounge, and they both stopped short when they saw me and Mason.

DS Harris looked from me to Mason and back to me again. Then she cast a brief look to her boss as if to say, *I told you so*.

'I'm glad you're both safe. I've been trying to find you all over the place,' she said to me. Then looked at Mason. 'And you're either a ghost or resurrected from the dead.' She shook her head slightly. 'This has been the weirdest two days of my career.'

'Weird doesn't even touch it.' Mason's voice cracked.

'Do you mind if we sit down?' DI Thornton eyed Mason carefully, as if he really was a ghost. 'We need to ask you some questions.'

'Fill your boots.' Charlie motioned to a Chesterfield sofa beneath the window. 'You might be here a while.'

Chapter 83

Mason held my hand tight and began explaining to the officers what had been going on. How he'd been in Narumbe because they were in desperate need of medical aid due to the civil war. 'Health International wasn't supposed to get involved in political issues, but when you're seeing the injured and mutilated and raped turning up at the health clinic half dead, it's hard not to want to do something. I got close to a local man named Adama, who was our contact out there, and I started asking him questions, because the thing that bothered me was that no children were coming out alive. Either the rebels were killing them or something else was going on.' Mason took a sip of his brandy and swallowed. 'Everyone was afraid to talk about it in case I was a spy, and Adama wouldn't tell me anything straight away. It took a while to build up the trust. And then he told me what was really happening out there.'

'Which is what? The drug smuggling?' DI Thornton asked.

'Sorry?' Mason's face scrunched up with confusion.

'We have reason to believe you were involved in a drug cartel operating from Narumbe. And that you faked your own death to cover up your involvement.'

Mason's jaw dropped open. 'I have absolutely no idea what you're talking about. There are no drug cartels out there, as far as I know. This is all about cocoa.'

'Cocoa?' DS Harris gawped at us.

'Yes. Cocoa beans. And the end product – chocolate,' I said.

DI Thornton leaned forward, elbows on his knees. 'Did you just say chocolate?' he repeated incredulously.

Mason nodded with a resigned expression of sorrow and told them how forty-three percent of the world's cocoa beans come from small farms in Narumbe. That Narumbean beans were found in nearly every bar of chocolate produced, and the global market for chocolate and cocoa products was worth hundreds of billions of pounds a year. 'That's a hell of a lot of profit to protect.'

DS Harris raised her eyebrows again and glanced at DI Thornton who still looked very sceptical, his mouth hanging open.

'The government is in complete control of the cocoa plantations and international distribution of cocoa beans,' Mason carried on. 'They set the prices they give to the farmers, which are barely enough to survive on, and they demand high taxes from them. Cocoa is the only export and industry in the country, and all the money ends up in the hands of corrupt government officials.'

He took another large swallow of brandy. 'Anyway, Moussa Damba was in charge of the rebels. He wanted to overthrow the president in a coup and take over distribution for the cocoa and make big fat profits to line his own pockets. But he knew he needed the people on his side, so he cooked up a scheme with the cocoa farmers, because there are thousands of small plantations out there. He offered them something to sweeten things so they'd give him their support for his eventual coup.'

'Child slaves,' I said.

'Child slaves?' DS Harris gasped.

'Yes, along with reduced taxes on their cocoa sales,' Mason added.

'I saw them,' I said. 'The children. The conditions they're kept in were horrific.'

'What?' Mason turned to me. 'That's where you'd been when I saw you at Heathrow?'

'Yes. I was trying to find out what was going on. I had no idea who was after me and why and thought it was the only place I'd get answers.' My gaze drifted to DS Harris as I relayed what I'd seen. When I got to the part where we'd witnessed that boy killed in front of us, I closed my eyes. I could still see his face. It would be seared into my brain forever. I bit back the tears and said, 'The rebels shot at us, but a friend of Adama's managed to get us out.'

'I had no idea,' Mason said to me. 'At that point, I thought you were already dead.'

'Sorry to break this personal conversation up,' DI Thornton said with an impatient tone. 'This appears to be a very strange situation, but I really need to hear everything right now.'

'Yes. Sorry.' Mason rubbed a hand over his face and blew out a deep breath. 'I started working with Adama. He had a network of people trying to help the slaves escape to an orphanage in Mali, but the scale of kids involved is unbelievable.' He paused, wet his lips. 'Child slave labour on cocoa plantations first came to light in 2000, but the chocolate industry tried to brush it off. Everyone along the chocolate chain passes the blame, but they're well aware of what is happening. In 2001, the chocolate manufacturers made a big show of signing the Harkin-Engel Protocol to get the press off their backs, which is a voluntary agreement made to eliminate child labour in cocoa production. But very little has changed since then.'

'So, let me get this straight,' DS Harris said. 'Moussa Damba's involved in a coup to overthrow the government and in arranging the massacres of villages and the kidnapping of children for slavery in the cocoa plantations?' She had a look of disgust on her face.

'Yes. But he wasn't working alone,' Mason said. 'As well as video footage I took of the inhumane and dangerous condition these children are kept in on plantations over there, I have audio footage that one of Adama's contacts recently obtained. Secret conversations between Moussa Damba and Julian Bolliger, the owner of Bolliger – a huge international chocolate company based in Zurich, with offices all over the world, including the US and UK. He was supporting Moussa's regime and giving him money to buy arms, in exchange for a deal to keep the cocoa supply costs low. Bolliger was fully aware of the child slaves on the plantations that supplied him with cocoa, even though he also signed the Harkin-Engel Protocol years ago.'

'Bolliger was helping Damba clear up loose ends,' I said.

'Meaning you?' DS Harris said to Mason. 'Moussa Damba tried to kill you in the plane crash, but when he realised you were alive, he came after Nicole and Isabelle to find out your whereabouts?'

Mason nodded.

DS Harris looked at her boss until he met her eye, then she peeled her glare away after getting her point across. She'd been right all along. DI Thornton adjusted his tie and coughed.

Mason told them how Bolliger was due to sign a merger the next day with Galleaux, who buy almost all of the Narumbean cocoa bean supply, and if it got out he was directly involved in supporting Moussa's actions and the use of child slaves, the merger would be called off and the public outcry would have a massive effect on his business.

Mason stared into his brandy and swirled the remnants around the glass. 'Late at night, Adama and his network of people would go to the plantations when the rebel guards were drunk on palm wine and they'd free the boys, one at a time. Any more than that was too dangerous to smuggle them across the border. I went with him several times and filmed it all. I spoke to the children who'd been rescued. It was utterly heartbreaking what they'd gone through.'

'We went to the orphanage where the boys were taken in Mali.' My eyes welled up with tears. I brushed them away with my fingertips. 'Honestly, you can't even imagine the half of it.'

'I'm sure,' DS Harris said. 'Did you tell Isabelle Moore what was going on out there?' she asked Mason.

'Yes, after I took film footage of the child slaves on the plantations. I called her two days before I was due home for my R and R. I wanted her to help me expose it. But she said she couldn't. It was HI's policy not to get involved in political and social problems in the country – they were purely an aid organisation. She said she couldn't risk being kicked out and undoing the good we were doing with the massacre survivors. I understood her position, but I couldn't go along with that.'

Charlie, who'd been watching us in silence by the fireplace with a clenched jaw, reached for a crystal glass decanter of brandy on the tray and filled up our glasses in turn. 'Do you want something to drink?' he asked the officers. If he was nervous about having a dead body in his kitchen, metres away from where they were sitting, he didn't show it.

'I would *love* a brandy after what I've just heard, but I'm on duty,' DS Harris said.

DI Thornton looked like he needed a stiff drink too, but he waved the offer away and said. 'Isabelle must've suspected your plane crash wasn't accidental.'

'I would imagine so. But she didn't know I was alive. I suppose she thought she was doing the right thing for the organisation. But she's paid a high price for it now. So many people have died over this.'

I clutched Mason's hand. 'Adama is also dead. I'm so sorry.'

Mason closed his eyes for a brief moment, pain etched all over his face. When he opened them again, his eyes were watering with unshed tears. 'He was a good man. The kindest, most compassionate man I've ever known.'

'We have someone in custody for the murder of Isabelle Moore,' DI Thornton said. 'The same man who tried to abduct you, Nicole.'

My jaw dropped open. 'So, you do believe me now, then?'

DI Thornton gave what looked like a sheepish look to DS Harris and a flush crept up to his cheeks. He cleared his throat. 'We've been investigating your claims while trying to find out your whereabouts.' He gave a standard non-committal answer.

I caught a slight raising of the eyebrows from DS Harris, as if this was all her doing.

'The person we have in custody for Isabelle's murder is a mercenary and professional killer,' DI Thornton said. 'He was booked on a flight to Zurich.'

'That's where I was going,' Mason said, startled. 'They must've worked out my new identity and wanted to follow me. It's where the merger is taking place. There's a famous world international chocolate exhibition where they're going to do the signing to give it extra publicity and kudos. There's a final bit of footage I needed to take for the documentary there. I decided that the only way to end this now was to get what I have out there and expose things. After I did that, I was going to turn everything I had over to Interpol.'

'You made your video and audio recordings into a documentary?' DS Harris asked.

'Yes. It will be explosive, that's for sure.'

'Do you have a copy of this documentary on you we can watch?' DI Thornton asked.

'Yes.' Mason slid his hands into the inside of his jacket where there was a zip compartment. He opened it and pulled out a USB stick. 'Everything's on here.'

'Have you got a laptop or something we can use?' DI Thornton turned to Charlie.

Charlie took the USB stick. 'You can watch straight from here.' He plugged it into the side of the huge flat screen TV in the corner of the room.

Chapter 84

We sat in stunned and sickening silence as we watched the footage on screen.

Mason and Adama had visited many plantations and videoed the brutal and hazardous conditions of the child slaves, working with machetes, carrying heavy loads, handling toxic pesticides with no protection, their injuries and scars from their dangerous work. The suffocating huts where they slept forty or more to a tin shack.

Interpreting through Adama, Mason questioned the children they had rescued, who bravely and sadly told of horrific experiences no one should ever have to suffer – some of whom had been kidnapped from the villages which had been massacred by the rebels, some – who had been tricked by traffickers in Mali, Burkina Faso, Niger, or Cote D'Ivoire – believing they would be getting a real job for real pay. In one rural village in Mali, a young boy told how he was one of a hundred and thirty children who had been lured away by traffickers without their parents' knowledge and sold to the cocoa farmers in surrounding countries.

They described the beatings they'd received, told witness accounts of the deaths of their fellow slaves, either through injury or at the hands of both the farmers and the rebel guards. They told of their stolen lives and despair.

Then came the damning secret recordings of conversations between Moussa Damba and Julian Bolliger, which documented Moussa's plans for a coup, and Bolliger's financial and moral support to him so he could keep the government sweet because of his plans for world domination in the chocolate sector. The global demand for cocoa beans already outweighed supply and nothing would stop him getting his hands on them. Given all the exchanges between them by phone, it was clear Bolliger not only condoned the trafficking and use of child slaves, but he was also involved in financing the rebels to supply arms to them so they would facilitate Moussa's take over of the country. There was also undisputed evidence that Bolliger was involved in the massacring of villages, war crimes, a conspiracy that spanned the globe, and mass murder.

When the film ended, we all sat in respectful silence for a moment. DI Thornton's face had drained of colour and DS Harris looked incensed.

DI Thornton pressed his lips together, deep in thought, before saying, 'You said things haven't improved with child slavery since this Harkin-Engel Protocol was signed, but … why not? Isn't the UN monitoring developments? Surely that would fall under their remit of enforcing international law regarding human rights.'

Mason took a deep breath and told them how the International Labour Organisation – who was part of the UN – was remitted with fighting child labour, slavery and trafficking, but as there were over two million children engaged in slave labour in the Ivory Coast and Ghana alone, their resources were stretched to the limit. It had been going on for decades with them barely touching the surface. And since cocoa wasn't as headline-grabbing as gold or blood diamonds, it wasn't exactly a priority for them. In the past, there'd been little international news coverage, in part due to the region's struggle with lawlessness and civil unrest, and the local journalists were just spies for the government with Moussa Damba controlling all the media getting out of the country. Mason named a French journalist who'd gone to Narumbe a year before to investigate what was going on. He'd been digging into corruption and slave labour in the industry for a big exposé, but he'd disappeared, and it was common knowledge out there that he'd been kidnapped in Lagossa and murdered by Moussa Damba.

'And then you've got the giant chocolate cartels with huge lobbying power denying any knowledge that child slaves are involved in their end products so they can keep the price of cocoa low,' Mason said. 'But everyone involved is very scared of it getting out, which could lead consumers to boycott their products or embargoes being placed banning exports from the countries supplying them with cocoa. They want to keep the beans coming, and they don't want people asking questions which reveal the true murky world of chocolate.'

'Why didn't you expose it before now? After the plane crashed, I mean?' DS Harris asked.

Mason turned to me. 'Because at that time, I didn't have enough evidence to prove both Julian Bolliger's and Moussa Damba's involvement and take them down. At first, all I had was footage taken of the slaves at the plantations, which the ILO wouldn't have done much about on its own because, as I said, they don't have enough resources to deal with the existing massive problems. They also threatened to kill Nicole. But what they didn't realise is, I had a copy of it all stored on a cloud. Adama smuggled me out of Narumbe into Mali, and I went into hiding until he could plant an inside man close to Damba to get the audio evidence against Bolliger and Damba that would be enough to get them convicted.'

He paused and ran a hand over his face. 'When I heard about the plane crash, I thought it was better for them to think I was dead for the time being. If they were watching Nicole to find out if I'd told her anything, it would be more realistic if they saw a grieving widow. I thought my silence then would ensure her safety. As soon as Adama sent me the final audio footage of secret conversations between Bolliger and Damba, I knew I had enough to expose everything then, which is why I was finally able to contact Nicole again. I was going to meet her and take her to safety before I went to Interpol.'

His face crumpled as he looked at me. 'I thought I was doing the best thing to protect you. But when I sent the photo, I didn't realise they'd found the plane wreck that showed I wasn't on it and they'd started looking for me anyway.' He shook his head solemnly. 'This has all been such a horrendous nightmare.'

'That sounds like a *massive* understatement,' DS Harris said. 'I'm glad you both managed to get out alive.'

DI Thornton stood up suddenly. 'Well, the other organisations might not have done anything, but they haven't seen us British police in action yet. You said you wanted some final footage for this?' He nodded his head towards the TV screen.

'Yes.' Mason explained what he wanted and what his plan was.

DI Thornton nodded. 'Okay. Look, I appreciate that this is an emotional reunion for you both, but there are some things we need to do right now. One, I want you to both come to the station and make formal statements. Two, I'm going to have to liaise with our Interpol contact to find out exactly which law enforcement contact we need to get in touch with in Switzerland. Three, we need to get you to Zurich for your final footage.' He smiled for the first time. 'I want to see those bastards pay for this as publicly as possible. I'll wait for you outside. I'm just going to call my boss and try to convince him to go along with my plan.'

Charlie retrieved the USB stick and handed it to Mason. He placed a hand on Mason's shoulder and said, 'Call me when you're finished at the station. I've got a spot of spring cleaning to do right now.'

I nodded at Charlie. 'You're coming to Zurich with us?'

He gave me a shark-like smile. 'I wouldn't miss this for the world.'

Chapter 85

DS Harris walked down Charlie's front steps with DI Thornton close behind. 'Christ. This was all about protecting the corrupt world of cocoa and chocolate? No wonder Fowler was so cocky. He probably thought with the connections Julian Bolliger has that it would be easy to pay someone off to get the charges dropped or tamper with a jury.' She shook her head, angry with herself for jumping to the wrong conclusions about a drug connection. 'I can't believe I got it wrong.'

'You got it half right. And we wouldn't even be here now if it wasn't for you. You did bloody good work. When this is over, I'm going to be putting you in for a commendation.'

A bit of a change of tune from disciplining her, she thought. She wanted to rub it in a bit, but she thought that might be pushing things too far.

She stood taller and grinned. 'Thank you, sir.'

'But first, we need to convince the Brass to let us go to Zurich. I want to be there when Julian Bolliger is arrested. And I'm sure you do too.'

'Do you think they'll let us go?'

'Child slavery, a corrupt corporation, a political coup, an international cover up, and a joint police operation?' He raised his eyebrows. 'It's a massive result and a huge scoop for British law enforcement. It'll be one of the most high-profile cases our force has dealt with, and the press coverage will be huge. They'll be wanting to milk the public relations angle for all its worth.' The excitement emanating from his voice and the animation in his eyes seemed to her like he was going to milk it to the hilt too, for a step up on the career ladder.

As he dialled the Detective Superintendent and put the phone to his ear, Becky leaned against the bonnet of the car, mulling over everything the Palmers had just said, anger swirling inside her body. It beggared belief the lengths some people were prepared to go to for greed. She doubted she'd ever get the footage of those children out of her mind. And, even though she was a self-confessed chocaholic, she knew she could never touch another bar as long as she lived. This was about far more than a high-profile case to her and an angle to get promotion, like she suspected it was for Thornton. And she desperately wanted to be there when Bolliger was arrested. She clenched her fists and chewed on her lip as she listened to Thornton's call.

When he finally got off the phone ten minutes later, Nicole and Mason were coming out of Charlie's front door.

'Right.' DI Thornton hurried towards them. 'We need to get moving. Everything's being arranged, but we've got a lot to do. We're going to Zurich.'

Becky did a fist pump in the air behind him.

'Thank you,' Mason said, clutching his wife's hand.

'And I also just found out that our technical department pulled some very interesting voicemail messages from Sean Fowler's phone, which basically order the hit on the both of you,' DI Thornton said. 'The number has been matched to an unregistered phone, so no trace on ownership details, but I'm betting voice analysis will prove it's Julian Bolliger. And with the footage we've just seen and heard from you, there's enough evidence to put him away for a long time.'

Chapter 86

After hours of taking statements and waiting around at the police station while DS Harris and DI Thornton liaised with their contacts in Zurich, we finally all arrived in Switzerland late that night. We'd been informed that DNA from Isabelle's body had matched Sean Fowler, and he'd now been formally charged with her murder.

As we took a minibus from the airport, Mason and I clutched each other's hands tightly. Now we'd found each other again, I wasn't going to let go for a long time. After Julian Bolliger was arrested, I was looking forward to us getting to know each other all over again, but there was something gnawing at me that I couldn't let lie. Something I needed to talk to Mason about in private. We hadn't really been alone since we were reunited.

'Sorry, it's not the Ritz,' DI Thornton said as the taxi pulled up outside a small city hotel. 'The Hertfordshire Constabulary budget doesn't stretch that far, I'm afraid.'

'Doesn't matter.' Mason squeezed my hand and smiled at me. 'We're together. That's all that matters.'

After checking in, Mason and I stood close together, hands still intertwined, desperately waiting to go to the room like a couple of frustrated teenagers.

'So, we've still got some last-minute things to sort out with our counterparts here ready for tomorrow,' DI Thornton said to us. 'But we'll see you for breakfast at seven sharp.'

'I'm heading to the bar.' Charlie grinned before giving me a tight hug. 'You did good, girl,' he whispered in my ear before giving the same treatment to Mason. 'Look after her now,' he said to Mason and walked off.

I giggled as we stepped inside the lift. It felt like a first date, which was ridiculous.

As soon as we got inside the room, Mason dumped the holdall on the floor and turned to face me. I dropped mine next to it.

He cupped my cheeks in his hands and said, 'I'm so sorry. If I hadn't taken the job, none of this would have happened. Adama, Isabelle, you nearly being killed. I can't imagine the pain you must've gone through thinking I was dead. It's–'

'And if I hadn't pushed you away, you wouldn't have gone. We could waste so much time talking about "if onlys" and blame, but none of that matters now. I spent so long pining for the future I wanted when I was going through the IVF that I forgot to concentrate on the present. From now on, I've made a promise to myself to live in the moment and appreciate what I have. I'm going to change. I'm never going to hold back again. I'm going to let you in completely.' I slid my arms around his neck and pulled him close.

My lips found his, and our tongues met in a gentle dance. I slid my hands underneath his shirt and sucked in a breath at the feel of his skin sending electric shockwaves trembling through every nerve ending.

When we came up for air he said, 'So if you don't want to talk, what do you want to do?' He cocked his eyebrow.

'I can think of plenty of things to do before seven am.' I laughed before pushing him backwards onto the bed.

Chapter 87

It was just gone nine am when we all stepped into the foyer of the luxurious and world-renowned Grande Hotel. There were signs pointing to a set of doors on our right for the International Chocolate Exhibition being held in their huge exhibition centre. In a few hours, Bolliger and Galleaux would be signing a merger at a podium on centre stage in front of a huge audience of spectators and press.

I was thinking about my future. About the plans Mason and I had made as we'd talked until the early hours of the morning. About a new life waiting for us when this was all over.

DS Harris and DI Thornton followed us surreptitiously, keeping us in their sights but not crowding us as we walked through the first part of the exhibition, which was an elaborate set – like something from a movie, decked out like the African bush. There were cocoa trees and pods scattered on the ground beneath them. The relaxing sounds of waterfalls trickling, and the occasional parrot call adding to the ambience. A small girl in a buggy being pushed along by her dad watched, entranced at the display of real-life stuffed animals.

A pathway led us naturally into another section, showing the history of chocolate production with old photos of plantations and tools.

We barely broke our stride as we meandered through the next area, which displayed famous bars of chocolate and rivers of liquid chocolate flowing into a rock pool. Two female members of staff dressed in traditional African costume handed out free samples to people. Parents and children jostled to get to the sweet treats, hands gripping complimentary bars with excited glee.

I thought about the children on the plantations. Children whose back-breaking, dangerous work and incarceration fed this industry. Children who had never even tasted a chocolate bar in their lives. And I thought about the privileged western world, who consumed the luxury item en masse with no idea what bloodshed really happened in secret to produce it. The sight and smell of the chocolate turned my stomach.

The final part of the exhibition housed the large chocolate companies' stands. I spotted a podium along one side of the large space which was being used for a demonstration with a young woman in a chef's outfit icing a luxurious chocolate cake. A large crowd had gathered around her, but we didn't stop, heading instead straight for the Galleaux stand.

A smart female dressed in a skirt suit of the company's maroon corporate colours stood behind it. Her hair was in a neat chignon, and she was fully made up, towering over me in her polished stilettos, a fake smile in place.

I looked at Mason. He smiled nervously at me. The disguised wide-angle camera he wore was attached to the side of his rucksack which hung casually on his right shoulder. Charlie had an identical camera and was working the other side of the room.

Behind the stand were displays of high end, luxury chocolates on one side and everyday bars that I'd seen thousands of times in supermarkets. Some I'd bought hundreds of times in my life.

'Hello.' Her smiled inched higher, displaying perfectly white teeth. 'Would you like a free sample?' She picked up a basket that contained a selection of mini-chocolate bars and held it out to me.

I gritted my teeth and said, 'No, thanks.'

'Nice display.' Mason made a show of looking at the chocolate.

'Thank you.'

'Where do your cocoa beans come from?' Mason asked casually.

'All our chocolate is made with the finest cocoa from West Africa.'

'From Narumbe?' Mason asked.

Her smile grew wider. 'Why, yes. Their beans are the most sought after and delicious. A little touch of gold in a pod.'

'Have you heard any rumours that those cocoa beans are grown as a result of child slave labour and child trafficking?' Mason asked.

That sent the smile sliding off her face. 'Absolutely not,' she said, wide-eyed at the suggestion. 'We ensure that our cocoa producers are of the highest integrity. I can assure you that there are no child slaves on any of the farms we use.'

'You're certain of that? Because I'd hate to think my money was being used to fund such operations.'

'Absolutely, sir. Some family farmers do use their own children to carry out light work on their plantations, which is a custom of the region and is perfectly normal. But child slaves? No. Absolutely not.'

'How can you be so sure of that?' Mason asked.

'Because we have offices in Narumbe, including a research and development centre, and we make sure we carry out inspections of plantations in the region. We always ensure people are paid properly for the cocoa beans.'

'Well, that's very good to hear. Come on, darling.' He took my hand, and we wound our way through the crowds to the Bolliger stand, which was even bigger. Giant TVs behind played adverts for their products on an endless loop.

A huge chocolate fountain display sat in the middle, oozing milky brown from the top into a bowl at the bottom. Next to it was a silver platter filled with strawberries on cocktail sticks. A mum picked one up and dipped it into the chocolate before handing it to her teenage daughter who wolfed it down, smearing chocolate on her upper lip, fawning over the taste.

A few more families were taking free samples from a woman dressed in an almost identical skirt suit to the Galleaux member of staff, but then they drifted away as one of their kids pointed out another well-known chocolate brand further down.

'Are you enjoying the exhibition?' the Bolliger representative asked us.

'Oh, definitely,' Mason replied. 'I've heard you're going to be announcing a merger with Galleaux in a few hours. It must be a very exciting time.'

'Yes.' She beamed at us. 'Bolliger Galleaux will be the biggest chocolate producer in the world. Have you had one of our samples?' She held out a basket with luxury truffles inside.

Mason shook his head. 'I've been hearing about the problem of child slavery on the cocoa plantations you buy your cocoa from in Narumbe. Are you aware of that happening?'

The smile dropped entirely. 'Oh, goodness, absolutely not. When we first learned of those issues in 2000, we made significant steps to address the problem.'

'What steps?'

She shifted from foot to foot, looking uncomfortable. 'We set up a stringent vetting and inspection process of all the plantations we purchase from to ensure those who were involved in such heinous practices were not associated with us. Our company does not stand for such deplorable behaviour.'

'You're certain of that?' Mason asked, his face impassive.

'I can one-hundred per cent guarantee it, sir. Our staff visit plantations personally to make sure.'

'So, what if I told you that it was happening now, in 2018, in Narumbe?'

She suddenly developed a pinched frown, her smile tight, looking over her shoulder as if trying to find someone new to talk to. 'I'd say that it would have to be an extremely rare occurrence. I've certainly never seen any evidence of it. There may be a handful of cocoa farmers who do this, but we don't own those companies and have no control over their cocoa farming and labour practises, so we can't accept responsibility for those few examples.'

'Okay. Thank you for your time.' Mason took my hand, and we wandered out of the exhibition. I glanced behind me and nodded at our police escort and Charlie who'd fallen in behind us.

When we reached the main reception area, DS Harris and DI Thornton caught up to us.

'Do you have what you need?' DS Harris asked while DI Thornton looked at his watch.

'Yes. I just need to add it to the beginning of the documentary.'

'We've arranged for you to use the business suite undisturbed,' DS Harris said. 'I'll show you the way while DI Thornton meets with the Swiss police officers for a final briefing.'

We followed her to a room decked out with laptops, printers, fax machines and several TVs. She unlocked the door with a key she'd got from the reception desk and we stepped inside.

Mason sat down at one of the desks, pulled his laptop from his rucksack and got to work.

Chapter 88

At quarter to two, we stood next to DS Harris and DI Thornton in the crowded exhibition hall. In front of us was the large stage with a podium in front centre of it. Behind it was a huge floor-to-ceiling projector screen with the corporate logos of Bolliger and Galleaux splashed across it.

The croissant I'd had earlier threatened to come back up as I stood nervously, waiting for the players to show up and sign the merger documents.

Mason looked calm, but I could tell how he felt by the muscle ticking away in his jaw and his palm sweaty in mine. Charlie had his hands in his pockets, grinning calmly.

DI Thornton's phone rang. He pulled it from his pocket and placed it to his ear, listening for a moment before hanging up. He nodded at DS Harris and then us. 'They're coming out.'

I took a deep breath and felt Mason tense beside me.

A dignified-looking Julian Bolliger walked up onto the stage, dressed in a very expensive charcoal grey suit with a sky-blue tie. He was in his late fifties, with salt and pepper hair and a neatly trimmed beard. His face was round, his blue eyes twinkling. He looked like a kindly granddad, rather than a mass murderer. Behind him was the CEO of Galleaux, Paul Wellington, who was dressed virtually identical in a well-cut suit, enhanced by trendy glasses frames that almost made him look young and fashionable.

The crowd clapped and cheered as both men stood in front of the podium and smiled beatifically at each other before turning to the audience.

Bolliger lifted a hand to call for silence, used to everyone doing his bidding. 'Welcome to the fifteenth annual Zurich

Chocolate Festival. I hope you're all partaking of the finest samples.' He lifted his hands in the air and surveyed his captive audience. The press took photos. The crowd roared with glee.

Mason looked at me with a raised eyebrow. I squeezed his hand.

'The name Bolliger has always been synonymous with luxury chocolate. For the past ninety years, my family has built up the company into the largest chocolate producer in the world.'

More flashes of cameras. More cheering.

'Today, Bolliger will sign a merger with Galleaux.' He turned and smiled at his counterpart. 'As you know, Galleaux is the largest cocoa mass producer in the industry. And today, we are involved in an historical event.' He gazed at the crowd, making sure everyone hung on his every word. 'An event which will make Bolliger Galleaux the number one global confectionary producer.' He raised his hands again, and the crowd took that as their cue to clap.

'Before we sign the merger documents, let's take a look at some of the groundbreaking and innovative history of our companies.' Bolliger smiled and turned around to the projection screen behind him.

Everyone was silent, eyes fixed on the screen, the broadcast media busy filming as their promotional advert started. Bolliger and Wellington smiled proudly, watching a montage of clips: Beautiful, lush green scenery of the plantations. Men smiling and laughing as they worked side by side, cutting down ripe pods from the cocoa plants, as if the day's work was nothing but a stroll in the breeze. The production line in their factories where men and women looked similarly ecstatic to work. The Western children devouring their products with glee. African children sitting in a classroom, answering questions from the teacher, and a hospital where mothers and children were being treated, inferring that Bolliger and Galleaux's money had helped fund local improvement projects for the communities.

Then the montage stopped, and the words: *And Now for The Truth…* flashed up on screen.

Bolliger frowned, confused, knowing that wasn't part of the footage. He looked at Wellington, who raised his eyebrows, not knowing what was going on. Bolliger stepped to the side of the stage and spoke with a female member of staff dressed in the corporate uniform. She shrugged her shoulders and disappeared into the crowd, presumably to find out what the technical hitch was.

And then the film started again, and I watched Bolliger smiling. But it wasn't what he'd been expecting, and the smile slid off his face when he saw on screen his member of staff being questioned by Mason earlier that morning about child slavery and denying all knowledge of it.

I watched Bolliger look beyond the crowd at who was manning the projection equipment, a confused look on his face. Then my gaze slid back to the screen. To the cocoa plantations, to the emaciated children, to their heartbreaking faces, to close ups of their injuries, to their stories.

Bolliger and Wellington were dumbfounded for a while, their mouths wide open. Until it hit them what was going on. Then Bolliger pulled himself together, his face a red mask of fury. 'Please stop the film!' he called out, waving his hands in the air in the direction of the projector operator who, little did he know, was with us. 'This is a complete fabrication by one of our competitors, trying to slur our name. Please turn it off!'

'This is an outrage!' Wellington blustered with what could only be described as a very guilty look on his face.

Just then, three police officers appeared from behind the screen, dressed in navy combat clothes and armed with handguns in holsters.

'What is going on?' Bolliger demanded as they stepped up on the stage, Mason's documentary still playing out behind him. The crowd were stunned into silence as they watched the damning evidence of Bolliger's deeds. Press video recorders filmed with excitement at the prospect of a huge scoop.

The air of charm had now disappeared, and Bolliger scowled at the officers. 'My event has been sabotaged by my competitors. I trust you're going to be taking action against them.'

A suited man stepped up on stage and joined his team of police officers. I don't know if he stood purposely next to the microphone at the podium when he told Bolliger he was under arrest for a multitude of crimes, but I think he probably did. DI Thornton stepped closer to the stage for a better look.

I threw my arms around Mason, my mouth stretched wide in a smile as the crowd continued watching with rapt attention, making collective noises of disgust and horror. The media went wild, cameras firing madly, flashing like a firework display.

DS Harris leaned in to us, a triumphant smile on her own face. 'Well, that couldn't have gone any better, I thought. I bet you'll be celebrating tonight.'

I looked at Mason. He looked at me. We both grinned stupidly.

Charlie looked at his watch. 'Well, sorry to be a party pooper, but I have to catch a flight. I need a bloody good holiday after all this.' He hugged me tight.

'What? Where are you going?' I asked, surprised. He hadn't told me he was going away and I was going to miss him.

'I'm joining your dad in Thailand for a bit. I need to square things up with him, because he's not going to be happy when he hears about all this. Especially me taking you to Africa. And besides, I need to lie on a sunbed on a beach and chill out for a while. I ain't getting any younger, and this has been a bit hectic for an old bugger like me. But I'll see you soon. Okay?' He let me go. 'You two look after each other.' He stepped back and turned to leave.

'You stay out of trouble now, Mr Briggs,' DS Harris said with an eyebrow raised.

'Always.' Charlie winked at her and disappeared through the crowd of excited onlookers as Bolliger and Wellington were led away in handcuffs.

DI Thornton appeared at DS Harris's side. 'Well, that's what I call a result. So, what's next for you? Now it's all over?' He looked at Mason and me.

'It's far from over.' Mason took my hand, and we slipped out of the hall.

Chapter 89

It was a moonless night, the darkness masking his approach to the back door of the palatial mansion. Not that he was particularly worried about being seen. He knew Fanta would've done what they'd asked of her.

He walked steadily across the lush lawn, up to the terrace and peered inside the patio doors that led to the lounge, behind which he saw Fanta coming towards him, her hand already outstretched to unlock the door. Her right eye was swollen almost shut, her uniform was ripped at the arm. No doubt Moussa had taken out his anger about Bolliger's arrest on her.

The shit was going to hit the fan big time when the news broke properly in Narumbe. This time, journalists would come and tell the *real* story. The bitter truth about what was going on out here. The UN, ILO, and Interpol were all putting together a joint operation to simultaneously storm the cocoa plantations and rescue the children. The political situation was more complex, though. Sorting that out would be a nightmare. He could only pray that, for once, the people were looked after. Until they were, he'd make sure he did what was necessary, and for that, he'd taken a detour on his way to Thailand.

'Are you all right?' Charlie whispered to Fanta.

'Yes. He never going to do it again to me.' She clutched the edges of her blouse together. 'Not to anyone. He never taste the drug I put in his cognac. He fast asleep now.' She nodded rapidly.

'Good girl.' He patted her arm and followed her down the hallway to Moussa's bedroom, pulling out the handgun from the small of his back and screwing on the suppressor.

She stopped outside the last door and tilted her head towards it, biting her lower lip.

Charlie stepped inside the room and walked up to the sleeping form of Moussa Damba, lying outstretched on the bed, still fully clothed, one shoe hanging half off. He was snoring peacefully.

Charlie wasted no time. There was nothing to say, and Moussa wouldn't hear him anyway.

He fired a shot in the centre of Moussa's forehead.

Moussa's body jerked with the force. Then … nothing. Stillness. Death. Hopefully where he belonged. In Hell.

Charlie grinned to himself as he unscrewed the suppressor and put it in his pocket, headed for the door.

Not bad for an old geezer, he thought.

EPILOGUE

It was the start of a new term with a new class of children. And for the first time in a long time, I was nervous as I sat in front of them, cross-legged on the grass. When I was a child at primary school, the classes I most remembered were the ones we took outside on the school fields when the weather permitted, and it was a glorious warm day as the children sat in a semi-circle under the shade of a tree, gazing up at me with rapt attention.

I held up a flashcard and smiled. 'Okay, what letter is this?'

'A!' they cried out.

'And what things begin with the letter A?'

'Apple.'

'Arrow.'

'Ant.'

'Aeroplane'

'Good.' I clapped my hands together. 'How does an aeroplane go?'

One by one, they got to their feet and held out their arms, zooming around on the grass, making aeroplane noises, giggling.

I grinned to myself and watched these children just being children. This class was unlike any other I'd taken before, and it was slow going, but that didn't matter. I had all the time in the world to try to make a difference to their lives. Instead of having my usual group of five-to six-year-olds, the ages of these children ranged from five to fifteen, and all of them had been rescued from cocoa plantations and had had no previous proper schooling.

Yes, I was at Oumar's orphanage. Sometimes, it takes a major event, a major heartbreak, to lead you on a different path. And some journeys you can never come back from.

I spotted Mason hurrying across the grass towards me, holding Sekou's good hand.

'Okay, class, that's it for the day.' I stood up. 'You've all worked really hard. It's play time now.'

Some of them scattered to go and kick a football around. Some ran to me and hugged me tight.

'Come on, let's see how Sekou got on.' I walked towards Mason and Sekou, my arms around two little boys.

I could see the difference in Sekou, even before we reached each other.

The children let me go, and I crouched down in front of Sekou, grinning from ear to ear. 'Look at this! It seems perfect.'

The two boys gasped in awe.

Sekou held out his new prosthetic arm proudly for inspection.

'How does it feel?' I touched his face.

'It feeling a little tickle.' Sekou smiled.

'This is a little tickle.' Mason tickled him under his chin, and Sekou squirmed and laughed and then fell into my arms.

I hugged him tight and looked at Mason over his shoulder, his smile as wide as my own.

'It's just temporary, until we can get one of the new prosthetics,' Mason said.

'You'll be like bionic man, then, won't you?' I stroked Sekou's head and stood up. 'Come on, let's get you a snack and a drink, you must be thirsty.' I took his hand in mine, held Mason's in the other as we all walked back towards the orphanage. 'Then we'll go home.'

'Home,' Sekou whispered as he squeezed my hand. He looked up at me with a huge grin that made my heart melt.

When I'd suggested to Mason about adopting Sekou, he'd been over the moon. And while the paperwork was going through, Sekou was staying at our new house in the village, a few miles from the orphanage.

I was finally about to become a mother.

Mason had set up a medical clinic in the village too. The desperate need for good healthcare in one of the poorest countries in the world meant he was already inundated with patients. Although not qualified as a nurse, Fanta was helping Mason out at the surgery. She was learning quickly and had a naturally caring nature.

As we approached the wooden picnic benches at the back-garden area where the boys ate, Sekou ran off to show his friends his new arm. My eyes watered with tears.

Mason slung his arm around me. 'He was very brave.'

I rested my head against his chest. 'They all are.'

Charlie came out of the back door with Yaya, carrying trays laden with fresh fruit and coconut milk for the children who were sitting, waiting. They placed the trays down on the long bench table, and the hungry boys pounced on them.

Sekou was too excited to eat, though. He took Charlie's hand and made him kick a football around with him. It tugged at my heart to see how much he'd come out of himself, how much happier he was since the first time I'd seen him here crying on the front steps.

Charlie roared with laughter as he fake-tackled Sekou for the ball, making sure Sekou kept control of it. I smiled and my heart soared, doing a happy dance beneath my ribs.

I wasn't the only one to find love again. Charlie and Fanta were taking it slowly, but it was obvious she adored him as much as he did her. So what if there was a big age gap between them? In this world, you should grab onto love and hold it tightly.

Charlie was funding the orphanage now, which meant Oumar could purchase better equipment for the boys and more of it. Dad was coming out for long spells to help out too, after deciding retirement wasn't for him. He needed something physical and mental to do to stop the boredom and a sedentary lifestyle, and he loved it here as much as the rest of us did.

So, life was good for all of us. We were all staying in Mali. For how long? Who knew? As clichéd as it was, I'd learned that life was too fragile to not live in the moment. Maybe clichés are just that for a good reason. I didn't need plans anymore. I just needed to live every day as if it was my last, because it very nearly was, for all of us.

A Note from the Author

Although *The Disappeared* is fictional, it was inspired by the documentary *The Dark Side Of Chocolate 2010* by Bastard Film & TV, which is available on YouTube. Narumbe is a fictional country, but in real life, West African countries (mostly from Cote d'Ivoire and Ghana) supply more than 70% of the world's cocoa that, in turn, supplies the majority of chocolate companies. After extensively researching the cocoa industry, and the child slavery/trafficking that goes hand in hand with it, I was horrified at what I discovered, and *The Disappeared* was born. There are too many articles I read during my background work to mention here, but if you're looking for some further reading on the subject you could start with *Chocolate Nations: Living and Dying for Cocoa in West Africa* by Órla Ryan.

I'd like to say a huge thanks to my readers from the bottom of my heart for choosing my books! I really hope you enjoyed *The Disappeared.* If you did, I would be so grateful if you could leave a review or recommend it to family and friends. I always love to hear from readers so please keep your emails and Facebook messages coming (contact details are on my website: www.sibelhodge.com). They make my day!

A massive thanks goes out to my husband Brad for supporting me, being my chief beta reader, fleshing out ideas with me, and generally putting up with me ignoring him when I'm writing!

Thanks so much to my beta readers Karen Lloyd, Sharon Bairden, Joseph Calleja, and Dianne Wallace for all your feedback when I was having huge doubts about this book. And extra thanks again to Karen Lloyd for your teaching plan advice!

Huge thank you to Ben Adam for all of his editing suggestions and for catching all the things I didn't.

Big, big thanks to all at Bloodhound Books for your help and support with this book.

And finally, a loud shout out and hugs to all the peeps in The Book Club on Facebook and to all the amazing book bloggers and book reviewers everywhere out there who enthusiastically support us authors with their passion for reading. It's so much appreciated.

Sibel xx

About the Author

Sibel Hodge is the author of the No 1 Bestsellers Look Behind You, Untouchable, and Duplicity. Her books have sold over one million copies and are international bestsellers in the UK, USA, Australia, France, Canada and Germany. She writes in an eclectic mix of genres and is a passionate human and animal rights advocate.

Her work has been nominated and shortlisted for numerous prizes, including the Harry Bowling Prize, the Yeovil Literary Prize, the Chapter One Promotions Novel Competition, The Romance Reviews' prize for Best Novel with Romantic Elements and Indie Book Bargains' Best Indie Book of 2012 in two categories. She was the winner of Best Children's Book in the 2013 eFestival of Words; nominated for the 2015 BigAl's Books and Pals Young Adult Readers' Choice Award; winner of the Crime, Thrillers & Mystery Book from a Series Award in the SpaSpa Book Awards 2013; winner of the Readers' Favorite Young Adult (Coming of Age) Honorable award in 2015; a New Adult finalist in the Oklahoma Romance Writers of America's International Digital Awards 2015, and 2017 International Thriller Writers Award finalist for Best E-book Original Novel. Her novella Trafficked: The Diary of a Sex Slave has been listed as one of the top forty books about human rights by Accredited Online Colleges.

For Sibel's latest book releases, giveaways and gossip, sign up to her newsletter at: www.sibelhodge.com

Also by Sibel Hodge

Fiction

Into the Darkness
Beneath the Surface
Duplicity
Untouchable
Where the Memories Lie
Look Behind You
Butterfly
Trafficked: The Diary of a Sex Slave
Fashion, Lies, and Murder (Amber Fox Mystery No 1)
Money, Lies, and Murder (Amber Fox Mystery No 2)
Voodoo, Lies, and Murder (Amber Fox Mystery No 3)
Chocolate, Lies, and Murder (Amber Fox Mystery No 4)
Santa Claus, Lies, and Murder (Amber Fox Mystery No 4.5)
Vegas, Lies, and Murder (Amber Fox Mystery No 5)
Murder and Mai Tais (Danger Cove Cocktail Mystery No 1)
Killer Colada (Danger Cove Cocktail Mystery No 2)
The See-Through Leopard
Fourteen Days Later
My Perfect Wedding
The Baby Trap
It's a Catastrophe

Non-Fiction

A Gluten Free Taste of Turkey
A Gluten Free Soup Opera
Healing Meditations for Surviving Grief and Loss

CPSIA information can be obtained
at www.ICGtesting.com
Printed in the USA
LVHW041719060219
606614LV00002B/165/P